Prince Otto and the Evil Mr Stark

Martin Parr

Published in November 2015 by emp3books Ltd
Norwood House, Elvetham Road, Fleet, GU51 4HL,
England

©Martin Parr

The author asserts the moral right to be identified as the author of this work. All views are those of the author.

ISBN-13: 978-1-910734-07-0

All rights reserved. No part of this publication may be reproduced, stored in a retrieval system, or transmitted, in any form or by any means, electronic, mechanical, photocopying, recording or otherwise without the prior written consent of the author.

To Katarina and our wonderful son Theo who both love stories.
To Lynn and also my dear friend John

To Lucy,

When she was growing up the queen was a kind and beautiful princess. She is now wise and majestic, maybe you will grow up just like her.

Best wishes.

Martin Parr

Contents

Chapter 1 A Dangerous Visitor and a New Tutor	1
Chapter 2 Trouble Arrives	9
Chapter 3 The Lady Who Lives in the Woods	21
Chapter 4 Full Steam Ahead	31
Chapter 5: The Student Prince	43
Chapter 6 A Small Expedition	57
Chapter 7 A Close Shave	69
Chapter 8 A Friend for Life	75
Chapter 9 A Wise Man's Early Morning Visit	89
Chapter 10 Winning over the Nobility	103
Chapter 11 A Big Secret Revealed	121
Chapter 12 Grand Progress	131
Chapter 13 Industrialisation	145
Chapter 14 Life and Death	157
Chapter 15 Light at the End of a Long Tunnel	169
Chapter 16 A Trip to London	183
Chapter 17 Trapped	199
Chapter 18 Some Things Will Never Change	215

Chapter 1
A Dangerous Visitor and a New Tutor

It was three o'clock on a cold February afternoon in Bavaria in 1858, there was a thick blanket of snow on the hills near Prince Otto's beautiful yellow castle and three boys had just set off from the top of a big hill on a new red sledge.

Prince Otto, a tall twelve year old fair-haired boy was at the front. Otto's two friends were sitting behind him on the flat deck of the big sledge, the plump and short George sat in the middle and the slim and dark haired Sebastian at the back.

Prince Otto pulled on the steering rope and set a course for the steepest part of the hill. The sledge slid over the deep snow well and gained speed, George and Sebastian held tightly to the sides of the sledge as the air rushed through their hair. Half way down the hill the sledge was going far too fast for the boys to control it.

"Help" shouted George. Otto had a good sense of adventure, but even he wished they had taken a less steep route.
"We need to slow down" shouted Sebastian.
"I'm trying" said Otto as he pulled the rope to the left and then the right to zig zag the sledge, but it really wasn't slowing them down very much ... all three boys shouted "Aaaaa" together. There was worse to come.

The sledge was starting to veer towards the woods at the end of the castle's garden. Otto steered to the right as hard has he could and they skimmed past a couple of small fir trees leaving the boys covered in ice and snow. Otto's plan was starting to work, they were turning away from the woods and heading towards the safety of the large castle lawn.

The three boys breathed a sigh of relief as the sledge reached the snow covered lawn, but their adventure was not over yet. The sledge was still going so fast that they wouldn't dare jump off it, and up ahead there was a narrow bridge across a stream that ran through the middle of the castle grounds. They couldn't risk going into the stream at this speed as the sledge would stop dead when it hit the opposite bank. So Otto set a course for the narrow bridge and all three boys again shouted "Aaaaa" together as the bridge loomed quickly up ahead.

Otto had steered perfectly and the sledge went onto the centre of the humped back bridge but, at the speed that they were travelling, the sledge was lifted into the air by the bridge as if it had been shot from a canon. The sledge was airborne for what seemed to the boys like two minutes and as they came in to land the three boys saw something that they really didn't want to see... a huge snowman that Otto had built that morning.

They were heading straight towards it. There was no avoiding the snowman. No matter where he pulled the rope Otto had no control of the airborne sledge's direction.

"Aaaaaaa" the boys shouted for the third time that day, but the impact was inevitable. The boys watched in what seemed like slow motion as they got closer and closer to the snowman. The sledge disappeared in a cloud of snow as it hit the snowman's body, Otto was sent tumbling to the left, George and Sebastian were flung over the snowman onto the snow covered lawn and the sledge embedded itself in the ground near to where the snowman once had stood. The most enormous cloud of snow was sent across lawn and over the side of the castle.

For a few fractions of a second there was calm, gradually the boys started to move and then they shook their heads to get the snow out of their eyes, mouths and hair. Each boy was white from head to toe. George turned to Otto and said, "What ever were you thinking, going at that speed."
"Just think where we would have ended up if it hadn't been for the snowman," said Sebastian, looking at the huge castle wall

just a few metres in front of them.

"Mmmm" said Otto.
"That was absolutely terrifying" said George to Otto. "It is the last time I am going to let you drive me on a sledge."
"It was a bit fast," said Sebastian.
"It was terrific" said Otto who had the sort of ear to ear grin that only comes from experiencing one of life's true pleasures.

The boys thought that if they cleaned themselves up all this would be forgotten, but in the distance a very English voice bellowed "What is the meaning of this?" Otto saw a figure just beside the castle door. The distant man was also covered from head to toe in snow. He was a thin man with round glasses and he looked angry enough to explode. Otto replied in a very flat tone, "I'm sorry."
"You could have all been killed," the man said.

Otto looked at him and again tried, with an insincere tone, "I am very sorry." Otto didn't recognise the man who was shaking his head, and then the stranger turned to go inside the castle. The three boys followed him and made their way down the stone corridors to the castle kitchen. Soon the boys and the man were all sat around a big kitchen fire.

When the castle cook, Mrs Gott heard about Otto's exploits she was furious with him, "Whatever were you thinking?" She passed the man and boys a pile of towels. "The speed you were travelling it could have been the end of all of you."

Mrs Gott was a short round lady and she pointed a particularly plump finger at Otto and said "You must be more careful, remember, you are the king's only son. Whatever would happen to the kingdom if you broke your neck?"

Just at that moment the kitchen door was flung open. The king and queen arrived and Mrs Gott and all the footmen stood up.

The king was a tall round man who filled any room that he entered. He was complimented the queen, who has long black hair and wore a big wide blue dress, pulled in in the middle so she looked a bit like an egg timer. "Thank goodness you are still alive." said the queen.

"What ever were you doing?" Bellowed the king, "When we saw you out of the window you must have been going at over 50 kilometres an hour down that hill, you were going faster than my carriage travels on the road to Vienna, AND you were heading straight towards a forest. What if your steering hadn't worked? If you had hit a tree you would all have been killed."

Otto looked as regretful as he could pretend to be and said "Sorry father," Otto knew that he should have taken a safer route, but he had enjoyed himself so much that day. Otto decided that he liked travelling fast and a bit of danger was just something that he and his family would have to accept.

In all the excitement everyone had completely forgotten that the new visitor had not been introduced. "Oh," said the king when he looked at the man. "Otto, this is Mr Higginbottom, your new tutor."
"Pleased to meet you sir" said Otto with a nervous grin, although neither Otto nor Higginbottom looked at all pleased to meet one another. Higginbottom stared in a cold way around the room and said nothing. Once the boys had dried off and warmed up they went to Otto's room where they could talk in private. "Did you know you were getting a new tutor?" Asked Sebastian.
"No".
George grinned "I hope he is more fun than he looks".
"So do I," said Otto.

Sebastian stood up. "It has been quite a first day with your new tutor, I mean demolishing a snowman and spreading its remains all over your him, not to mention coming within a few metres of annihilating him, all of us and your sledge on the south wall of the castle."

"Mmm," replied Otto.

George still had his grin "Do you think your tutor will hold it against you?"

Otto smiled. "I'm sure he will have calmed down tomorrow and all will be fine."

At seven thirty a gong was rung. "That is for dinner," said Otto, "We had better not be late." A vast meal had been prepared by Mrs Gott, which was served by the servants for the three boys, the king and the queen. The king began the meal with a speech "To celebrate our son's twelfth birthday we originally planned a big party, but Otto decided that he had too many social events this year and wanted just his two best friends to join us for dinner. So, thank you George and Sebastian for coming today, and it just remains for me to wish my dear boy a very Happy Birthday."

Everyone raised their glasses and said "Happy Birthday Otto." The meal began with chicken soup and bread. This was followed by chicken, potatoes and cabbage. A desert of ice cream was prepared for the boys. Once they had eaten as much as they could, a birthday cake that was almost half the size of Otto was brought to the table. The king helped the boys demolish a big chunk of it.

"Time for the presents," said the queen as she caught her husband looking at the cake again. "Open this one, you might find it useful," said the king as he and one of the footmen carried a long heavy present for Otto that was wrapped in red paper. "Wow" said Otto as he unwrapped the present "This is one amazing set of skis."

"I wonder whether he will be any safer on skis than he is on a sledge?" George whispered to Sebastian.

"I doubt it" replied Sebastian.

The boys went to Otto's room to talk after dinner. Soon the queen came in. There was lots of grinning and giggling from two of the

three boys, "What is so funny George?" Asked the queen.
"We were just talking about the snowman."

The queen did not look amused, "It is very late. Sebastian and George. Your parents will be getting worried about you." Soon Sebastian and George were both sat in a carriage drawn by four black horses, waving to Otto and beginning their journey back home. The king came to say goodbye to the boys.

Once George and Sebastian had begun their journey Otto decided to talk to his father about about the stiff looking English tutor.
"Father do I really need to have another tutor?"
"Of course you do."
"But you, mother and Mrs Haase from the village have been teaching me since the last tutor left."
"Yes," replied the king, "but we can only teach you the bare foundations of an education. A good prince needs to understand the world. Higginbottom is an excellent tutor, he comes very highly recommended and he will teach you many wonderful things. One day you will be king and you need to be able to control complicated and difficult situations, you need to know about politics and particularly history."
"But history is so dull," protested Otto.
"Dull it may be, but history is important for a new king because, without an understanding of the mistakes of the past there is a very good chance that you will end up repeating them."
"But," the prince continued to protest, "you know that I am clever and I can just learn my history and politics when I need it."

The king had a warm smile "My son, you will not have time to learn when you need to. Let me give you an example. Two years ago I borrowed a sum of money from a man called Mr Ivan Stark. The Bavarian economy and the castle desperately needed money. Mr Stark had agreed to lend the money for at least five years but Mr Stark knew exactly the moment to ask for his money back, just when I had invested the money for a long while and could not repay it. Mr Stark is coming to the castle tomorrow, on a Saturday of all days; do you have any idea what I should tell him?"

Otto looked very surprised. "I had no idea that you were in trouble father. I really don't know what to suggest."
"Well, that makes two of us. I have no idea either. Stark will demand something other than his money, lets just hope that he doesn't want this castle or we will all have to find somewhere else to live," said the king with a smile.
"You seem to be taking this well father, are you sure it will be all right?" Asked Otto.
"Of course," replied the king, "I am sure that Stark is a reasonable man at heart, and we can find a reasonable solution."
"So that just leaves one problem, what about this English tutor?" Asked Otto.
"Well," said the king, "you had better get yourself well rested. Your lessons start at eight o'clock on Monday morning."

Chapter 2
Trouble Arrives

The next day was Saturday and the sun shone on the yellow stone walls of the castle and the red brick turrets stood out from the blanket of white snow. The castle nestled near to a big clear lake, that was frozen for half of the year. In the distance there was a huge white mountain range.

At precisely two o'clock Mr Stark arrived to see the king, who had been waiting nervously. Mr Stark arrived dressed completely in black and stepped out of his dark carriage, passed his top hat to the butler and was shown to the king's study.

Very soon a huge argument developed between Mr Stark and the king. The king raised his voice to a level not heard since the butler dropped a dish on the king's foot five years ago. All the servants heard the king's words echo through the castle... "I will NOT sell it... under no circumstances ... HOW DARE YOU."

Mr Stark replied, "very well ... you leave me no choice ... I will have to foreclose on the loan."
"All right," snapped the king, "... I see I have no other way out of this ... but you will have no further hold on the kingdom."
"Of course" replied Mr Stark with a cold smile, "I have no problem with that."

Mr Stark stayed for little more than ten minutes and left the castle in the same quiet and sinister way that he had arrived. He showed no emotion in his face as he walked past Otto in the hallway. He got into his carriage and the four white horses pulled the dark carriage away from the castle, along the gravel driveway and towards the open road. The queen and Otto went to the king's study and found the king in a very different state to Mr Stark's calm appearance. The king had a red face and sweat dripping from his brow, "That evil man made me sign away the navigation rights to all the rivers in the kingdom to repay a five year loan that we had agreed two years ago." Otto had never seen his father look so angry.

"Father, I promise I will find a way to help you," said Otto.

The king replied "there is no way to help. We just have to accept what that evil man has done to us."

*****

There was worse to come for Otto on Monday. Mr Higginbottom began his the day with a hoarse voice "Welcome to your first history class with me, your royal highness."

It was precisely eight o'clock and the classroom was set out just like any other school room, except that there was just one desk. Otto had a wooden desk with a lid that lifted so that he could store some of his writing books, he had book shelves around the room with text books and there was a big blackboard at the end of the classroom which Higginbottom wrote on as he spoke, "do pay attention, your royal highness, you will have some work to do this evening on this subject".

In fact Otto was given work to do in the evening on every subject that day: History, Politics, Maths and Science. He was given so much work that he couldn't get to bed until eleven o'clock.

The next morning Higginbottom arrived with a very bad cold. His nose was red and he coughed and sneezed all day and sounded terribly unwell. The morning lessons were punctuated with Higginbottom's nose being blown.

"Maybe you should take the afternoon off to recover," said Otto helpfully.

"I don't ... achoo... need time off I just need you to do your ... achoo ... work."

"Please Mr Higginbottom, on the subject of work," Otto tried asking as politely as he could, "I would like to have a little less homework."

"We would all like a little less of something," replied Higginbottom. "I would like to have had a less stressful and more relaxing afternoon when I arrived here... achoo ... without fear of being killed. I would like to have a little less of this cold which undoubtedly came from being covered in a thick blanket of ice and snow three days ago. so you ... achoo ... you *can not* have a little less homework, I will not allow it."

There was a knock at the door. "Come in" said Higginbottom. A young girl with long blond hair and a calm looking face came into the classroom and spoke to Higginbottom in a quiet voice. "Excuse me for interrupting your lesson. My name is Katarina and I was told that you needed a tonic to get your cold better." Katarina handed Higginbottom a cup of dark brown liquid.
"I am ... achoo ... fine," replied Higginbottom, looking distrustfully at the contents of the cup, "I don't need anything."
"Yes you do!" Said Katarina in a firm tone. "Look at you. You have a white face, a red nose and puffy eyes. You need to get your cold better quickly before you get really ill."
"Who are you?" Asked Higginbottom, "I don't remember meeting you before."
"My father is doctor Fabian and I help my father by using herbs to get people well."
"You seem very young to be an expert on herbs." Said Higginbottom, still with a suspicious tone.
"Well, I am not an expert. I am only twelve, but my father has been teaching me about herbs for six years."

"Katarina may be young but she does a splendid job," said the queen as she entered the classroom. The queen continued, "Katarina sorted out the king's bad knee last month and he can walk on it perfectly now."

Higginbottom looked like he no longer had the energy to argue. He sniffed at the thick solution in the cup. "What is in this?" He asked.
Katarina quickly replied, "It is a combination of herbs that will get your strength back and calm down your swelling."
"Drink it" said the queen impatiently, "it will get you better."

Higginbottom drank a mouthful, and immediately an expression of disgust came to his face, the tonic must have tasted absolutely terrible. Higginbottom had great difficulty swallowing his mouthful. Otto thought that this was very funny. When Higginbottom eventually swallowed the tonic his face relaxed.
"That tastes revolting," announced Higginbottom.
"Well all the best tonics do" said the queen. "Now drink up and you will be better by the afternoon." Higginbottom drank the remainder of his tonic, struggling to get each mouthful down due to the appalling taste. Once he had finished he handed his cup to Katarina and said, in a weak voice, "thank you, I do hope that this will make a difference."
"Oh it will" replied Katarina. "By this afternoon you will feel like a different person."

Sure enough, when the afternoon came Higginbottom looked much better. He was not sneezing as much and his face had more colour. "I must find out what was in that tonic," said Higginbottom. "If I get a cold again I will need some."

The days passed by and Higginbottom kept giving Otto hours of work each evening. Otto decided that the best plan was just to do as he was told and take his punishment, as his dad would say, "Like a man." After all he really didn't have anyone but himself to blame for the situation. Otto was certainly making good progress with his studies and what was clear to him was that the regime of constant work was just as wearing for Higginbottom as it was for Otto. After two weeks Otto looked in much better shape than Higginbottom, who was now thinner and more white in his face. Otto tried everything he could think of to get to know Higginbottom and reduce his workload. He tried being nice to Higginbottom and helping him set up and clear things away after the day's tuition. Otto tried to talk to Higginbottom about his family and where he grew up but none of this yielded anything that you could describe as a good working relationship. Higginbottom seemed to be a man on some particular mission. Quite what that mission was and whether this could benefit Otto was still unclear. What was certain was that this stand-off could not go on indefinitely, Otto was not the sort of person to live like this for very long, he had a good sense of right and wrong. Otto also could play practical jokes better than anyone else he knew, so if Higginbottom though that he would keep the upper hand with Otto for long, Higginbottom was going to be deeply mistaken.

Higginbottom was surprised by the speed that Otto could pick up new skills although he was also surprised that, for a prince, Otto did not seem to have very good social skills. Otto did not use his voice to great effect and was unwilling to make a lot of eye contact when he spoke to Higginbottom. Otto observed that Higginbottom was a proud man who thought he knew his place. He felt that he was above the servants, well below the king and queen and also below the many guests that visited the castle each week. It was easy to see when Higginbottom was in the presence of someone he thought was above him – he became a little bit wooden, with extended gestures and jerking movements from his arms. In Higginbottom's world Otto certainly fell into the 'well below me' category. When Higginbottom was with Otto he was a tough taskmaster who demanded results and there was no sign of the slightly 'wooden' Higginbottom anywhere at all.

Otto decided that his best chance of shocking Higginbottom out of this state of continual work was to show him that he should take Otto more seriously.

Otto's chance came late one Friday afternoon. A ball had been planned for Saturday at the castle in honour of a duke's wife's birthday. The duke's wife was not a very popular lady and so the king had invited everyone he could think of just to make up numbers. Higginbottom was very pleased with an invitation to this party and he spent some of the time while Otto was working on his maths problems, repairing an evening suit jacket which had a few hanging threads. Otto knew that the evening would include lots of eating and dancing. Otto also knew the band who were going to play always rounded the evening off with a lot of Hungarian music.

That Friday Otto had been left alone in the classroom while Higginbottom went to talk to the queen. The queen always like to talk about Otto's progress and Otto knew that he had a good five minutes before his tutor returned. Otto could see the black suit that Higginbottom would wear to the ball hanging in the corner of the classroom along with some black thread, a needle and a pair of scissors. Otto couldn't pass this opportunity by. He took the scissors and cut out three sides of an oblong on each side of the back of Higginbottom's trousers, leaving only the lowest section connected. He took the thread and sowed two very weak stitches to connect the top of the oblong section with the trousers. He quickly put back the thread, needle, scissors and trousers exactly as they had been placed on the hanger.

Otto finished his maths work and Higginbottom returned. Otto could hardly contain himself. He would occasionally grin during the remainder of the afternoon but always said that it was because of a very funny joke he had been told. Higginbottom didn't ask about the joke, he just got back to work. At five o'clock the day finished. Otto left the classroom and Higginbottom took his suit back to his room and hung it in his wardrobe.

On Saturday evening Otto was the first to come to the castle ballroom. The servants had lit all the candles on all the lights in the ballroom and the pictures on all the walls were illuminated with an even and gentle light. Otto was very disappointed that Higginbottom had not yet arrived. A few guests arrived slowly, and then suddenly Higginbottom joined them. As Higginbottom turned around Otto was overjoyed to see that the 'adjustments' to Higginbottom's trousers were still in place. Higginbottom had obviously not noticed that they had been adjusted when he put them on.
The evening got off to a good start. The guest of honour arrived and the meal began. After dinner the musicians began to play in

the castle ballroom ... it was going to be an unforgettable evening for everyone. Gentle waltzes began the evening's music and progressed to some sequence dances. As the night went on, the music became faster and soon things began to get interesting.

As the end of the evening approached the tempo increased and Otto was just hoping that Higginbottom would come back to the dance floor. For a while there was no sign of Higginbottom and Otto was starting to think that his plan was never going to work, but suddenly the last dance of the evening began and sure enough it was a Csárdás, a dance that starts very slowly and then builds up to a fast speed. The dance involves lots of kicking of the knees and feet. Otto grinned as he saw Higginbottom make his way towards the dancers.

Higginbottom thought of himself as an excellent dancer. Otto watched and watched, all the time thinking that he had probably made the threads too strong. Otto was about to give up hope when, during the last fling of the dance, Higginbottom's thread gave way and one side of the back of the trousers unrolled, this was quickly followed by the second. Otto could not believe his eyes, the top of Higginbottom's hairy legs were now on public display, accompanied by the bottom of his white underpants. For a few seconds no one noticed, then there was some mild laughter from the men and a couple of shrieks from the ladies. Higginbottom continued to dance, unaware that that he had suddenly become a public exhibit. As the music reached its peak Higginbottom got a tap on his shoulder and one of the noblemen whispered something in his ear, but the music was very loud "my ackside is uncovered?" Higginbottom repeated "what on earth is an ackside?"

"No, you fool" the gentleman said, "your BACKSIDE is uncovered." Higginbottom quickly put his hands down behind his legs and found that his trousers were indeed missing some important pieces. He turned bright red and, walking backwards like a spider that had lost its web, he swiftly made his way to the back of the ballroom and found a door to the hallway.

Higginbottom did notice one person in particular as he left. Out of all the gentlemen who were laughing gently there was one who was beside himself with laughter, to a point that he looked like he would soon need medical assistance, and that was Otto. The musicians had stopped playing due to a fit of the giggles. Higginbottom hoped that at least the king and queen would have been too busy to notice, but the final insult of the evening was dealt when, just as Higginbottom had stepped into the hallway, the last thing he heard from the ballroom was the king's deep voice, interrupted with bursts of laughter, "Higginbottom – you do need to get yourself a better tailor ... the queen does not wish to see that sight again."

"What an evening" said Higginbottom to himself as he made his way sadly back to his suite. "What an evening," said Otto with a broad grin, "I really am good at practical jokes." Otto turned around as he was about to leave the ballroom and a familiar girl appeared beside him, "poor Mr Higginbottom, whatever must have happened to his trousers," said Katarina in her soft gentle voice.

Otto replied in between giggles, "Higginbottom's trousers met with an accident involving a sharp pair of scissors and some very weak thread."

Katarina's voice was no longer soft or gentle "You did this?"

"Well ... yes. He deserved it. He has been awful to me ever since he arrived ... he finds every opportunity to load me up with work morning, noon and night and it is about time he had a bit of hardship."

"A bit of hardship!" replied Katarina in a severe tone. Her cheeks starting to glow red with anger at Otto's lack of any care or concern for his tutor. "From what I understand Higginbottom has put every bit of strength he has into teaching you. He works long hours and still marks your work in the evenings. How could you play such a cruel trick on poor Mr Higginbottom?"

"That was not not a cruel trick, that was just a bit of fun." Said Otto.

"Well, you may have had a bit of fun but how do you think Mr Higginbottom would have felt?" Otto was silent for a few seconds. "Well ..." He began.
"Well, what? The poor man will be feeling terrible. He was so embarrassed. You should go up to his room now and apologise." Said Katarina in an insistent tone.
"I will do no such thing. I am a prince and I don't take instructions from anyone."
"Well then, if you can live with your conscience after this, that is up to you. I will go and talk to the poor man myself and make sure that he is not planning to jump off the castle roof."
"Jump off the castle roof?" replied Otto "I really don't think that is Higginbottom's style."
Katarina was so angry with Otto that her face was red and she was shaking with rage. Despite the fact that Otto was a prince, and Katarina would probably be in all sorts of trouble later on for this, Katarina decided that she would tell Otto exactly how she felt "How would you know what is anyone's style? You treat your tutor appallingly and you leave the poor man on his own without a thought for his well-being. You seem to parade around this castle as though the world was just put here for your amusement. Well, other people have feelings you know. You may not care about them but some of us do."

Otto looked at Katarina with his mouth slightly open. Otto was completely lost for words. No one had ever spoken to him that way in his entire life, even a telling off from the king was usually more gentle than this. Katarina realised that she had probably said more than she should. Otto and Katarina moved uneasily away from one another, they turned looked at one another as if to say something, but no words were spoken. Otto went to his room and Katarina went to find Higginbottom. Once Katarina was out of earshot Otto shook his head and muttered to himself, "sometimes she is scary."

*****

Otto was beginning to forget about the weekend's excitement by

Monday morning as he sat at his school desk, rubbing his eyes and waiting for Higginbottom. Suddenly a red faced Higginbottom arrived and thrust the cut trousers in Otto's face bellowing "what is the meaning of this? You had access to the suit, the scissors and the thread. I know it was you. I saw you laughing at the end of the evening. You might just as well admit it was you or else ..."

" Or else what?" said Otto defiantly, "or else you will give me piles of work, tons of your stiff English attitude and little time to rest ... oh no you can't, because you have already done that".

"I will do worse than that. I will send you to your father."

"Good, then I will tell him how you have treated me these past two months and you will be looking for a new job by the end of the week."

"You insolent brat. I came here to help you and I am treated like a servant by you and like a manual worker by your father who refuses to accommodate my wife."

"You have a wife?"

"Yes," said a slightly calmer Higginbottom, "I have a wife who is living alone in England waiting to come to Bavaria and live with me."

"But that is terrible why is my father not letting your wife join you, you have a big enough suite in the castle?"

"I have no idea" sighed Higginbottom, "it was promised in my letter of employment, but every time I ask, the king refuses to discuss it."

"Well that is appalling, leave this with me." Otto replied.

"But what about my trousers" Higginbottom mumbled as Otto left the room.

"I will order you some new ones" shouted Otto from the corridor.

Otto was gone for no more than five minutes and he returned with a big smile, "he said that she can come and live here."

"Who said that who can come and live where?" Asked Higginbottom looking confused.

"The king said that your wife can come and live here in the castle with you," explained Otto clearly.

"How did you manage that? What did you say? I have been asking him to change his mind for months now – why did the king suddenly have a change of heart, and why would you do that for me?" Asked Higginbottom.

"Never mind about that, let's get on with the lessons. The sooner we start the sooner we finish," said Otto.

Higginbottom tried all day to get Otto to tell him what he had said and done to change the king's mind in an instant, but by the end of the day Higginbottom was still no wiser. By five o'clock Higginbottom finished his last lesson and gave Otto his usual Monday evening homework of English, maths, Latin and geography. There was still no let up in the homework schedule, but Otto had a feeling that help would soon be at hand. A contented tutor might be less willing to inflict hardship on a pupil, but on the other hand there had been no sign of Higginbottom softening so far, why should he change in the future?

"Just look at the amazing stitching on these trousers, and they match my jacket perfectly" said Higginbottom on Friday morning when Otto presented him with his new trousers.

"They really are fantastic" continued Higginbottom "you wouldn't be trying to get me to ease back on the homework would you?"

"The thought never entered my head," said Otto as he tried to make sure his face didn't give the game away, "what happened to your trousers was my fault and so I owe you a good pair of trousers."

"Well thank you, these are much appreciated."

"You are welcome," replied Otto. The day passed by just like any other Friday with a full day of lessons. Classes finished as usual at five o'clock and Otto went to his room to rest for a few minutes before he got changed and went downstairs.

Chapter 3
The Lady Who Lives in the Woods

It was April and the warm spring sun had finally returned to Bavaria. Otto had a big day planned on Saturday. He asked Mrs Gott to make a big packed lunch with all of his favourite sandwiches and enough food for three very hungry boys. The three boys were of course Sebastian, George and Otto who had planned a big adventure, they were going to walk to the other side of Deep Wood and see what was there.

The Deep Wood was more like a forest, it was about eight kilometres long and three kilometres wide. When the boys set out early on Saturday morning it was very cold, they wore big coats, hats and gloves. They walked for five kilometres before they stopped for an early lunch, by this time each boy had got warm enough to take off his hat, coat and gloves.

They had reached a big clearing and dark pond near to the other side of the Deep Wood. The boys unfolded their picnic blanket and sat down to eat – very little conversation took place while the three boys ate. They were much too tired to say anything, other than to utter the odd satisfied grunt when they came across a sandwich that really hit the spot. Once the food had been eaten and everyone had rested Otto looked up and said, "that's the way we should go now" pointing to a path beside a stream that flowed into the dark pond. The path led to a particularly dense part of the wood.
"It is a bit dark in there" said George as he looked at the path.
"I thought that we wanted adventure" Otto said with a grin, "all we have done so far is to walk."
"There is no harm in taking a look along that path" Sebastian replied "if we don't like what is there we will just come back here again."
"Have you any idea what is there?" Asked George timidly.
"No idea at all. That is part of the adventure," Otto replied as he

collected his food bag, "are we ready?"

Otto was in front and he suddenly stopped "This is amazing – don't you think George?"
"I don't know – I would much rather we went somewhere where there was sunlight – it is like night in here."
"But look at the trees, they are huge and have amazing branches that just go up and up" Otto replied "what do you think Sebastian?"
"I have never seen anything like this in my life" Sebastian replied as he put on his coat and hat. Otto and George also put their coats and hats on. It really was cold in that part of the wood.

The three boys kept to the path, and seemed to be more worried by each bird or small animal that they met. Finally George had had enough "I want to go back to the pond, there is nothing to see in here except darkness and trees." Otto was not so sure "let's just go around that bend in the path and see what is there. I can smell something different in here." As they got to the bend they could all smell a fire and after another bend in the path they could see that the fire was coming from an old cottage that was situated in a small clearing beside the path. George could not contain himself any longer "let's go back before whoever, or whatever, lives in that place eats us all for dinner."

Otto wanted to take a closer look, but this was too much even for Sebastian "if you go any closer to that house you are on your own. There is one thing for certain, anybody who lives this far away from civilisation does not like company."
"That's fine" Otto replied "you go back to the clearing and I will meet you in a few minutes."

George and Sebastian pretended to walk away but they knew that they couldn't leave their best friend somewhere where he could be eaten by a monster or have something worse happen to him. They followed the path until they got to a bend, then they hid behind a big fir tree and watched as Otto approached the house.

"HELLO" Otto said, George and Sebastian held their breath. "HELLO" Otto shouted "is anyone there." Suddenly a small wooden door creaked open and even Otto wanted to run away. A short lady appeared with long white hair that was untidy. She was wearing an old blue coat and a grey skirt. "Why are you disturbing my peace and quiet?"
"I just wanted to know who lives here ... I'm Otto, I live at the castle."
The old lady's face changed to a gentle smile. "Your Royal Highness, I'm sorry, I didn't recognise you. My name is Fiona and I am a member of your family."
"You are?"
"Yes. My father was a duke and he owned a wonderful big house not far from here ... would you like to come in? I have a warm fire. It is very cold out there."
Otto replied, "would you mind if a couple of my friends joined me – they were too frightened to come to your door?"
"Please do bring them in your Royal Highness."
Otto smiled at the gentle old lady and said, "Please don't worry about the 'royal highness' stuff, you are my family and they are my friends. Everyone just calls me Otto."

Otto whistled and waved, he couldn't see his friends but he knew that they would be somewhere nearby. Sure enough the two boys walked timidly towards the cottage. Once they arrived outside the cottage Otto said "Boys, let me introduce you, this if Fiona, she is a duchess. Fiona, meet my best friends in the entire world George and Sebastian."
Fiona looked very pleased with her unexpected guests "Pleased to meet you boys. Do come in and have coffee."

Inside the cottage they found a very neat and tidy house. There was a small kitchen with a stove and fire at one end, at the other end of the cottage there were some chairs and a table. Fiona brought the chairs into the kitchen area so that the boys could sit beside the fire. Once they had drunk their coffee and eaten some cake Otto asked the question that he had been itching to ask ever since he learned that Fiona was a duke's daughter.

"What happened to your father, the duke?"
Fiona looked very sad "He was robbed. Not by a highwayman or a common thief. My father was robbed by a very clever and evil man who now seems to want to own most of Europe. You are all young, you don't want to hear about old history."
Otto looked curiously at Fiona "My father keeps telling me how important history is. I would very much like to know what happened."
"Please tell us" said Sebastian.
"Very well then, I will tell you. But I warn you this is not a story that is going to bring you any joy at all."

Fiona smiled when she talked about her childhood. "I grew up in a huge house – I always called it the palace. Every day I would thank God that I lived in this wonderful place with the two people I loved most, my mum and dad. My dad was exceptionally kind to everyone around us, he was deeply religious and he always told me that I should love God more than anything else. My dad looked after the servants well, the lords all looked up to him as an example of kindness and goodness and everyone who visited our home always left saying to me "you have such a kind father." Those were good times. We lived our lives according to the seasons, joining the community harvest festival, I helped the poor at Christmas and my mother gave so much help to people who were suffering. We often had people staying in our house when they had nowhere else to live."

"When I grew up my parents always wanted me to marry well. They had chosen a boy called Philip, the son of a lord. Philip was great company and good fun, but on my sixteenth birthday someone else joined the party who was one of the fastest man on horseback in the kingdom. He could hunt, shoot and drive his carriage better than anyone else. I begged my parents for two years to let me marry him. When I was eighteen we were engaged and we married almost twenty years ago on my nineteenth birthday." The boys looked shocked that the lady with grey hair could be so young. Seeing their faces Fiona said "I don't really look like I am 39 years old do I?" No one answered.

"Where is your husband now?" Sebastian asked to break the silence.
"I have no idea. All the time that we were engaged he was setting up one business venture after another. My father was involved in most of them, and my father never checked what he was getting himself involved in. My father trusted the people around him, particularly his future son-in-law, and father wanted everything to be fantastic for me. After the wedding my husband started travelling a lot. He was always away on business in Vienna or Prague. People kept coming to our house complaining about a business that didn't work or money being lost. We had no way of knowing what was going on and when we tried to sort things out my husband just refused to discuss these things.

All the tension started to make my parents ill. My father had been so well and young when I was married. I don't remember him being ill in my life, but just two years after the wedding he looked like an old man. He was only 48 years old, he already had white hair. His skin was dry and old and he was often so unwell that he had to stay in bed for many days. One of the last things that dad said to me was how much he enjoyed being in his bed because he couldn't hear the people coming to the house asking about their lost money or their businesses. Dad died when he was 51. That was terrible for my mother and me, but there was much worse to come.

My husband inherited all the money and the land and he ordered a vicious reorganisation of the estate when he took it over. Many servants lost their jobs and many farmers lost their homes but my husband didn't care. My mother took in every one of the people who lost their homes, and soon our house was full of people. My mother had also aged and got ill. Within two years of dad's death my mum was frail and unwell. Her last words to me were "I am so sorry I have no more strength left. I don't want to leave you in this place – run away now." Even in her last minutes she was absolutely correct. I thought that by helping the people who were living in our house I would somehow forget about all the hardship but this was not the end of the story. My husband had used our house to guarantee loans he had made. He had not repaid the loans and the house was sold just six months after my mum died."

Otto looked surprised "Could the king not have stopped this?"
"I asked your granddad, who was king at the time, for help. He couldn't help me because the debt was a legal debt that my husband was allowed to have. Creditors needed to be able to get their money back and the king could not show one rule for a duke's daughter and one for everyone else in the kingdom."

There was a silence while Fiona dried her eyes. "How did you end up in this cottage?" Asked Sebastian.
"I ran away from the house and took anything that I could carry with me. When I had no more energy to run I walked and as I was walking along the path through the woods the old lady that lived in this cottage said that I could stay here. She was very kind and looked after me so well. I was delighted not to have anyone coming to the house asking about debts or money."
"What about your husband?" Asked Otto curiously.
"I have no idea where he is. That man just wanted daddy's money and he didn't care what he had to do to get it. I am a Christian and I can't wish any harm on anyone, but this man that I once trusted, I can now truthfully say that I really don't care whether he is alive or dead."
"What was your husband's name?" Asked Otto.
"Ivan Stark," replied Fiona. Otto felt a chill in his spine "not the Mr Stark that is buying up the kingdom's waterways and holding us to ransom over them?"
Fiona turned quickly to Otto "I don't know – what does he look like?"
"A tall thin man who always wears black."

"He certainly has always worn black, and for good reason. It is a dark day when he comes to visit you. If this is my husband, be very careful. He has no compassion at all. He will take everything he can from you and leave you with nothing. I would not be surprised if he managed to rob a king. He has certainly done this for a duke, and reduced his family to beggars."

George looked out of the window, "its getting a bit dark, shouldn't we start walking home now or we will have to get through the woods in pitch black without a lantern."
"Good point, lets go" said Otto. He turned to Fiona "It was lovely to meet you. Thank you for the coffee and cake. Would you like to come to the castle at some time?"
Fiona hesitated. It had been a very long time since she had been part of any social event. On the other hand Otto looked like a wonderful and kind young man. Fiona smiled as she replied "I would love to come and see you and your family." Fiona waved to the boys as they left "see you again soon" she said.

The boys made their way back through the woods and arrived at the castle just before it was completely dark, George and Sebastian stayed at the castle for dinner that evening.

They were about to go through to the dining room when a tall and slim lady entered the drawing room wearing a very smooth blue dress, the king announced "we have a new guest joining us at the castle. Welcome to Amelia Higginbottom", Higginbottom's wife had finally arrived from England. Otto was the first to shake her hand and welcome her to the castle. "It is a great pleasure to meet you Otto, Michael has told me a lot about you."
Otto looked puzzled "Who is Michael?"
"Michael is Mr Higginbottom" said the king with a grin.
Mrs Higginbottom smiled "I keep forgetting that students always have to call him Mr Higginbottom … but Mr Higginbottom does make him sound like he is a hundred years old."
"Have you seen very much of Bavaria from the carriage on your journey?" asked Otto.

"Not very much, I was very tired during the last day of my journey and I slept for much of the day. The castle and the lake certainly look amazing."

Otto pointed to a big map on the castle wall "you really must see the island in the lake – it is beautiful. You and Mr Higginbottom could borrow my boat and go and see it tomorrow."

Mrs Higginbottom replied "I would like that, are you sure you don't need the boat?"

"Not tomorrow – I still have lots of work to finish for Monday."

"Are you working him too hard?" The new guest asked her husband.

"No" replied Mr Higginbottom, but they could both see Otto nodding.

Amelia looked sympathetic "Michael is a tough taskmaster."

Otto nodded "I know."

"Higgie – give the poor lad a day off so that he can show us the island tomorrow." Mr Higginbottom sighed "all right – no homework for tomorrow."

Otto was overjoyed "Thank you" he replied and thought to himself. 'Higgie', I really must remember that.

Amelia looked at Otto "Would you be happy to show us the island tomorrow?"

Otto smiled "Yes, of course."

*****

The three of them set off early in the morning in Otto's rowing boat with a picnic packed by Mrs Gott. Otto was very strong and was used to rowing to the island with the king and queen. It usually took half an hour to row to the island, but with Otto on one oar and Mr Higginbottom on the other the two of them made the journey in just over twenty minutes.

They tied the boat up to the small jetty on the island. The island had sandy beaches in all directions that led down to the water, there was a grassy area that was perfect for picnics and then a large wooded area. In total the island was about 2km long and half a kilometre wide. "What a beautiful island" said Mrs Higginbottom "I can see why you love to come here. What is that little wooden house?"

Otto replied, "It is said that this was once home to a king who went mad for a few months. His son ruled the country and kept the old king here on the island where he was most content. The king was brought a daily delivery of food and water, and as soon as he was well enough the king was taken off the island. They say that after a few months the king made a full recovery and was very soon ruling the kingdom again."

Mrs Higginbottom was very surprised. "It must have been very lonely to live here for many months."

Otto replied "It is said that crowds of people upset the king. Once he was brought here he became much calmer."

The Higginbottoms had a wonderful morning on the island with Otto. They had brought some tennis rackets and a croquet set. It turned out that both Otto and Mr Higginbottom loved sport and they both loved to win. Otto had become a strong tennis player but he was no match for the power of Mr Higginbottom's serve. A few points were deliberately lost by Higginbottom when Amelia was looking, when she was not, he went back to an Otto demolishing game through the sheer power of his serve.

When it came to croquet Otto was the superior player and he won both games, easily working out how to get an advantage from the uneven surface that was last mowed when the castle gardener visited the island three weeks before.

Once the games had been played it was time for lunch. Otto was very curious about Amelia. "What did you do before you became a tutor's wife?"

"I studied history and was a teacher. I taught Queen Victoria's children in England."

"Did Mr Higginbottom also teach the queen's children?"

"No he was tutor to Viscount Hill's children in England, you are the first prince he has tutored."

"He says he is so delighted to travel in this job as Viscount Hill never travelled beyond the shores of England. Some say that is because Viscount Hill loved England so much he refused to leave it, other say that it is because Viscount Hill gets terribly sea sick!"

"What do you enjoy about history?" Asked Otto curiously.
Mrs Higginbottom replied "I like the way that society adapts to whatever comes along, in England we have adapted to domination – the rule of the Romans, we adapted to freedom and self rule. I also admire people for being able to invent amazing new things. Take paper for example, the new ways we have of making paper. Now our paper is so much whiter and clearer than it ever was."

Otto was enthralled "I like inventions too. Tell me, is Bavaria really lagging behind Europe?"

Mrs Higginbottom didn't really know how to answer this question. "There is still a lot of Europe that makes its living from farming. Gradually countries gain industry and people stop working as much on the land, people move to towns and cities and work in factories. England has more of this, but I don't think that Bavaria is behind the rest of Europe."

Chapter 4
Full Steam Ahead

The early morning sunlight streamed into Otto's classroom. The day's lessons started with English, German and Latin. Higginbottom was in full command of the lessons he had planned and Otto answered his questions faultlessly. Higginbottom smiled "I think that you are making fine progress your royal highness." It was unusual to get praise from Higginbottom.
"I am just doing what I usually do."
"But you are doing it very well. You have answered all my questions perfectly today and we are now making good progress with your work, so I have decided that there will be no work for you this evening." Otto thought that Higginbottom had really changed his ways. A few weeks ago Otto was loaded up with work for the evenings and for Saturday and part of Sunday, Otto was lectured day in and day out by Higginbottom without a single word of praise. What could have affected this transformation he thought?

Higginbottom announced "Tomorrow the king has asked that we both go to the touring industrial exhibition that is coming to Füssen and that you open the event in his place, how good are you at making a speech?"
"The exhibition could be a lot of fun, but a speech ... I have never made a speech before in my life ... what should I say?"
"You need to welcome everyone to the event, thank the organisers and say how pleased you and the king are that the exhibition could come to our local town. It is quite straightforward."
"It may be straightforward for you, but I am just a young boy, why should anyone listen to me?"
"They will all listen to you if you have something good to say. You are a wise and kind young man, and you are also their prince, so they have to listen to you!" Higginbottom had really changed ... a wise and kind young man ... Otto knew he had to

find out what was going on. "Is everything all right Mr Higginbottom?"

"What a strange question. Yes, everything is fine."

"You are not diagnosed with some strange and incurable disease?"

Higginbottom looked uneasily at Otto. "Why are you asking such questions?"

"You just seem, well, different."

"Oh do I" said Higginbottom with a grin. "Excellent. I am not unwell, nor am I at death's door. Now that we have cleared that up we need to get back to thinking about tomorrow – what are you going to say?"

Otto shrugged his shoulders, "I really have no idea."

"You need to have something. You will welcome a group of people to the exhibition; they will expect their prince to be kind and charming."

Otto was worried by this public appearance. It was one thing to stand next to his father and look smart, but quite another to be delivering a speech. Otto decided to write his speech while he was eating lunch so that he could memorise it later. It was more comfortable to know exactly what he planned to say. He wrote one draft after another and finally settled on a version that he could talk Higginbottom though. Higginbottom cancelled the first class of the afternoon so that they could work on the speech. He found Otto a chair that he could stand on and Higginbottom stood at the back of the classroom.

"Pretend that this room is full of people. You will need to raise your voice and speak slowly and clearly."

Otto began at full speed "Ladies and Gentlemen, welcome."

"STOP!" shouted Higginbottom "That was too fast and you are looking at your notes and not looking at the people."

Otto began again more slowly "Ladies and Gentlemen, welcome...."

Higginbottom interrupted. "That was better but it needs to be much louder."

Otto tried to get his voice to be louder but it sounded more like shouting than talking.

Higginbottom tried to encourage him "I can see we have some work to do here."

"Why don't we just get someone else to make the speech?" Said Otto sadly.

"Because you are a prince and you need to be able to talk to a crowd. Let's work on some exercises to build your voice up."

Higginbottom found the ideal phrase to build up Otto's confidence. "Try reciting this as you breathe out 'I am your prince and you need to listen to me'." Otto recited this over and over as he went through the breathing exercises and very soon his young voice was a little bit deeper and had lots of rich colour in it.

"Good" said Higginbottom, you are developing your voice. Now let's try with the speech. Put the paper down, stand on your chair and repeat slowly 'I am your prince and you need to listen to me' and then go straight into your speech." Suddenly Otto's voice sounded confident and sincere, it was a rich loud voice that could be heard well. There were still a few lines that needed polishing but Higginbottom knew that this was more like the voice of a leader. Higginbottom was delighted "What a difference. That was so clear and so well delivered, the king will be very proud of you." They worked on the speech for the rest of the afternoon and Higginbottom made sure that Otto looked into people's eyes as he spoke. After a last couple of rehearsals the speech was ready and Otto was very confident to deliver it.

The next day the exhibition had drawn a huge crowd from far and wide. The town hall was full and people were standing in it to hear the speeches. The mayor welcomed the prince and then it was time for Otto's speech. Otto stood confidently on his chair in the middle of the crowd, smiled at Higginbottom and then began slowly and calmly with a voice that filled the room.

"Ladies and Gentlemen, welcome to this exhibition. This is a unique event for all of us and today we will see machines that have the power to change our future, in Fűssen, and in Bavaria. I am delighted to see so many of you here today and I am sure that you are looking forward to seeing these machines of the future. My father, the king, is sorry that he is not able to join you today. The king hopes that this event will be a great success, and it only remains for me to say a very sincere thank you to the mayor and the many people who have made this event possible. Ladies and Gentlemen, on behalf of the king, I am proud and delighted to declare this exhibition open." The applause that followed took Otto by surprise. The mayor shook Otto's hand and said "Excellent speech your royal highness." It then seemed as though everyone in the crowd wanted to meet Otto. Otto knew some of the local noblemen, others introduced themselves to him.

Suddenly Otto looked up and a familiar face was in front of him. "Katarina" Otto said nervously. Otto was not sure what to expect after Katarina had told him off so severely in their last meeting, he tried to think of something to say, all he could come up with was "I didn't know you were interested in machines of the future."
Katarina replied with a smile, "nor did I until I came here. My father wanted to see the exhibition."
"What do you think about it?" Otto enquired.
"Well," said Katarina, "I like the idea that machines can save people doing heavy or boring work but I think that most people don't want these machines, so this is exhibition is important to help people understand what Bavaria is doing."
Otto was surprised by her reply "Why don't people want them?"
"Because they think that if a machine does a man's job then it is taking the job away from the man, and so they think that ordinary people will not have work and will be hungry. But that is not true. These machines will help Bavaria do more work and become wealthier – don't you agree?" Katarina said.
Otto quickly replied "Yes, of course that is how it works. But how can anyone be foolish enough to think otherwise?"
Katarina started to get red cheeks. She was getting annoyed with Otto again. "Because, your royal highness, they have not had the privilege or the time for an education. Things may be obvious to

you, with your full time tutor ... but the rest of us just manage with whatever education we can get. And you don't even seem to feel any gratitude towards the people who provide your education."

Now Otto was getting annoyed. "We are not talking about that again are we? It was one evening and one pair of Higginbottom's trousers. I bought him some new ones and I have helped him bring his wife here – what more can I do for the man?"

"You should make him feel comfortable and valued," replied Katarina.

Otto looked blankly at Katarina.

"Well, you could start by just saying thank you for his help. I think that you are very good at making speeches but I think that a prince needs more than this. Any good leader needs passion and a love of the people around them and a love of what they are doing.

Otto again looked blankly at Katarina, "I ...I do love this country. Every prince loves their country. Father always tells me that this is important."

Katarina replied, "But, what is it that you love about this country and want more of here? Find that and you will find your passion."

The mayor interrupted the conversation. "Your royal highness, please could you join me?" Otto introduced the mayor to Katarina and then apologised that they had to leave.

Otto walked around the exhibition with the mayor. There were a few models of static machines in the town hall and the town square was full of engines that had their fires lit and were running big machines from a factory. There was a railway engine from England, a small factory engine that had been made as a demonstration engine in Munich and there was also an English steam powered car. After his initial tour Otto went for lunch with Higginbottom, the mayor and a few of the noblemen.

"I am amazed by what I have seen so far," said Otto, "machines that can do the work of so many men, machines that can transport us at high speed across countries, maybe even continents. I think this is an amazing time in our history and I think that Bavaria must play a part in this revolution."

The mayor looked admiringly at Otto "Well said your royal highness." But among the noblemen a few were less welcoming. Sebastian's father was amongst those that did not like what was happening. "You talk about these machines as progress, but when people move from the villages and towns into the cities to work in the new factories, no one will be left to work on my fields." Most of the other noblemen nodded.

Otto quickly responded "Barron von Staig, we can all share in this industrial future. Look at the steam powered car, imagine that this replaced your carriage. You don't then need your groom and stable hand, you could even drive the car yourself and then the labour of three men has been saved by just one machine."

Von Staig replied "What will happen when that machine breaks down, I will still need a man to repair it?"

Otto smiled. "But that will not happen very often and the repairer can be shared by everyone who owns a car. We haven't even mentioned machines that can help with farming. Imagine if your crops could be planted and harvested by machine – on your estate you would save the work of hundreds of men."

Von Staig decided to be mischievous. "If you can show me one of those steam powered contraptions that will climb my apple trees and harvest the apples I will gladly eat my hat, but until then I say that these machines should not be welcomed to Bavaria." Looking at the other noblemen, he said "the machines could mean that we will all be forced away from the land that we have farmed for centuries, and we will not stand for it no matter how much you and the king want to be left alone to farm your own land with just some fancy apple picking machine as your labourer." The other noblemen were looking very red and nodding at every sentence. Higginbottom thought that it was time to do something. He could see Otto was itching to counter Barron von Staig and the other noblemen. "Gentlemen" Higginbottom began "I believe that this year is particularly warm and that the farmers have managed to get their spring crops in early. Is that right?"

"Oh yes, it promises to be a year of magnificent yields" said Barron von Staig. All of the redness had gone from his face and he talked with pride about how some of his farmers had managed their land particularly well and, despite their land having drainage problems, some of his farmers achieved the best yield of crops in the entire district. Otto got bored with this line of conversation, he would dearly have liked to take on Barron von Staig and his old fashioned ideas, but every time the conversation headed in that direction Higginbottom cleverly changed the subject again.

After lunch Otto had a little time to walk with Higginbottom around the exhibition. As soon as they had moved away from the noblemen Otto asked "why would you not let me take on Barron von Staig. His attitudes are out dated and stupid."
Higginbottom replied. "He is a nobleman, an elder of this community and he is much older than you. While you out rank him socially you must be very careful to be seen in public to support the noblemen, however out-dated their attitudes are. If you do not support him in public he has the power to undermine you and therefore your father's power. Ultimately if the king and the noblemen have a big public disagreement it is likely that the king will no longer be able to govern the country."
Otto looked sceptical. "How is that possible? A king is a king. He rules a country for his lifetime."
Higginbottom smiled at Otto. "Remember your history? A king will always be a king in an entirely autocratic country when the king simply tells everyone what to do and the army makes sure that the king's orders are obeyed. We no longer live in those times. If you want to remain as a king you will have to govern with the consent of the people because, once thousands of people no longer want you as their king, it will be impossible for you to stay."
Otto was genuinely surprised by Higginbottom's reply. "So you are saying that progress is not possible, we have to live with the backward attitudes of people like Barron von Staig and leave Bavaria unchanged, just farming its land just as it did in the

middle ages."

"No, you can take on Barron von Staig and anyone else, but you have to do it on your terms, in a way that they will follow you."

Otto looked confused. "What does that mean?"

Higginbottom explained. "If you got an expert to tell Barron von Staig that the rivers were about to swell and change course meaning that half of his farm land was going to be under water next month, Barron von Staig would be the first person in Bavaria to buy a steam pump."

Otto grinned. "So we need a clever lie?"

Higginbottom said calmly, "no, you need a clever truth, you can't continue with a lie for very long, but once people see that they have no choice then they soon will change."

Otto looked at his tutor in a very different way. Remembering what Katarina had said to him he said, "Higginbottom. Thank you for everything you are doing. You are such a fantastic tutor, some days I wonder what you are doing working here. You should be running a country yourself."

Higginbottom gently glowed with pride at the compliment and replied, "I like my work just as it is."

Otto spent the rest of the day at the exhibition and by five o'clock he and Higginbottom got into their carriage and began the journey home. Otto could hardly keep his eyes open, he was so tired from the day's activities. "Well done with your speech" said Higginbottom.

Otto yawned and said "I do think that they liked my speech, but it was a very long day just to open one exhibition don't you think?"

Higginbottom corrected Otto. "You didn't just open an exhibition: You played to a crowd. You have helped people to know a little more about the royal family and reassured them that you are a king in waiting. People now know that the royal family, and the country are in safe hands in the future."

"Did I do that?" Asked Otto.

"Certainly. This was a most important day."

Otto replied "Higginbottom, I couldn't have delivered that speech without you. Actually I am not sure I could have delivered any speech without you."

"What did you like most?" asked Higginbottom.

Otto replied. "The best thing for me was the railway engine, it was amazing. Just think, if we had one of those here we could be back at the castle within minutes, rather than spending an hour in a coach."

"You would need some track to put it on."

Otto said, "Yes, but once you have built your track then you can travel very quickly. Roads also need building so it doesn't seem to be much more difficult to put in a track than a road."

The next morning Otto waited in his classroom. Higginbottom arrived just a few moments after Otto. Higginbottom started the lesson with his usual enthusiasm "I have been thinking about that chat we had after you were talking to Barron von Staig. You have worked so hard at your lessons, why don't we spend just an hour or two a week talking about how you can work with lots of different people, I think it might help you as a prince and a king."

Otto smiled. "I am happy to do that, but what will we do?"

"Lets start now and I will show you. We can take Barron von Staig as an example. How well do you know the baron?"

Otto replied "Not well, he is Sebastian's father but I very rarely have chance to talk to him."

Higginbottom asked, "If you needed to get to know him quickly what would you do?"

"Find something interesting to talk to him about."

Higginbottom said, "Pick a subject."

Otto replied "Fishing."

"Fishing? What do you know about fishing, and why do you think he will know anything at all."

Otto looked puzzled. "Well, it is something that people usually talk about isn't it?"

Higginbottom sighed "Only if they are interested. It is pointless having a conversation to build up trust with someone and talking about something that you, and probably he, are not interested in."

"What did von Staig mention when we talked to him that could be useful?"

Otto struggled for an answer, "that machines are bad for Bavaria."

"No. He mentioned that he was proud of the yield of crops his farmers had delivered. I would start by asking him about that. What happened to change this? How did they get that yield?"

"I see" said Otto who was clearly being enlightened by the conversation "so I should look for something that they are pleased about as a topic?"

Higginbottom continued wisely, "yes, this is a good starting point. What would you do next?"

"It depends what I want to achieve."

"You want von Staig to like you and work with you." Higginbottom said.

"Then I would ask him about his family and his work." Otto replied.

"That is good, so why would you do that?"

"Because that is probably also something he is proud of."

"Excellent." Replied Higginbottom "I think you are getting this."

"And when von Staig comes to you and says that he doesn't like your machines, what do you say?"

Otto grinned, "Well, I know what you did. You talked to him about the weather. A very English tradition I believe."

Higginbottom smiled. "It was one way of bringing him back to something that we could all agree on. What else is there that we can agree on?"

Otto thought deeply. "There are lots of things: The traditions of Bavaria, The need to maintain great farms and the rights of the noble men …"

Higginbottom looked very pleased. "You learn quickly, so there you are. Some ways of getting people to like you and talk to you."

It had been a long day of lessons and by five o'clock Otto really wanted to go and rest, but he couldn't rest though until he had asked Higginbottom for just one last bit of help.

"Higginbottom, I really do think that the engines we saw are the way of the future, but I understand why von Staig is scared of them. I would be scared as well if I couldn't see what they were capable of. You talked about winning von Staig over, but what should I do next?"

Higginbottom replied, "You would have to spend time with him and get him to realise that these machines will really help us. He would also have to feel that he couldn't continue as he is. It is as simple as that."

"That is all you need to do?" Asked Otto.

Higginbottom replied "Yes, but doing this is more difficult than it seems and it all boils down to one thing – how do you get someone to change?"

Otto looked blankly at Higginbottom. "I don't know."

"They have to want to change – it is the only way," replied Higginbottom.

Chapter 5: The Student Prince

It was a dull Monday morning in April and Otto looked strangely at Higginbottom. "Again you give me such simple exercises to do. This mathematical differentiation is as simple as the work you gave me last week on series, which was as simple as the work you gave me on complex numbers. Please can you find me something that is more challenging and fun?"

Higginbottom replied, "You need to have the basics of your education before you can move on"

"I have the basics – you can see that. Can't I have something a bit more difficult from time to time?" Otto asked.

A smile crept across Higginbottom's face "I can help you there. I have some mathematics papers from university – how would you like to have a go at those?"

"If I can borrow your text book to help me with the methods, I would love to."

Higginbottom left Otto with the papers for about half an hour. He came back expecting to find Otto confused and willing to go back to basics again. But Higginbottom was quite mistaken. Otto looked up, "I have a solution for questions one to five and a partial solution for questions six and eight."

"And what about question seven" said Higginbottom trying not to sound surprised.

"Ow that's obvious." Higginbottom checked Otto's working and could find little fault, some of his ways of getting to the answers could do with polishing but he was only twelve and this was a paper that nineteen year old university students struggled with. Higginbottom said, "all right, I can take a hint. You are really good at mathematics." Now it was Otto's turn to be surprised, this was the first time he had ever heard Higginbottom say that anyone was really good at anything. Higginbottom said "We can do a bit less mathematics in the future so that you can concentrate on your weaker subjects."

"I don't have any weak subjects," Otto said.

"Everyone has weaknesses. Maybe we should find out what they

are."
Otto was not happy with this approach. "That is surely a waste of time, you teach everything in the curriculum and I learn fast so I must be strong at everything ... unless, of course, you are weak at teaching it." We will see" said Higginbottom, ignoring the last part of Otto's sentence. "Lets test English, Geography and French today – I have some papers that we can use as exam papers in my study. I will set some tests tomorrow for Latin, German, Science and on Wednesday for Politics, Art and Music. I think this is a very good idea."

Otto warmed to the idea. He liked a good contest and he thought that there could be nothing in Higginbottom's tests that would be difficult for him. Otto completed the English, Geography and French tests by four o'clock and then he went to see Mrs Gott for an early supply of coffee and cakes while Higginbottom reviewed his work. When Otto returned to the classroom Higginbottom was delighted. "Amazing results, really amazing. Sometimes I am such a good teacher, I surprise myself."
"Anyone would think that you had taken the test" muttered Otto.
"What was that?"
"I was just saying that it was getting late and you should be taking a rest."
"Goodness, look at the time," said Higginbottom. "We need to stop for the day." There were times when Otto wondered just how good Higginbottom really was, but then Higginbottom suddenly would have an ability to see things from different perspectives that Otto hadn't thought of and so it was very difficult to tell whether Higginbottom was clever, lucky, or a combination of the two.

Higginbottom continued the testing of all subjects. He asked Otto to play to him on his chosen instruments, the piano and the flute. Otto played pieces he knew very well, he was good at sight reading music and he could pick up tunes by ear after listening to them a couple of times. "All good" said Higginbottom proudly at the end of the music tests. "It is clear that you are learning well but perhaps need stretching a little more."

The next set of tests was about physical endurance. Higginbottom knew that Otto loved outdoor sports and so he timed him running, swimming and rowing distances. For his age Otto did well in all his sports but Higginbottom knew that he could help Otto do much better in swimming. Higginbottom had swum very well when he was in England, and he had no problems in helping Otto to perfect his swimming style, getting him to think about the finish line and power himself forwards more carefully. Even after a few weeks of training Higginbottom could still beat Otto, but his lead was reducing. Otto started to learn that Higginbottom was really good at some things and he became very impressed that Higginbottom could swim with immense power, particularly as he was a thin man and didn't look like an athlete.

Finally, after a couple of weeks, Higginbottom had completed the testing and marking work, he gave Otto a puzzled look. "You have done well in many of your tests but you have some interesting gaps in your thinking. Your mathematics and languages are excellent. You can remember dates and times so the details of your history results are good, but there is something unusual. How can you remember all that knowledge and not be able to tell me how king Harold Hardrada felt as he went into battle with William, the Duke of Normandy – the man who would win the Battle of Hastings and become King William I of England. I am really surprised."
"I just don't pay much attention to feelings. Why would I?"
Higginbottom was more intrigued. "I see. So how does your father feel about being king?"
"He is content"
"Content. What in the world does that mean?" Said Higginbottom in a frustrated tone.
"It means that he is happy with his situation."
"You mean to tell me that every moment of every day he walks around 'contentedly'?" Higginbottom was getting more and more

impatient with Otto, for all the amazing things that he was and for all that he could remember and do, the world of emotions was like another dimension that Otto had not even begun to explore.

Higginbottom went back to something more straightforward, here is a very simple question for you, "How do you feel right now?"
"I ...I feel ...um ...er … content...happy with my situation... good."
"Content, good … just like your father?"
"Yes"
Higginbottom asked "Are you always content and good?"
"I don't know. Sometimes I am, sometimes I feel like I should feel something else." Replied Otto.
"Do you know how your friends feel?"
Otto replied, "They are always good – George and Sebastian never feel bad"
"Never?"
"No, I have never seen them feel bad"
Higginbottom was astonished. "So, how about one of your bad times? Tell me about how you felt when your grandfather died four years ago?"
"I felt alone."
"Did you not get on well with your grandfather?"
Otto stared at Higginbottom with a cold gaze. "I got on with him very well, he was an amazing man." Higginbottom had never met anyone who would not even say that they were sad when a close relative died.
Higginbottom could see that there was only one way of showing Otto what he was missing. "Let me tell you how I felt when my grandfather died: I was shocked, I couldn't feel anything for a few hours, part of me wanted my granddad just to be in the next room and I would even open his study door sometimes just hoping that he would still be there. Then I became very angry, so angry that I would cry, I was angry that this could happen to him, I was angry with myself that I didn't do more to help him and I was angry with God that he had not helped me more. I remember

feeling so angry and so empty at his funeral. The anger lasted many weeks and then I just became depressed and exhausted, I was too tired to be angry. I just wanted to be left alone. After a few months I would have a good day and then I would feel guilty for my granddad that I had not been sad. After many months there would be more good days and less bad days, I would still feel guilty, but less guilty than I did and the guilt would pass more quickly. Eventually, after many years the guilt has all but gone, the anger and the sadness have mostly gone and I can look at a picture of my grandfather and say, we had some amazing times together. I miss you and still love you every day and feel a bit sad for you just for a few moments, but I can accept that you have died."

Otto looked like someone had shone a bright light into his eyes.
"Thank you" he said.
"For what"
"For telling me about your grandfather"
"I wasn't telling you about my grandfather, I was telling you about how I felt"
"Yes, thank you for that," replied Otto.
"So, what kind of emotions do you think people have?"
"What do you mean?"
"How would you describe how people can feel, what words would you use?"
Otto again looked blankly at Higginbottom, "Um ...Happy....Sad"
"Any others?" Asked Higginbottom.
"You mentioned some... how about angry and depressed"
"Any others?"
"I don't know, I wish I knew more." Otto looked as though he had met his match on this subject.
Higginbottom had red cheeks and an exasperated expression on his face. He picked up the chalk and began to write on the board "Here is my list as a starting point he said – make sure you write them down: Happy, Sad, glad, surprise, anticipation, revolt. How would you use this list to help you in conversation?"
Poor Otto was really struggling, "I don't know."
"Find out how the other person is feeling, and then you can talk

about what really matters to them."

"Thank you Higginbottom, how are you feeling?" Asked Otto politely.

"Good question, I am feeling exhausted."

"Good." Replied Otto.

"What do you mean good? Is it good to feel exhausted?"

"It is after exercise." Higginbottom's face started to get even more red, he felt like Otto had landed from another galaxy.

"No, it is not good to feel exhausted just from having a conversation. Exhaustion is a sign that the conversation is not easy." Higginbottom had really found a blind spot for Otto, Otto was completely unaware of how he felt or how other people might be feeling. "Good feelings are happy or surprised, when people tell you about a good feeling then you can say something like 'I am glad you are happy, what is the reason for this?' when someone tells you about a bad feeling you could say 'I am sorry about that, why are you feeling sad?' If you start a conversation like this it is much more likely that people will talk to you about what matters to them. You will get people to talk honestly with you." This triggered something within Otto; it was as though a light had been turned on.

Otto replied, "thank you Higginbottom, This has been a really fascinating lesson. I am so grateful. You really are the best tutor ever Higginbottom."

Higginbottom smiled. "Thank you. I think I am going to give you very different homework today, perhaps even show you a very different world. Your homework is to pick as many of the list of emotions as possible in telling me tomorrow how you felt since I saw you this afternoon. You also need to find out how other people are feeling."

Otto seemed willing to have a go as he packed up his books and papers for the day. "I can do that homework, I know I can. Have a good night" Otto said as he left the classroom.

Otto went straight to the kitchen as always after his lessons. "Good evening" he said to the servants. "What's on the menu tonight?" He asked Mrs Gott.

"Beef stew and dumplings"

"It smells incredible, could I have a taste please?" Asked Otto.

"Just take a bit, we don't have very much to spare tonight and you need to save your appetite for later." Otto took a couple of ladles of the stew and filled a small bowl. He left it to cool and then started to think about his homework. "How do you feel?" He asked Mrs Gott.

"I'm exhausted," she replied, "I have been on my feet since six o'clock this morning and I am looking forward to dinner being served so that I can eat and have a rest. These days I live for my evenings. I have a drop of wine, only because the doctor recommends it, and I talk to some of the footmen for a little while. We share a story or two about the day or some gossip from the village and then I read a good book. That's my idea of a pleasant evening"

"I am sorry that you are so tired, it is good that you enjoy your evenings though. What do you enjoy about your work?"

"My goodness, you are in a mood for asking difficult questions this evening... I enjoy blending the herbs and spices together to form a really tasty meal. I love to see everyone enjoy a good lunch or dinner."

Otto became more curious. "Is there anything else you would have liked to do rather than this job?"

"I don't think so. I don't really know anything else, I have always cooked. My sister runs a boarding house in Füssen and I sometimes think that she has a better and easier life, but I am very happy here. What about you master Otto, why are you asking so many questions this evening? Is there some job you would rather do?"

"I had a difficult homework problem and it helps thinking about other people's lives"

Mrs Gott was surprised. "That is the first time I have heard you say that you have had anything difficult as homework, old Higginbottom is working you hard then?"

"Well not so much hard ... as making me think. You asked a very important question a moment ago, would I like to do something else. Yes, I think I would, I would like to be a university professor."

Mrs Gott laughed, a very deep laugh from her belly. "It could be a bit difficult to do that, especially with your other job."

Otto sighed, "I know, being born to be king does have some disadvantages."

"But it also has lots of advantages. For one thing you get paid whatever you do … goodness, look at the time. I need to get this food ready for the table or I will be looking for a different job."

Otto smiled. "Thank you, you have helped me a lot with my homework"

"Not sure how I helped, I have seen some of the mathematics that Higginbottom teaches. It makes my head hurt just looking at these pages of funny symbols … I don't think that talking about my job can have helped with that." Mrs Gott continued to prepare the dinner while the footmen waited to carry it up to the table.

Otto quickly went to his room and changed his clothes for dinner. On his way to the dining room he saw the king. "Good evening father."

"Good evening."

"How are you feeling today?" Asked Otto.

"I'm … I'm all right thank you."

"What has been good about your day?"

The king replied, "Well, the chancellor has finally got the tax changes put in place that we wanted... and the stable roof has been fixed"

"That's good father, I'm very happy that you had a good day." Once the dinner had been served Otto turned to his mother, "How are you feeling today?"

The queen was much more articulate than the king. "I am confused. We need to go to Munich next week but there doesn't seem to be a spare day to make the trip. I think we will have to let someone down, I always feel terrible whenever we have to say that we are not going somewhere because people go to such trouble to entertain us when we come and see them."

The king didn't look up from his food, he replied, "they have to

understand that plans sometimes change."
The queen was unhappy about this comment. "You have never been in the position of having a royal party arrive on your doorstep and then having to entertain them. My father was a lowly lord who didn't have much spare money and he often hosted your father and his friends and servants, inevitably their plans changed and we ended up managing as best we could. Every time the royal party arrived my father had to command an operation like a general commanding a battlefield. Three times as much food needed to be brought to the house, prepared and cooked. There were rooms that needed tidying and cleaning. Just lighting all the candles in the house in an evening took one of the footmen over an hour, when it was just our family at home we only lit a small number of the candles, it saved time and money. I don't think that you realise that when we arrive as a royal family we put people under pressure and I know that we have to do it because we have to be seen to be staying with our our lords and dukes, but I don't like causing them more work than is needed."

The next morning Otto rushed into his classroom.
" Higginbottom, I think I am beginning to see this different world that you mentioned ... and do you know, some people really seem to talk to me when I ask them about their feelings."
Higginbottom smiled. "That is great; tell me what you have learned."
"Well, last night I felt great sadness and fear at having to do something new. I was really scared about asking how someone felt."
"Why?" Asked Higginbottom.
"I was just concerned that I wouldn't be able to deal with the reply."
"How would that be possible?"
Otto continued, "Well, what if Mrs Gott had said that she felt hatred today because ... I don't know ... for example her sister had been poisoned by an evil client who refused to pay his bill."
"It is a bit unlikely."
"But what if she did?" Said Otto as he tapped his fingers on the

desk.

"You would say how terribly sorry you were."

"Is that what I should say."

Higginbottom smiled again. "No, there is nothing that you should say in that situation, but it is one of the things that you could say."

Otto's puzzled expression changed as he thought about the evening. "All the things I was scared of did not happen. I felt like I was speaking a different language with Mrs Gott when I was talking to her about her job, she really likes her job and all the wrinkles on her face smooth out when she talks about her work. I think that she is a very sincere person. I was really sad when I spoke to my father and the best thing in his day was a tax change and a repaired stable roof, I think he should do something about this ... this is not a healthy state of mind. My mother was amazing. She said that she was confused, which is something that I have never heard her say before. She was confused about a trip and when my father tried to make this less of a problem for her she got angry with him. It is the first time I have seen her being cross with father for a very long while."

"What did you learn?" Asked Higginbottom.

"That I have been missing something, and that I have not listened very well to how I feel or how people around me feel. I...I was also working on something else ..."

"Go on" said Higginbottom encouragingly

Otto continued, "Harold Hardrada, would feel scared and maybe a bit sad because battles, especially at that time, were very dangerous."

Higginbottom smiled. "Great progress. For your next task I want you to work on what really makes you happy and what makes you sad. You can tell me on Monday. Next we are going to start work on mathematics, some more of the university course." Otto was glad to get back to the familiar world of mathematics that day. It had been interesting for him to see this word that he had not seen before, but Otto also found it took a lot of his concentration. It was like trying to speak a new language for the first time.

Otto did not get a very long break before he was again plunged into unfamiliar places, this time by his Friday afternoon lesson on politics. "So Otto, what do you want your kingdom to be?"
"Well ... excellent, having healthy people who are working hard and very content."
"Content again?"
"Well, happy, joyous, enthralled, captivated and enriched." Replied Otto.
Higginbottom grinned. "I see you reached for the thesaurus yesterday ... but what would make you enthralled and enriched if you were an ordinary man in this kingdom?"
Otto said, "well I think is starts with having the basics: Enough food for my family, plenty of clean water, a warm house, having a healthy family. Then it is important to have something useful to do that holds your attention and keeps you busy and interested, but what can a king do to change this?"
Higginbottom replied, "Let me explain."

Higginbottom launched into a lecture on one of his favourite subjects, economics. "Right now most of Bavaria's money comes from farming. In England they have found that you can have more wealth if your country's money comes from industry and the English towns and cities are now full of factories that make all sorts of things from cotton, metal, wood and many other things. Huge steam engines power these factories and thousands of people work in some of the buildings. If you want Bavaria to do well you probably need follow what was done in England."
Otto liked the idea of changing his country. "What can we do to be more industrial?" He asked.
Higginbottom replied, "You can invest money in things that are important to people and generate wealth. So what can you buy that will help your country?"
Otto replied, "Transport, a king could invest money in boats to move goods around the kingdom using rivers and waterways so, for example the people who make nuts and bolts in Munich can sell them easily in all the towns in the country."
Higginbottom smiled, "very good example. This is the 'free

market' at work where people decide what to make, where they sell these things and how much they should charge. You are right, you need a transport system that will move goods around, but it doesn't have to be on water; what about roads or rail?"

Otto was intrigued. "So what controls the free market? How do the right things get to be made and sold?"

Higginbottom was in his element, he loved economics and he continued, "the controls are very very simple ... price. When there are not enough bolts in the kingdom the price for the bolts that have been made goes up. Other people then think it is worth making bolts and so the supply of bolts increases and the price reduced. If you have too many bolts and they need selling they have to be sold more cheaply."

Otto was amazed. "So price controls the entire market and neither the king nor the government have to do anything."

Higginbottom continued. "Well, it is not quite that simple. You do need to do some things .... someone needs to make sure that people have the skills needed. If there was only one person in the kingdom who could make bolts then the price of bolts would become so high that few could afford them, then your free market breaks down because you need nuts and bolts to make almost everything... if the people who make nuts and bolts can't get metal then they can't make bolts. If the people who make boats can't get craftsmen to make them or designers to design boats then the entire system falls apart. So what do we do?"

Otto scratched his head, he was rarely at a loss for words but finally he said, "Someone needs to plan what skills are needed?"

Higginbottom loved the subtleties of economics, he replied, "No not exactly plan. If you plan that you need four tilers, ten builders and eight carpenters what will you do when things change? You need to plan to give people a good basic education from which they can do many things. Those people who are good at making things may decide to lean how to build houses or make bolts, but the people who would rather think about the world may become tomorrow's university professors. So it it will be your job as king to make sure that people have a good basic education and then

they can be trained to do many things."
Otto replied, "Higginbottom, I like that. I think that the free market is what we should have in Bavaria."

Otto thought more about what Higginbottom had said. "Higginbottom, there are so many things that a king could do. A king could build new waterways, he could educate people more, he could help people to have warmer houses. How do you decide what to do?"

Higginbottom replied, "you are right, a good king must choose between many things he could do and these things compete with one another."

"So how can a king have it all?" Otto asked.

"You have seen some nineteenth century thinking about the free market, lets take you back to some older ideas - do you have any idea who said 'The end justifies the means'?"

"No idea at all." Replied Otto.

Higginbottom had more ideas on what Otto should consider. "'The end justifies the means' was said by Niccolo Machiavelli who was the brains behind an Italian ruler called Medici. Machiavelli wrote a classic book called The Prince which shows a prince or a king how to build and maintain power within his kingdom, don't worry about how Machiavelli suggests you do this because his methods are a probably too charged with ambition and deceit to be of much use in this day and age, but what is important from this book is the answer to your question, how can a king 'have it all'? Machiavelli talks about how new princes can act such as 'putting down the powerful people' ... the point is that you begin with a plan or a strategy and it is never too early to think about this. History helps with these and it is much better to pick a plan that has worked for someone under similar circumstances than to take a chance with a completely new plan. When you start to think about what you love and what you dislike, keep on thinking about what you would love to see in your kingdom and what you would dislike."

"Thank you" said Otto "that was an immensely fun lesson."

"Remember Machiavelli is just an example of the way that a

strategy can be built, his methods would be condemned by many so please don't base any plan on these ... one or two have merit such as 'one should make sure that the people need the prince, especially if a time of need should come along' but his idea that you can do whatever you like just to get what you want would be absolutely barbaric in these times. Machiavelli wrote his book at a time when kings routinely killed people that they didn't like."

Otto replied, "We still kill some prisoners, but only those who have killed others."

"Is this right?" Asked Higginbottom.

"We remove people who kill from society and keep ordinary law abiding folk safe. What is wrong with that? Surely this is what people want from their royal family."

Higginbottom was not so convinced. "It is just that the bible says fairly clearly 'Thou shall not kill'. It doesn't say 'Thou shall not kill unless the person has killed someone else ', it says just 'Thou shall not kill'. Our Lord Jesus once found some men who were about to throw huge stones at a lady to punish her for her wrong doing, Jesus said 'let he who is without sin throw the first stone'. No one threw a stone and the lady was saved. This is a message from almost 2,000 years ago. We need to be forgiving."

Otto looked confused, "so you think that we shouldn't kill even people who have killed someone else?"

Higginbottom replied very strongly, "yes, people should not kill anyone. It is wrong to kill. I am not saying that we should let people who kill out of prison, no they should be locked up, but we do not have the right to kill them. I am really sorry, we have run out of time. We must stop here for the week. Good night Otto and have a great weekend."

Otto replied, "good night, do enjoy your weekend."

Chapter 6
A Small Expedition

Otto arrived for his class on Monday morning. He was full of energy and his cheeks positively glowed. "I have told father that I want him to remove the death penalty so that in Bavaria we don't kill prisoners regardless of what they have done."
"How did the king react?" Asked Higginbottom.
Otto replied, "My father said that it was impossible to do this."
Higginbottom shook Otto's hand. "Well done. You are standing up for the things that you believe in. Of course the king would say it can't be done, It is a lot of work, but keep going on this and he will get the point in time."
Otto also wanted to talk to Higginbottom about the book. "I read Machiavelli's book, The Prince from cover to cover, and I think I have got it."
Higginbottom wasn't entirely sure whether by 'got it' Otto was referring to the narrative of The Prince or Otto's plans but Higginbottom said "Tell me all about it" as encouragingly as he could.
"The things I love: Travelling very fast, dangerous hobbies such as climbing tall trees and exploring new places, learning new things and working with new and exciting inventions ... I love industry and the amazing new machines that we can make in this country. I dislike conformity, the days when you have to dress up and pretend that you live a boring life"
Higginbottom asked, "Why would you pretend that you live a boring life?"
"It is what some of the visiting noblemen seem to expect, mother is always telling me not to go sledging in the winter when we have visitors."
"Perhaps that is just for their own safety" said Higginbottom with a wry smile.
Otto ignored the comment, realising that Higginbottom hadn't completely forgotten about the incident involving the snowman.
"Anyway," Otto continued, "what I want for the country is very

much what I want for me. I want Bavaria to have an exciting and amazing time building new inventions when I am king. I don't want it to be a boring place to the point when you wouldn't know whether you were standing in a town in Bavaria or in Saxony."

Higginbottom replied "This is excellent. You have been thinking about what is important to you. We usually do very well at the things we think are important, so the more that your work is just like something that you would do for fun, the easier work becomes."

Otto looked very seriously at Higginbottom. "So you really think that this is the way I should run the kingdom, abandon father's slow and steady taxation and alliance plans and run the kingdom in my own way."

Higginbottom said, "I think that if you understand what you are doing, follow your own heart and make sure that your plans are based on something that has worked for someone in the past you will not go far wrong. If you are really serious about doing something different you will see how this could work tomorrow. We are going on a small expedition together."

Otto could hardly concentrate on his studies for the rest of the day. He was so happy to have a plan that was interesting and someone who was a talented as Higginbottom to work with him.

*****

The carriage arrived at eight o'clock the next morning. Otto and Higginbottom were off to Füssen to meet people and see what was really happening in the kingdom. Their first visit of the day was to a watermill. The miller greeted Otto with a deep bow and said "Welcome to my mill your royal highness." They were given a tour of how the mill worked, Otto was so surprised by how old fashioned the mill seemed to be. The only mechanical help the miller had was that the mill stones were turned by the waterwheel from the stream. Apart from this all the grain had to be lifted into the mill by hand and the flour had to be lifted out from the mill. "You seem to work very hard here milling the grain, what would you need to help you?" asked Otto.

The miller looked confused, he didn't know how to answer Otto's question. "We manage well given all the things we have to do."
Otto continued, "But if the king could do anything different, what would you like him to do?"
"Well … it would be great if he could reduce the taxes a little."
"Yes, and what else?" Asked Otto politely.
"I don't know, we manage quite well"
"Are you sure, how about the way that you transport the grain. Could we improve this?"
The miller smiled, "well, if you can fly it here that would certainly speed things up"
"How much grain do you mill in a day?" Asked Higginbottom with a little frustration in his voice.
"Usually we do thirty to forty bags each day, unless something in the mill breaks."
"How long does it take you to repair a breakage?"
"Sometimes a couple of days if I can just make a new wheel or free up a bit of the drive system. Once we had to stop for three weeks to get the waterwheel replaced."
"How do the local bakers manage if you can't make flour for all that time?"
"They have to transport the grain to the windmill in Kempten, that wastes a lot of time and it costs everyone extra money. I lose money for each day that I don't work and the bakers lose money transporting the grain a longer distance. "Do you not have people who can repair your mill locally?" asked Otto.
"No, there is no one in this town that knows how to repair the mill. The blacksmith will have a go at making fittings for me but he doesn't know anything about the mill, I just have to repair it myself if I can, or wait until someone can travel to the mill."

Otto and Higginbottom then went to see the local bakery just as the manager was selling the last of the day's bread. They found a very similar approach from the baker, if anything broke he just tried to fix it himself, and if he couldn't he would wait until someone from another town or city could be found to help. Finally they went to see the town major who told them about the real effect of this way of doing things. "People in this town go hungry often just because of simple things. The mill keeps breaking down, the bakery does not work for a day and people have to go without. There are more serious problems, our river keeps flooding and we lose crops every few years. There never seems to be in a time when everything works well. None of these things are difficult to deal with, but there is just such a lot to do that usually the really big problems like flooding do not get sorted out."

"It is all so inefficient" Otto said to Higginbottom when they were back in the carriage.

"I know, " replied Higginbottom, "that it why I wanted you to see it. You are used to a castle that runs like clockwork, you don't go without bread just because the baker's oven is not working or the millers cogs have jammed."

"Why do these people put up with this?" Otto asked.

"Because they feel that they have no choice. They are much better off than when they had to farm alone, we have communities now that help one another, they just don't have enough tools and skills to make a really big difference to the way that they live."

"What can I do, I really want to help these people?"

"Continue your studies, keep thinking about your plan and ask God to bless what you do."

"Will that be enough?" Asked Otto.

Higginbottom replied, "I think so. You have the ability to be a great king and to transform the lives of the people around you into something much much better."

Otto had to take a breath. He had never heard Higginbottom speak so passionately about anything. With a grin Otto asked "Who are you and what have you done with Mr Higginbottom?" Higginbottom smiled. "Otto, I think you may well be a kindred spirit" Higginbottom replied.

Things were not as friendly when they arrived back at the castle. The king was stomping around like a demented elephant, he was exasperated. As soon as he heard the front door open the king

roard "Higginbottom I want a word with you ...several actually."
Higginbottom walked into the king's study and closed the door. The king continued his monologue, "What do you mean by taking Otto to see a miller, a baker and the town mayor without my knowledge and agreement? The lords are furious."
Higginbottom replied, "I am sorry that you feel so angry but it was important that Otto should see ordinary people without the lord's knowledge or the people we came to see would just be told what to tell Otto, and this would do no one any good. Otto needs to see real people in this kingdom and hear what they really have to say if he is to become a good king."
"Your job, sir, is to teach him about real people from real text books not to go parading about on 'informal' visits and upsetting all the local lords."
Higginbottom tried to apologise but the king was not having any of it. Higginbottom said "I am very sorry that the lords are upset. I didn't want this to happen." Finally the king started to calm down and he replied, "All right, but will you promise me never to go on a visit like this again?"
Higginbottom wanted to please the king but he had no intention of promising something that he could not deliver. "No I will not promise you this, it is an essential part of Otto's education that he is allowed to visit the kingdom, how else will he find out what really goes on?"
The king was not used to other people telling him what was to be done and he said, "well sir, you had better choose which you would prefer. Would you like to continue as Otto's tutor without the 'informal' visits, or would you prefer not to continue your employment?"
Higginbottom refused to back down, "I can't work in an environment in which I am constrained in this way. I will educate your son to the best of my ability but I cannot and will not be told how to conduct something as simple as a visit to the local mill."
"Well then," the king bellowed as he summoned himself to his full height, "I suggest that you seek a new employer, good day to you."

The queen had heard all the commotion coming from the king's study, she arrived just as Higginbottom left. The queen flung the king's door open saying, "Whatever is going on?" When the king explained that Higginbottom was being unreasonable and trying to tell him how to run his kingdom the queen replied "You pompous old fool. Don't you see how much good that man is doing for our son? Otto adores him and Higginbottom is the best thing that could have happened to Otto. You go and apologise to Higginbottom right now."

"I will not be told what do do in my own castle" bellowed the king.

The queen looked straight at the king, "Well if that is the way you want to behave Otto, Higginbottom and I will be leaving for Vienna in the morning."

The king refused to change his mind, "Go if you like, I will not change my mind." Otto heard all the commotion from the hallway and was getting concerned. When the queen left the king's study Otto talked to her in the hallway, "Mother, are you really sure that father will change his mind. I like it here. I don't think I want to live in Vienna"

The queen smiled a gentle smile at Otto. "The king will change his mind. He is just being a cantankerous old so-and-so. You leave your father to me."

The next morning the queen and Otto had prepared their trunks and the trunks were placed in hallway by the servants to be put into the carriage. The king saw the trunks and went immediately to find the queen.

The king said "You can't be serious that you will leave this wonderful castle over a tutor?"

The queen replied, "I certainly am. You really don't get it do you? Higginbottom has taken fantastic care of your son for months now. He was worked with him come rain or shine, he has never taken a day off. Higginbottom has coached Otto in sport, pushed him in his classroom subjects and he is now trying to help him understand how this kingdom works ... a job that you seem to be too busy to do. Most importantly if it wasn't for Higginbottom goodness only knows what would have happened to Otto. You know how reckless he is when he is left to himself. Without good guidance our son will kill himself on a mountain or get blown up by a steam engine, or come to some similarly sticky end. If you want someone to blame for yesterday's debacle blame the way you have let the lords walk all over you. Why on earth shouldn't you, me, Otto or Higginbottom go to meet people in our own kingdom. This really is something that you should fix."

The king rubbed the back of his neck as though he had been bitten by a wasp, "all right, all right ... You win. Mr Higginbottom can stay."
The queen smiled, "I thought you might come to your senses... and while we are on the subject of Otto, you have been absent from his life for far too long. Now it is your turn to show him what men do and particularly what a good king does. You will find him something he can help with this week, something useful he can do."
"All right," sighed the king. He knew when he was beaten.
"And while you are at it, find a way that we can all visit our own kingdom without anyone's permission. I also would like to go and visit some places in the town." Seeing a smile coming across her husband's face the queen quickly said "and don't even think of giving this problem to Otto ... this is your problem, you need to fix it. He is twelve years old and he needs a problem that he can really solve and help you with. He must be able to do whatever you give him by himself, not fail to solve something that you can't do." It really was not the king's day.

The queen went to tell Higginbottom and Otto that they would still be working together at the castle, the king went to his study to calm down and think about how to manage the lords and the servants brought the trunks back upstairs, making sure that the king did not see that they were all completely empty. Later that morning the king went to find Otto. He found him studying English with Higginbottom.

The king unusually knocked on the classroom door (he usually just flung the door open). "Excuse me, I am sorry to interrupt," said the king. "I just need to ask Otto for some help for a couple of minutes." The king had never once asked for help. Otto was very excited.

The king took Otto to his study and on the way Otto said, "I would love to help you, what can I do?"

"Well," said the king, "it is a problem that you found yourself when you visited the town, the river in Füssen keeps flooding the town. We have been trying to solve the problem for years but all the obvious solutions can't be taken forward for all sorts of reasons. We need a solution and I would like to help but I just don't have the time to get involved. The best person to talk to about all the ways we have tried to improve this is the mayor – he will tell you about the past and why we are still struggling with this after two years."

Otto's eyes were bright with joy at the prospect of doing something useful for the kingdom, "thank you" he said cheerfully to the king.

The king replied, "You may not thank me when you see how difficult this is. Don't expect to find a quick solution" warned the king."

Otto wanted to make a start immediately and that evening he asked Higginbottom to come and see the mayor with him. They arrived at the mayor's stone house which was built high up on the edge of town. "I guess that you don't have problems with flooding here?" asked Higginbottom.

"No" replied the mayor, "I am a bit too high to get flooded, but let me explain why the town does. This should be a simple problem," explained the mayor as he unrolled a beautiful old map of the town on his large oak table and pointed to the river as it runs into the town. "We have three ways to stop the town from flooding, firstly we could dig the river bed deeper, but this is a lot of work, it would mean that the bridge would need reinforcing and it will only help for a short time as the river bed will fill up again soon with silt. Then we will have to dig it out again.

Secondly we could dig another channel around the town but this would be difficult to do in a number of places as we would need to remove lots of trees and it also involved building another bridge to the town, so this is far too expensive. Thirdly we could widen the river, which works well at the edges of the town but not in the centre as there is not enough space for widening."

Otto looked closely at the map, "very interesting, is there any other way?"

"Not unless you can evaporate the water or get it to flow in a tunnel underground" said the mayor.

Otto replied, "but the flooding is only at its worst for a few days a year, what about using the lakes and ponds further upstream to manage surges of water, and then you can use a combination of all the other methods to keep the town dry when there is not a surge?"

The mayor was very surprised "We have had engineers from Munich working on this last year and they didn't come up with anything like this ... but they also didn't look beyond just the small section of river as it flows through the town. I don't know if it will work though... do you think that this can work?"

Higginbottom smiled "I am no expert in river flows but the idea has a lot of merit. If you can take some of the pressure off the town by regulating the flow of water, then this is good. You already have a series of ponds upstream, the millpond being the biggest, the only problem is that the mill pond would have to be emptied before the flood water arrived and I don't think that the miller will feel very comfortable about this."

"The miller shouldn't feel too bad about it," said Otto "he just needs to stop work a few hours after a big rainstorm, he will only need to stop for a few days a year, and paying the miller money for his idle mill would surely be cheaper than rebuilding sections of the town."

The mayor looked like a man who was itching to go and ask people to start work that evening "So how do we do this?" he asked impatiently.

"You need one person who will manage the sluice gates on all the upstream ponds. As soon as any heavy rain has been falling for more than half an hour he needs to empty all the upstream ponds gradually into the millpond. Then, once the water level has stabilised he needs to begin emptying the millpond. As soon as the town's river level rises above two metres he will put the sluice gates up gradually on the mill pond and then put the gates up on the higher level ponds. If we get the timing right the surge should be relieved … it should at least help until the rest of the river can be improved."

"How would we improve the river?" Asked the mayor.

Otto replied, "as soon as the river is down to its summer levels we would dig under the bridge and re-enforce the sides of the river channel and the bridge supports. We can then widen the stretch of river on one side before the bridge and dig a second channel just after the bridge around the woods and create a woodland island. The ponds can help catch the remaining water and for a while and it should be possible to work on this with the river bed dry. How do you feel about this?"

The mayor was astonished "I feel overjoyed. You are the first person who has brought me a solution, not just more problems … have you been studying rivers?" He asked.

"No" replied Otto "… it just seems like common sense."

The major smiled, "well I am glad that you brought your common sense here this evening, thank you very much your royal highness," said the mayor, "we will start work on the plan this week."

Otto smiled, "please can you let me know how it develops."

"I would be delighted to, your royal highness." Said the mayor.

When Higginbottom and Otto returned Otto made Higginbottom promise not to mention the evening's events with the mayor to the king just in case Otto's great plan did not seem so great in practice. Two weeks later though, the next big storm hit the kingdom and Otto couldn't resist going to see the mayor just as the waters were at their highest. When he arrived at the mayor's house he could see that Füssen was indeed remarkably dry. The mayor enthusiastically shook Otto's hand. "It is working" he said "your plan with the ponds is really working, look at the river

levels, not one drop of flood water has touched the town today."
Otto looked so happy "I am very glad" he said.

The castle was full of guests that evening, a group of visiting noblemen had arrived in time for dinner and they passed on the good news to the king. The king managed to find time to talk to his family during the meal. "Astonishing" said the king and he turned to Otto "how did you come up with this plan?"
Otto replied, "it just seemed like common sense."
"Well, I am glad that you have such good common sense."
The queen stared at the king, and the king turned to Otto "I think I need to get you involved in more of the running of the kingdom" said the king.
The queen smiled "It will be good for both of you."

Chapter 7
A Close Shave

It was a bright Saturday morning in late April and lessons were finished for the week. The sun shone as it rose above the lake, the ripples of the water made whirling patterns on Otto's ceiling, and he thought it was a like being under water and looking up at the surface. Otto heard the birds singing loudly in the early morning sun and he could not stay in bed for much longer. Mrs Gott had just started making breakfast for the king and queen, she made Otto a quick breakfast of toast and jam in the kitchen so that he could go and enjoy the day. Otto finished his toast, drank his water and put the plate and glass in the sink. "Thank you Mrs Gott" he said cheerfully as he left the kitchen. Otto walked down to the boat house. The king was happy for Otto to take out the boat on his own as long as someone knew where he was going, but in his excitement he had forgotten to tell Mrs Gott as he left the castle, and now there was no one to tell in the castle garden."Oh bother, what a nuisance" Otto said to himself as he remembered that he should have told someone where he was going. He thought about just going out without telling anyone but this would have been very silly. If anything happened to his boat no one would even know where to look for him. He walked back to the castle and half way across the lawn Otto met Higginbottom.

Otto smiled, "hello Higginbottom, what are you doing up so early?"

"I could not sleep and decided to take a walk on this magnificent morning."

"It is such a great day, the spring is certainly here. I am just going to take a boat out for an hour or so, please can you let mother and father know."

Higginbottom looked concerned. "Are you sure you will be all right rowing the boat on your own?"

"Don't worry, I will be fine." Otto replied.

"I can come with you if you like?"

"Thank you for your kind offer, but you enjoy your walk Higginbottom."

Higginbottom walked back to the castle and asked Mr Benn to tell the king and queen that Otto was out rowing on the lake. Higginbottom decided to go back outside, although it was a very pleasant day there had been a lot of rain in the past weeks. The lake was now very full and the rivers that flowed into and out of the lake had fast currents. Higginbottom spent a few minutes looking across the lake for Otto, the sun light shimmering on the water made it difficult to find a small rowing boat. Soon Higginbottom saw the silhouette of Otto's boat, it was heading towards the weir. Higginbottom ran along the path beside the lake, through the large wood until he was much closer to Otto. Higginbottom shouted from the bank "OTTO BE CAREFUL, ROW AWAY FROM THE WEIR". The weir was a place of fast flowing water that flowed out of the lake. The weir consisted of one large waterfall out of the lake and then four smaller falls further downstream. There were three signs in the lake that said "Danger, Weir" but there was no fence around the weir and any boat that got too close would be sucked in towards the waterfall by the current and would be broken into a thousand pieces as it crashed down into the rocks at the sides and bottom of the waterfall. By now Otto could see the danger, he was rowing away from the weir as fast as he could but the current was so strong that the boat was slowly being pulled towards the weir, despite Otto's efforts. "Row harder" Higginbottom shouted, but it was no good, Otto was getting exhausted and the boat was still being pulled slowly toward the weir by the current.

Two fishermen came running to Higginbottom to see what they could do, but no one could think of anything that would get Otto out of danger very quickly, so Higginbottom took off his shoes, socks and his jacket. He jumped into the cold water and swam in an almost straight line towards the boat, despite the immense power of the current pulling Higginbottom sideways. Otto was amazed, there were very few people who would be able to swim in such difficult conditions. Higginbottom reached the boat and said to Otto "keep rowing" as he pulled himself in. Once Higginbottom was in the boat he said "right, when I say go you will let go of the oars and I will take over ... ready, steady, GO". Otto left the oars, quickly got up and let Higginbottom sit on the boat's seat and row. In the time that it took for Otto to swap to Higginbottom the boat had got to within five metres of the weir, Higginbottom took the oars and rowed with all his might, slowly the boat started to move away from the weir and as they moved away the current reduced a little so that they could move away more quickly. It took about five minutes for Higginbottom to row them both out into the lake where they could safely stop rowing and catch their breath. Otto looked at Higginbottom, "that was incredible, how did you learn to swim so well?" Higginbottom just nodded, he was too cold and exhausted to reply.

Otto rowed them both back towards the boathouse. The fishermen had gone to the castle to let the king and queen know what was happening. By the time that Higginbottom and Otto reached the castle boathouse a crowd had gathered. The king and queen were at the front with all the servants around them, everyone wanted to make sure that Otto was still in one piece. The king grabbed Higginbottom's hand and shook it strongly "Thank you" the king said in his booming voice "you have saved my son today I will be forever in your debt." The footmen were carrying blankets and passed them to Otto and Higginbottom so that they would warm up a little on their way back to the castle. Once Otto and Higginbottom were back in the castle kitchen warming themselves by the fire, Otto again asked "so, how did you learn to swim so well?"
Higginbottom replied, "I swam a lot when I was at school and then joined the university swimming team. I am not that good. I just learned to swim in a powerful way."
"Would you teach me how to swim like you?"
"I think that would be a very good idea. With the things that you keep getting yourself into, being able to swim well might just save your life at some time." A footman arrived back with the

rest of Higginbottom's clothes and his shoes. "Thank you" Higginbottom said "I will be needing those." Higginbottom turned to Otto, "Let's start those swimming lessons next week, the weather is warming up and we can do this as one of your lessons."
"Thank you" said Otto.

A week passed quickly. It was two o'clock in the afternoon and it had been agreed that once a week Otto would have an hour of swimming lessons with Higginbottom. Otto was very excited to start swimming. They began their lake swimming near to the shore and Higginbottom worked on Otto's style of swimming, getting him to keep his head lower and put more power into his arms. "Head down" Higginbottom kept shouting. Otto tried but he was struggling not to keep breathing in lake water with his head further down. After half an hour Otto had finally mastered keeping his mouth just below the surface and then turning and lifting his head for each breath. "You look exhausted" said Higginbottom. "The water is cold today and I think it is time to stop now." Higginbottom and Otto went back in to the castle to dry off and drink a warm cup of peppermint tea.

While Otto and Higginbottom were drinking their tea in the kitchen a delivery of meat arrived. Mrs Gott talked to the man who brought the meat who said "beef is becoming more and more expensive, because so many of the fields are flooded."
Otto listened more carefully. The delivery man continued, "the river in Fűssen has flooded again, despite all those modern things that some clever chap has put in." Otto went to the store room.
"Where did it flood?"
"Your royal highness," said the man, looking astonished "It... it flooded right through the town again, just the same as it always used to."
Otto looked confused, "I just don't understand. The rivers were well managed, how could they flood?"
"Well, water levels are very high your royal highness."

Otto went back into the kitchen. Higginbottom looked at him and said "you want to go to Füssen don't you?"
"Yes, we need to go now." They both finished their tea and got straight into the carriage. Within an hour they were able to see the flooding for themselves, water was flowing right through the town and people were getting on with things in the best way that they could. The market was still held in the centre of the town and big wooden boards had been put down that were standing on piles of bricks to help people to get to the stalls without getting their feet wet. Finally Higginbottom and Otto reached the major's house "What happened?" Otto asked. The major was a wise old man.
"It seems that some people didn't like what you had done, some people wanted Füssen to get wet each spring and they have damaged the sluice gates so we can't manage the water flow any more."
"Why would anyone want that?"
"I am not exactly sure but the people who sell wood sell a lot more wood when doors get wet and need fixing and people need wood to stand on to get to the market. All this water damages walls and so the builders and brick suppliers get a lot of work with each flood."
Otto was astonished "This is terrible. I still don't understand how people can make other people's lives so much worse just because they want some more business."
Higginbottom smiled "this is human nature, if the merchants or the builders feel that their business is not as good as it was they will do everything possible to get business back, including vandalising those sluice gates."
Otto looked very sad "what can we do about this?"
Higginbottom replied, "I don't think we can do very much at the moment. We have tried to give the town a solution, but until people in the town see that it is worthwhile keeping the town dry then there is no point in trying to force another solution on them."
Otto shook his head "That is terrible" he said again.
Higginbottom smiled "that is politics." They thanked the major

and returned to the carriage.

Otto had a lot of questions. "Higginbottom I still can't see why anyone would leave the town in this position."

"When men need to earn money for their families they will do many things to keep their income. They are not able to look at whether their actions are good for everyone, the men who supply bricks and wood will do whatever it takes to increase supply. You live in the most privileged position, your castle is safe and warm, you have food and your family is happy. Imagine what would happen if you could not afford to feed your family this week. What would you do?"

"Surely people are not in this situation?" Otto replied.

"Some people are very poor, and those that are not know that they are lucky and they know that they need to keep working hard so that they have food and a warm house." Otto was silent for the rest of the journey home. He had never thought that people in his kingdom could be so poor that they would not have food. He thought about all the wonderful meals he ate and then wondered what these poor people would be eating tonight.

Chapter 8
A Friend for Life

It was a Friday evening in late April. The king, queen and Otto were enjoying their dinner of roast chicken when the king announced, "the queen and I have to go to England early next week, and we are going to be away for over a month."
"I will be coming to England with you, won't I?" Asked Otto.
The queen smiled gently at Otto. "Not this time, it is a long journey and we do not want to interrupt your studies."
"But I am doing well in my studies, and a few days of interruption for the journey will not cause a problem. Higginbottom can come with me so I can study in England, and it would be good for me to see more of Europe and understand how England is managing their industrial revolution." The king looked calmly at Otto, "all in good time, we can perhaps take you on the next trip but this time we need to talk to Prince Albert alone." In a sombre voice the king continued, "Prince Albert may now be the only person left in Europe who can help us."
Otto was so shocked by both parts of this announcement that he didn't know what to say. "Why is Prince Albert the only person who can help?
The king replied, "As the husband of England's Queen Victoria, prince Albert is one of the most powerful men in Europe, he was born in Saxony and he has always been very helpful to us. Many countries have been corrupted by Mr Stark and few European countries are now willing to help us."
The prince protested, "you are going to go and travel through France and England for over a month and you can't take me, just because you need to talk privately with Prince Albert, this makes no sense. I could wait in the carriage if it is such a big problem."
The queen looked very sad. "I am so sorry that things are so bad for us, we really can't take you on this trip because we will spend all of our time in England trying to find help, but we promise to bring you something wonderful tomorrow that will mean that the time we are away passes more quickly."

Otto looked sadly at his plate and said ungratefully, "I doubt that there is anything that I would describe as wonderful now."
The queen tried to seem encouraging, "You just wait until tomorrow."
The dinner was finished and nothing more said about the trip that evening. Otto said a simple goodnight as he went to bed early. Otto was used to his parents going away on a trip for a few days, maybe even a week, but not months.

The next day, Otto went to the kitchen for breakfast before the king and queen got up and then he stayed in his room in the morning reading books and drawing pictures. Otto still felt terribly sad. At eleven o'clock Otto got a knock on his door, it was one of the footmen, "your royal highness ... please come downstairs quickly. There is something that you should see."
"I am very busy, I will come later." Replied the prince.
"But, your royal highness, Mrs Gott says that you will love this."
"I am sure that it is the best food imaginable, but I am not hungry and I want to be left alone." The footman went away and Otto continued reading for a few minutes, until he heard a scratching and whimpering noise just outside his door. "Who is there?" he asked. There was no answer but the scratching and whimpering noise continued. Otto got up and went to open his door. Suddenly it was as though a hurricane of energy had been released into the room, the most excited big white puppy with black markings bounded through Otto's open door. The puppy was a huge German Mastiff with short hair and had a tail that was never still. The puppy wiggled excitement with all of his body as he rushed to greet Otto, licking Otto's hands and face. Otto cuddled the puppy for the few seconds that he would remain still before the puppy set off to have a good run and sniff around Otto's room, returning triumphantly with one of Otto's socks in his mouth. "Bring that back" said Otto as he gave chase. The puppy's tail was now wagging even more rapidly and Otto chased the puppy out of his room and down the stairs into the hallway, just managing to grab the end of the sock before the puppy could go into the dining room. Otto pulled the sock as hard as he could

and the puppy slid forward, unable to grip with his paws on the stone floor. The puppy growled playfully as he tried to pull the sock back. Soon the puppy's erratic pulling gained him a few extra centimetres of sock before the sock started to tear. Otto pulled it back in one last attempt to free the sock, but it was no good. It had ripped from one side to the other and Otto was left with about one third of a sock while the puppy was joyfully chewing the remaining two thirds. "I think you may need some new socks," said the queen as she walked into the hallway.
"I think so too" replied Otto with a big grin.
The queen mentioned Otto's comments from the evening before, "So there is nothing that you would describe as wonderful now, is that right?"
Otto gave the queen a smile and said, "Well, no ... so who does this gorgeous puppy belong to?"
"Well you, if you want him. We thought that he might be fun to take with you on your adventures, and he is also big enough to keep anyone bad out of the castle while we are away."
"What is his name?" Asked Otto.
The queen replied, "He is your dog, you can choose his name."
"I would like him to be called Rufus."
"Well," said the queen "Rufus it is then."

The rest of the morning was spent with Otto running after Rufus or Rufus running after Otto. Both boy and dog got so worn out every half hour that they had to sit and rest for a few minutes, Rufus would then get a cuddle from Otto, and as soon as either the boy or dog had recovered some energy the running would begin again. By lunchtime there were protests from the boy and the dog about Rufus needing to be cared for by a footman while the king, queen and prince had lunch. Then, right after lunch, Rufus and Otto went to the garden to have a walk. Rufus loved the garden and ran into the clear waters of the lake across the sandy beach as often as he could. As soon as Rufus felt wet he would shake himself dry over anyone who was nearby. Higginbottom was also out for an afternoon stroll. Rufus was a gentle dog who had seemed to get on well with all the servants and so far he seemed to like everyone he met. Oddly, Rufus did not seem to like Higginbottom. Rufus bared his teeth at Higginbottom and growled at him. Otto found a large stick and threw it for Rufus to chase so that Higginbottom could continue his walk. Higginbottom just wished everyone a good afternoon and continued his walk towards the castle.

That night Rufus was supposed to sleep in the room next to the kitchen but he made such a lot of noise when he was left there that Otto said he could sleep for the first part of the night on a rug on Otto's floor. When the footmen went to bed they would take a big bone and bring Rufus into the downstairs room. Otto awoke on Sunday morning and was greeted by lots of licks from his new best friend Rufus, who had clearly not spent any part of Saturday night, or Sunday morning, in the downstairs room. Otto got dressed and went downstairs. He then asked the footmen what happened; their explanation was simple, "we are very sorry your royal highness, we tried to take Rufus downstairs but he made such a lot of noise every time we tried to move him that we were sure he would wake you up."

"I see, it seems that I have a room-mate," Otto said with a large grin as he patted Rufus' head. "Thank you for trying to take him to his bed downstairs."

The king and queen spent Sunday instructing the servants on how to pack for the trip. By eight o'clock in the evening the trunks were finally placed in the hallway and dinner was served. Otto tried one last time to persuade the king and queen to take him to England but it was no good, he was told to stay and look after Rufus and the castle. Rufus slept on Sunday night on his big rug in the corner of Otto's room. Just after breakfast on Monday Otto sadly waved goodbye to the king and queen. He knew that it would be a long time before he saw his parents again. "How do you feel?" asked Higginbottom.
"Empty." Replied Otto.
"Empty and sad?"
"Yes, that's right."

Higginbottom tried to make Otto feel better, "I'm sorry that you feel so sad. I will help you as much as I can." Just at that moment Rufus managed to get away from the footman that was looking after him and came bounding out of the castle towards Otto. Rufus jumped as he reached Otto putting his front paws up on Otto's chest, Otto rubbed Rufus' ears and then took a step back so that Rufus would return to having four paws on the ground. It was then that Rufus noticed Higginbottom and bared his teeth and growled again. Otto grabbed Rufus's collar and said "No."

Monday's lessons went by slowly. Otto was not concentrating well and Higginbottom really did try to help him feel less sad. Rufus was supposed to spend the daytime in a room near to the kitchen, but the moment that there was some activity going on and no one was watching the dog he would walk around the castle until he found Otto's smell. When Otto was studying Rufus would curl up and sleep just outside the classroom. This was starting to make things very difficult for Higginbottom. When Higginbottom wanted to leave the room, Rufus would stand up and growl, Otto would say "no" and then Higginbottom would slide along the corridor while Otto held on to Rufus's collar. For the first time ever, Higginbottom decided to stop work at three o'clock that day. Otto was not concentrating and Higginbottom had had enough of running past the dog. He left Otto and Rufus to play together outside in the afternoon sunshine. Both the boy and dog ran so much and got so exhausted that they fell asleep while taking a rest on the lawn. When Mr Rott found them at half past five Rufus was lying on Otto like a giant blanket. As Mr Rot laughed, Rufus lifted up an ear and then started to wiggle and wag his tail. Otto woke up just as Rufus gave his cheek a lick with a giant tongue, Otto pushed Rufus away to stop him licking any more of his face and then stood up, and seeing Mr Rott Otto said "we were just ...um ...having a rest."
"So I see."
Otto continued, "Puppies get exhausted very quickly, they can dehydrate if they don't get proper rest."
"I am sure they can. I just came to make sure that you were all

right"
Otto smiled. "We are absolutely fine."
"Excellent your royal highness. I will leave you to it."
"Mr Rott" called Otto, "I will take a short walk with Rufus very soon … I will be back in time for dinner."
"Very good your royal highness."

Everything seemed to be doing so well in the countryside in late spring as Rufus and Otto walked. The wild plants were flowering, the trees were growing thick leaves and the rabbits played on the distant hillsides, until Rufus came close and chased them away. Otto and Rufus returned to the castle at seven thirty. Rufus was taken downstairs to keep the footmen company while Otto changed for dinner. Dinner time that day was very unusual. It was decided that Otto should not eat alone so Mr and Mrs Higginbottom both came to join him for dinner. Despite Otto feeling low they all had a very merry evening, Otto was telling them about things that he and Rufus got up to and Higginbottom talking about the lengths he had to go to to avoid the dog. The evening was filled with joy and laughter, exactly what the young prince needed to take his mind off the situation.
Higginbottom recounted "I think I will soon need to get a fresh bone from the butcher each day if I am to stand any chance of getting to the loo unscathed."
Otto replied, "I really don't know why Rufus does not like you, it is very odd. Did you have a dog when you were young?"
"No, we never had any animals at home."
Otto said, "That's a pity, perhaps you just need time to get to know Rufus, lets give it a try tomorrow."

The conversation continued on to other subjects. "I gather that you two recently saved the local town from flooding?" Mrs Higginbottom said.
"Yes we did for a while," said Otto, "Fűssen was not managing its river very well, but after Higginbottom and I helped they improved things."
"You seem to enjoy a good challenge."

"I certainly do." Replied Otto.

"What challenges are you working on now?" Asked Mrs Higginbottom.

"I don't really have one. Looking after Rufus is, I suppose, a new challenge but I don't have anything else at present."

"There must be something that you want to do," she asked.

Otto replied, "Most of all I would like to travel and help to solve some of the real problems in the kingdom and in Europe."

Mr Higginbottom looked at Otto "All in good time" he said. "It is important to have strong foundations to build on … when I was your age I made the garden my universe. I designed and built a tree house. It was huge, so big that my father was afraid that it would bring the tree down on a windy night."

"Did you bring the tree down?" Asked Otto inquisitively.

"No," replied Higginbottom, "it was a very strong English Oak."

"So, how did you build it." Asked Otto.

Higginbottom replied, "A tree house is really quite simple, you just need some strong wooden beams at the bottom that you secure into the tree and then some solid wood to form a floor and some walls, and then a few beams and some flat wood for the roof. The most important consideration is how high you make it. If it is too low it is no fun at all, and if it is too high then you will be forbidden to enter it by your parents."

"Mmmm" said Otto, with a bemused expression on his face. "Do you have any drawings of your old tree house?"

"I'm sure I do, I will have a look for them tomorrow." Promised Higginbottom.

Lessons began at eight o'clock the next morning. As soon as Otto was set his first piece of work he turned to Higginbottom and said "could you find me the set of plans for your old treehouse please."

"Of course, I will go and look for them now." It took Higginbottom a good ten minutes before he arrived with some old looking papers and gave them to a very excited Otto. "Thank you Higginbottom, I will take great care of them."

"Never mind the drawings, the main thing is that you take great

care of yourself. Only build a few metres above the ground and get someone to make sure that your structure is safe."
"I will" promised Otto.

First thing on Saturday morning, Otto and Rufus walked to the village to see Mr Adler the carpenter.
"We would like to buy some wood and nails to make a tree house at the castle. I have a list of what I need here – would you be able to find these for me please?"
"I am very happy to your royal highness, but I don't have time to build this for at least two months."
Otto replied "I don't need you to build it … I just need the wood and nails."
Mr Adler looked very puzzled, "so who is going to build it?"
"I am," replied Otto.
"Have you ever built one before?"
"No, but Higginbottom found me some plans and it looks simple enough."
"Right you are" said Mr Adler with a smile, "when would you like it all to be delivered."
"Could you drop it in this afternoon please?" Asked Otto.
"I had planned to finish the church porch, but the priest won't mind if it takes an extra day. I will bring this to you this afternoon. But make sure that you take care building this, we can't have your royal neck broken."
"I will." Promised Otto.

When they returned to the castle they found Sebastian waiting in the drawing room. In amongst all the excitement Otto had forgotten that the queen had organised for Sebastian to stay for a few days.
"Sorry Sebastian, I just had to dash out to see the carpenter, it was very urgent" said Otto importantly.
"No problem, I have just been drinking that very delicious herbal tea that Mrs Gott always makes for us."
Otto replied, "I think I need one of those, I have just had a very busy morning." Just then Rufus bounded in and tried to jump on

Sebastian's lap "This is Rufus" announced Otto.

"Good morning Rufus" said Sebastian.

"Down!" Otto said has he grabbed Rufus' collar to save Sebastian having his tea poured all over him.

Sebastian grinned. "You are so lucky having a dog like that."

"You are right, I am lucky, being here with you and Rufus for company is great."

"So, what are we doing for the next few days?" Asked Sebastian.

"Let me show you, just wait a moment" said Otto as he went upstairs.

When Otto returned he handed the tree house drawings to Sebastian, "we are going to build one of these," Otto said.

Mr Adler delivered the wood in the afternoon and said, "Once you have finished your tree house, let me know and I will make sure it is safe for you. We can't have a prince falling from a tree house can we."

"Thank you Mr Adler" replied Otto. "Have you put anything like this together before?" asked Sebastian.

"No," replied Otto, "but I read a few books last night on how you join wood together. I think it is fairly simple." Rufus was keen to help, but Otto asked the footmen to find him a nice bone to keep him happy for a few hours while they worked on the tree house. The boys found some tools in one of the sheds in the garden and soon they were measuring up the wooden beams and marking cuts on each one. They began their first cut. It was much harder work than either of them had imagined. They kept swapping the sawing work between them. After half an hour they had only got about one quarter of the way through their first wooden beam. Otto was starting to doubt that they would finish the tree house at all. "At this rate it will take us two weeks just to get a floor put up." Higginbottom happened to walk past and smiled when he saw what they were doing. "That looks a bit tough" he said pointing to the beam, "Let me have a go for a moment." The boys happily gave Higginbottom the saw. Higginbottom thought it was quite amusing that the two boys had never sawed anything before, "as I suspected, this saw is so blunt that I doubt you

would get it through cold butter. Do you have anything better?"
"I'm not sure" said Otto, "I will go and look."

Otto returned a few minutes later with a saw that was so big you could use it to cut a tree trunk. "Well that one is worth a try" said Higginbottom. "You just need to get one person on each end of the saw and pull the saw through so that it stays running straight. If you force the saw through and it bends then the saw will get hot and it will be very difficult to use." The boys gave it a try and within five minutes they had cut straight through the big beam. An hour later all the beams were cut to length. The next job was to climb the tree and pull each beam into place in the tree. Otto went up and set up a pulley so that the beams could be lifted easily. Sebastian stayed on the ground so that he could tie the rope to each beam before they were lifted into the tree. Gradually the beams were put in place in the tree and Otto started nailing them together. The nailing was almost has hard work as the sawing. The wood beams were very hard and Otto had to hit each nail many times with his hammer to drive it in, suddenly Otto missed the head of one of the nails he was holding "Awww" he yelled as the hammer hit a finger nail.
"What did you damage?" Asked Sebastian.
"Just a finger nail." Replied Otto.
"That hurts."
"I know." Otto put his finger into cold water for a few minutes to reduce the swelling and then carried on nailing more carefully. By the end of the day the boys had built a level platform as a floor for the tree house. Mr Adler the carpenter called in and took a look at the platform "Very good" he said. "It is big enough that you will be safe here. Well done, it is also strong enough that it will carry anything that you can put up there. It might even carry a grand piano."
"I don't think we will take one of those up" said Otto. Both boys were so tired at the the end of the day. They hardly spoke as they ate dinner and then they went straight to bed after they ate. Otto had just enough energy to rub Rufus's ears for five minutes before he lay in his bed. Rufus then went to his rug and walked

in a circle a couple of times before lying down and going to sleep for the night.

The boys went to church on Sunday morning and had to promise that, as it was a Sunday, they would not work for the rest of the day. They ate cream cakes in the kitchen and Mrs Gott served tea. As the small kettle that was hanging over the fire boiled Otto noticed how the steam made the kettle move backwards away from the jet of steam.
"Do you have an old kettle?" Otto suddenly asked Mrs Gott.
"Somewhere in the pantry I think" she replied "do you need one?"
"Oh yes" replied Otto with a big grin.
"What are you planning?" asked Sebastian.
"Wait and see."

Once the boys had eaten as many cream cakes as it is possible to eat in one morning Otto went upstairs and returned triumphantly with a large wooden boat that he had been given when he was five years old. Otto smiled "It is good that we never get rid of anything in this castle."
"What are you going to do with that?" Asked Sebastian.
"Wait and see." said Otto to the obvious annoyance of his friend. The boys spent the rest of the morning putting two wooden posts onto each side of the boat with a chain between them that the old kettle could be hung from. Otto took a hammer and squashed the spout of the kettle a bit so that there was a very much smaller hole for the steam to come out through. Rufus was finally convinced that the boat was not edible and so he lay down on the floor. Sebastian still had no clue what Otto was making "Is this going to serve tea to us while we row to the island?"
Otto grinned again and set off towards the big garden shed "No" Otto called as he was walking away, "... and rowing will soon be a thing of the past."
Sebastian shook his head, "Will you tell me what you are doing, this is getting very boring." Otto appeared from the shed with a small metal box and a chain to secure the spout of the kettle in

place. "The final parts" Otto said. "Come with me and see if it works." They went to the kitchen to get some small pieces of wood to act as kindling for a fire and some matches. Otto gently poured some water into the kettle and they took the boat to the lake and floated it beside the jetty. Otto lit a fire in the metal container which was placed just below the kettle. Nothing much happened for a few minutes while the water got hot, and then as steam started to come from the spout of the kettle, which was pointing to the back of the boat, the boat began to move forwards very slowly into the lake and then as more steam was produced the boat moved faster. Otto and Sebastian got into the rowing boat to follow their craft but soon they couldn't keep up. The lake was very calm, there was no wind and so there were no big waves and the toy boat and kettle were propelling their way faster and faster across the lake. "We need that boat back" said Otto.

Sebastian shouted "Row faster." Otto tried to row faster but the little boat was now moving so fast that no rowing boat would ever be able to catch it. Otto was getting very worried about losing his craft "What do we do?" he asked.

"Wait and see what happens," came the reply. As they watched the little boat whizzing along the lake it suddenly hit the wake from another rowing boat and turned over a few times before coming to rest upside down. Otto rowed as fast as he could and they caught up with the little boat within a couple of minutes. Otto pulled it out of the water. The boat was intact apart from losing its firewood. By now the kettle had been cooled by the lake so the entire boat was cool enough to touch. Sebastian offered to row back. As they arrived at the jetty Higginbottom was walking by. "Take a look at this" said Otto. Sebastian went in to the castle for more wood and this time Otto rowed out into the lake before pointing the little boat towards the shore and lighting the fire. Higginbottom was astonished. "That is incredible; I have a friend, professor Ritter of Engineering in Munich. You must show him this – he will be amazed." The boys returned to the castle and had a fantastic lunch. They talked about nothing other than the boat as they ate. Otto was determined to use this craft for something interesting.

After all the excitement of the morning the boys decided to enjoy their treehouse in the afternoon. Otto brought some books and some paper up and Sebastian brought some cushions. The idea of reading seemed like a good one but Rufus was not pleased and whined and barked at them from the bottom of the treehouse – he wanted to be wherever Otto was. "Shhh" Otto kept saying but Rufus would not be quiet. "I have an idea" said Otto, and he dashed down the rope ladder and attached the hook from the pulley to a wide cloth sling that he wrapped around Rufus's tummy. He pulled the pulley rope and an uncomfortable looking Rufus began to go up. "Sebastian, please steady him as he arrives." Otto said. Rufus whimpered occasionally as he was lifted two metres into the air but as soon as Sebastian pulled him into the tree house Rufus walked around and sniffed for a couple of minutes and then curled up and slept. Soon both boys fell asleep in the middle of the large tree house floor and awoke as Rufus began to whine. It was near to dinnertime and a dog always knows when it is nearly time to eat. Otto lowered Rufus down again using the pulley and the two boys and the dog went into the castle to get ready for dinner.

The weeks flew buy as Otto was busy playing with Rufus and tinkering with his little boat to get it to run faster. Otto had one major job to do in May, he was determined that Rufus should get to like Higginbottom. One evening he made up his mind that the dog was going to be trained properly. "Higginbottom is an acquired taste," Otto told Rufus sincerely "but you will like him, he really is great." The next day Otto put Rufus on his lead and asked Higginbottom to walk towards them. Rufus did what he always did and growled. Otto had been reading about how to train a dog and he said "NO" in a strong voice and gave Rufus a gentle smack on his bottom. Otto repeated this six times until Rufus stopped growling. Next Higginbottom picked up a big juicy bone and held it out to Rufus. Otto gently let Rufus walk towards Higginbottom and sure enough Rufus was easily bought

… the dog made no protest at all and he took the end of the bone gently from Higginbottom and then lay on the ground in a Sphinx position to gnaw at the bone. While Rufus was busy Otto asked Higginbottom to gently rub Rufus's back and then rub his head. For the next week Higginbottom made sure that whenever he saw the dog he had some king of canine treat on him.

All it took was one week and Rufus never growled at Higginbottom again, he wagged his tail most of the time when he saw Higginbottom because he was now sure that Higginbottom was going to feed him.

Chapter 9
A Wise Man's Early Morning Visit

It was six forty-five in the morning and Mr Benn the butler knocked on Otto's door. Mr Benn came in to Otto's room and announced "I am sorry to wake you at this hour your royal highness but you have a visitor, an Englishman. He says that he has important news about a dangerous situation in Bavaria and he needs to see you, he is insisting that he must see you now."
"Thank you" said Otto "please can you wake Higginbottom and ask him to come and see me as soon as he can." Otto got dressed and waited for Higginbottom. They agreed to see the man together just in case this was part of some sinister plot. Otto walked nervously down to the library with Higginbottom, Otto worried about whether this was part of the threat that they already knew about or something more dangerous.

Otto caught a glimpse of an older well dressed gentlemen sitting in the library drinking tea. He had a rim of white hair around an otherwise bald head and his round glasses complimented his very round face. The man looked kind and Otto took a deep breath before he walked in to the library, lowered his shoulders and raised his head as he walked forward. "You royal highness" the visitor said "I am terribly sorry to disturb you at this hour, but I have important news for you. My name is Sir Harold East, I am the British Ambassador to Vienna and I am travelling through Bavaria to London today." Sir Harold showed Otto his badge of a Knight Bachelor, he continued "I know that the king and queen are away but I wanted to deliver this news to you as quickly as I could."
"Thank you for taking the trouble to come and see me" said Otto, who still looked puzzled. This is Mr Higginbottom my tutor. "Higginbottom," replied Sir Harold, "I am sure I have met you before somewhere, but I can't quite place you."
"I think you must be mistaken" replied Higginbottom, "I am merely a tutor to his royal highness." Higginbottom examined Sir

Harold's badge, then passed it back to Sir Harold who gave Higginbottom a confused look, but then turned to Otto. "Your royal highness, I will come straight to the point but I need to talk to you in private." Otto turned to Higginbottom.

"Thank you Higginbottom." He said and Higginbottom nodded, got up from his place, left the room and closed the door behind him. Higginbottom waited just outside the door in case the visitor turned out not to be the gentle and kind man that he appeared.

Once the library door was closed Sir Harold looked very sombre as he turned to Otto. "Prince Albert asked that my embassy in Vienna keep an eye open for any threat to Bavaria and I know that you have heard about the threat that your father's kingdom faces because the king told me, when we last met, that you had discovered that our adversary Mr Stark has a wife."

"Yes, I know about Mr Stark and his evil deeds." Replied Otto.

"Well, things have developed. I can't tell you how I know this but I know that Mr Stark intends to cut off almost all trade through Bavaria, maybe as early as next week by putting huge charges on the transport of goods on the waterways, and he will demand a king's ransom to remove this charge. Stark will want a fortune from you once he has this hold on the waterways. Stark is just now buying waterways in Vienna and Saxony so that he can cut off your international supply routes.

Sir Harold had brought with him some copies of documents that showed Stark's intent. Sir Harold continued "Stark has influence everywhere now and has bought ministers and state employees, I cannot trust anyone but yourself with this news."

"Thank you for telling me, but while the king is away I am not sure what I can do, unless I can warn the government or ask my father to come back home quickly."

"By the time your father returns it will be too late. You will need to decide what you can do and who you can trust with this news. I have tried to get the sale of both waterways held up so that I can give you more time, but Stark is a slick advisory and he will find a way to buy the waterways very soon whatever I do."

Otto was lost for words. For a long time he had wanted some responsibility, but not anywhere near this much, and certainly not all in one morning. How was he to decide what should be done next if he couldn't trust anyone with any of the details of this?

Otto decided that his visitor was a wise and kind man. While he had never met the ambassador in person the king had always spoken well of him and Otto was convinced that the information was genuine. "Sir Harold" Otto asked "what would you do if you were me?" Without a second of hesitation Sir Harold said "I would find a confidante, it must be someone that you trust the country and your life to. I would tell that person about all of this and ask for their help in managing this situation. Do you have a minister or a nobleman that you know well and completely trust?"
"No, I don't have anyone in a powerful position that I know and trust."
"That person does not need to be powerful, they just need to be trustworthy, wise and helpful so that you can talk to them about all the things that you can do." Otto knew that only one person fitted this description, and he was waiting just outside the door.
"Yes" Otto said, there is someone who is wise, completely trustworthy and helpful that I can turn to."
Sir Harold replied, "I would talk this over with that person, and then find a way to minimise the damage to Bavaria. You will not get out of this easily but I am certain that a major crisis can be avoided, and, of course, I will help you and England will help you, as much as we can."
"Sir Harold, what will we need to do to really escape from the grip of this evil man?" Asked Otto. Sir Harold's face lit up and a smile grew. "They told me that you were good at asking questions, this is an excellent question, your royal highness, one that I have pondered for a while now. Stark has limited means. All this evil work of his, buying up waterways and paying off governments is costing him a great deal of money, like anyone else he can run out of money. You just need to engineer a situation so that when he stops your country trading through the

waterways he runs out of money before you do."

"But how can we do that, if he has cut off our trade we will not survive?"

Sir Harold replied, "Yes, you are right, if he manages to cut off your trading you are ruined, but look at what is going on in England, we are building railways – these are the transportation links of the future. Maybe even roads and cars will be the way forward. The world will not be using slow river and canal boats very much longer. If you really want to finish Stark you need a plan that will take him by surprise."

Otto still looked unhappy. "But railways and roads cost a lot of money. We already have canals and we are about to see our trade cut off. How can we afford to do this?"

Sir Harold proved to be a wise man, "There are plenty of wealthy people in Europe who can help you still, even your own barons could finance this if you persuade them that they have no choice, just show them that you are serious about your future and that you take pride in this beautiful country of Bavaria … and that they and you are ruined if you do not!" Otto was surprised. Sir Harold knew so much about what was happening in the world, half an hour with him was like having the useful parts of dozens of text books copied directly into his brain. "One other thing," said Sir Harold, "do not write about this to anyone. We believe that Stark is managing to read your mail, probably the mail from other noblemen as well. This is why I have called here at this hour today. If you want to talk about what Stark is doing just send a letter and say 'I would like to meet you'." Sir Harold drank up the last of his tea and prepared to leave.

"I am sorry to have to bring you such bad news in this way, but I thought that I should tell you about it first hand while I had an opportunity."

Otto replied, "thank you. I sincerely appreciate your visit and your words of encouragement. Please do come and see me whenever you are nearby."

"I will, thank you your royal highness." Sir Harold got into his carriage and set off on his long journey back to London.

"What was all that about?" Asked Higginbottom.
"I will tell you all about it, but first I need to have a cup of coffee. I feel like my brain is not working at all well today."

Over his coffee Otto told Higginbottom all about Sir Harold's message. "Let me see if I have the situation in my head" Higginbottom said to Otto. "According to Sir Harold, Stark is going to buy two more waterways so that he can cut off Bavaria from most of its international trade. The embassy in Vienna and Britain are doing all that they can to help but nothing is going to hold up the sale forever. In the worst case the sale will go through next week. Stark will then own enough to be able to cut Bavaria off until you offer him whatever he wants, gold, silver, perhaps even the king's throne. Is that the situation?"
"Exactly" Otto replied.
Otto turned to Higginbottom, "Are we are convinced that this was Sir Harold, not someone sent by Stark to frighten us?"
Higginbottom was convinced. "Sir Harold's badge looked genuine. You can't buy those, so the man is genuine and Sir Harold would have no reason to bring you this news as a false story."
Otto replied "So we are convinced that this is true?"
"Oh yes." Replied Higginbottom. "So Sir Harold says that you can't even warn your own government because Stark will then find out that the British know about his plans. So the next question is who in Bavaria would have most to lose if Stark does this?"
Otto replied, "Father has often mentioned that Count von Schwarz is the nobleman who trades a lot of goods overseas."
"Do you trust von Schwarz?" Asked Higginbottom.
"I only know him slightly, but father has always told me that he is a good man and a strong leader."
"Then von Schwarz is the man you need to see, where can you find him?"
Otto replied, "He has a castle in the Alps like us, but he is almost always in Munich."
"Then you had better pack, we are going to Munich as soon as

we are ready."

Otto gave Rufus a big cuddle and then the carriage set off. Otto remembered how much he loved travelling in the summer, it was a warm day and he could see the light green grass at the base of the mountains meeting with the dark green of the trees leading to the grey of the mountain tops and then finally the blue sky. As the carriage made its way towards Munich and the landscape changed to a flatter and duller outlook, the pressures of the morning took their toll on Otto and he fell asleep. When he awoke they were already in the busy city streets where carriages clattered over the cobble stones and people pushed their way through the crowded pavements. Otto closed the window. He was used to pure mountain air, for a few minutes the stench of the city was too much to bear. As they turned into a more leafy area and stopped at the Grand Hotel the smell subsided. Otto and Higginbottom were shown to their rooms at the top of the hotel.

It took most of a day to track down von Schwarz and set up a meeting in his house in the city. Otto and Higginbottom met a very exuberant red faced plump man who was clearly enjoying every moment of his life in this expanding city. Once they had explained the situation to him, and made von Schwarz promise not to tell another person, they left and agreed to meet him the next day to plan. As they were leaving von Schwarz looked like he had suddenly been given all the problems of the world on his shoulders. The meeting the next day was tense. Von Schwarz had clearly not slept well and he really said out loud exactly what he was thinking. "I don't understand why the king has not come here to tell me this in person?"
Otto replied, "He would, but he is too far away to get back to Bavaria in time."
"So you are telling me that the three of us are the only people in Bavaria to know about this and, out of the three of us, I am the only person who is able to do anything, so what you are really saying is that this impending national disaster is all my problem."
"We will help in any way we can" Higginbottom said sincerely.

"The way you can help is to bring the king here."
Otto stood up "It would take at least four days and by the time he arrived there may be little that can be done. We thought, since you have a lot of international trade we should let you know as soon as possible"
"I am really unhappy that it is left to me to deal with this," although a more hopeful look suddenly came over von Schwarz, "but I am willing to help." He smiled at Otto. "I am grateful that you thought of me. I will go to Vienna and try to buy the waterways in place of Mr Stark. I will leave this afternoon."
"Thank you" said Otto.
"Now gentlemen, I have some packing to do so if you wouldn't mind I would like to get on with it."
"Thank you" said Higginbottom, and he and Otto wished von Schwarz a safe journey.

Otto and Higginbottom were very quiet in the carriage on the way back to the castle, they both knew what was at stake and neither of them wanted to guess what the outcome of the trip to Vienna would be. Von Schwarz had promised to call in to the castle once he had some news. Once they reached the castle Rufus saw the carriage coming from almost half a mile away, he ran straight towards the carriage and the driver had to stop as the dog approached for fear of running him over. Rufus made such a noise that he had to be lifted into the carriage and was not content until he was sprawled over Otto and the seat beside him.
"Man's best friend" said Higginbottom with a smile.

It was almost a week before any more news came. Time passed by very slowly during Otto's lessons and history seemed more boring than ever. Suddenly one wet morning a familiar sound broke the monotony. Both Higginbottom and Otto raced to the window when they heard a carriage on the driveway to the castle. Sure enough it was von Schwarz and by the speed of his exit from the carriage he had some news. Higginbottom and Otto made it to the library just as Mr Benn was showing von Schwarz the way through the hall. As soon as the library door was shut von Schwarz looked like he was going to burst, he couldn't contain himself any longer. "I have come up with the most brilliant plan, it won't get rid of Stark but it will delay him by months ... let me explain: We have bought an option on those two waterways."

"We have bought a what?" asked Otto.

"You know ... an option" repeated von Schwarz.

"Higginbottom" said von Schwarz "what have you been teaching this boy in economics?"

"We haven't got to economics yet" said Higginbottom in a crusty way. He turned to Otto "an option is an agreement to buy something in the future, so I could buy an option now on all the apples in your orchard for a certain price. I would give you a small amount of money now and would have the option to buy them for a certain time, perhaps in a few months. When it gets to harvest time I can decide whether to buy the apples at the price we have agreed or not."

Otto finally got the point "I see so you, or we, could buy those waterways in the future ... but we don't have to."

"Exactly" said von Schwarz. "It is brilliant isn't it?"

Otto didn't look convinced "I don't know."

Von Schwarz answered his own question "Yes, it is brilliant because for the next nine months the rivers can not be sold to anyone, and after that we can decide whether we want to pay the king's ransom that we will have to pay to buy them or not ... but most importantly they can not be sold to Stark or anyone else in the meantime."

Higginbottom looked pleased "that is excellent news."

"What did it cost?" Asked Otto.

"Well if we both share the costs, one thousand guilders each. I assume that the king will pay his half?"

"Of course he will" said Higginbottom not wanting to offend their guest. Soon Mr Benn was summoned and he served tea in the castle's best tea set.

"This is a very English tradition" said von Schwarz.

Higginbottom smiled, "We try to maintain the best traditions from right across Europe."

Once the tea had been finished von Schwarz announced that he should continue his journey home.

"Thank you" said Higginbottom, and Otto together.

"It was my pleasure." Said von Schwarz.

As soon as von Schwarz had left Otto turned to Higginbottom "Was that really the most sensible thing to do?"

Higginbottom replied, "I think it was the best that we could have hoped for. At least we have nine months to get out of this, rather than just a couple of weeks."

"But it did come at a huge cost." Said Otto glumly.

"A cost that I'm sure the king and von Schwarz can afford. Anyway, what is done is done. We asked for von Schwarz's help and he has helped us in the best way he can. He put a lot of his own money into this, so he must think it was the best deal that we could have secured. Now it is time to look to the future."

Otto's eyes lit up "that is the fun part" he said. "We need to find out about the transportation systems of the future. Sir Harold told me a lot about this but we need to know how to build railways and roads in Bavaria, and we need help with this right now."

Higginbottom seemed happy to help "I think that we will need to go back to Munich to talk to professor Ritter."

"When can we go? Is tomorrow possible?"

"No, leave me to make the arrangements. Maybe next week … anyway you have a lot of studies to catch up on." Higginbottom said.

Otto replied, "We are in the middle of a crisis, so this must take priority. And anyway, this is much more fun than my studies."

The next week passed by quickly. Otto completed his lessons during the week and before Otto had time to think about anything else he was back in Munich with Professor Ritter. Higginbottom had reminded Otto to pack his small modified toy boat that had been given the kettle for a propulsion system. They had arranged to meet the professor in a very strange place, a huge brick building on the edge of the city that was the home of the Munich iron works. The professor and the works' manager were waiting to greet their young royal visitor. The professor was a tall thin man with a white beard and white hair, while the works' manager was a round short man who had hardly any hair at all. Otto and Higginbottom walked with the two men to the back of the iron works where, to Otto's amazement, a long U-shaped section of railway track and been laid across a field at the back of the works. A steam engine and a steam car were waiting for them in the yard. Both vehicles had their fires lit and within two minutes Otto was standing on the footplate of the early steam engine being shown how to drive it by the works' manager. Otto practised going gently forwards and backwards on the straight section of the track, and he then turned to the works' manager and asked "would you mind if we go a bit faster?"

The reply was "not at all your royal highness, we have about a mile of straight track but please go steady when we reach the turn." Otto once again developed one of his ear to ear grins as he got the engine up to 30 KPH. They then approached a turn and the works' manager said "gently here please your royal highness." Otto slowed the engine down and it went smoothly around the turn, he then sped up as they were on the return straight track and stopped the engine again when they reached the back of the iron works. Just as it stopped, there was a big hiss of steam being released. Otto thought that the engine was the most impressive thing he had ever seen. Higginbottom and the professor were waiting to talk to Otto.

"What do you think?" Said the professor.

"That was amazing" replied Otto "Completely amazing. Imagine if we could have come to Munich on this engine, it would have been much more fun and would have saved hours."

"Shall we try the car next?" asked Otto.

"No" replied the professor "it is an early prototype and is not able to be driven at present."

"That is a shame, but anyway, I think it is unlikely to be as impressive as the steam engine." The three men and Otto then went to the manager's office and were served coffee.

Higginbottom wanted to get straight to the point, "Professor, you know why we are interested in transport. What would it cost to build and equip an east-west road or railway across Bavaria?"

The professor paused for a moment and thought. "It is a long distance and there are many hills so a railway could be more difficult than a road, unless a suitably level route could be found."

"What about equipping the route? Can enough steam trains or cars be built?"

"Cars are more difficult at the moment, building small engines is proving more complicated than we first thought and I have no idea how long it will be before a fully working steam car is available to the public, but building say twenty engines for steam trains seems quite possible."

Higginbottom continued asking questions, "so what would it cost for an east-west railway and how long would it take to build?"

The professor paused again. "I can't tell you straight away, it is not something that I have done a lot of research on. I would need to consult some other engineers about the route … but I can get you a rough costing within a couple of days."

"Thank you" said Higginbottom.

"Thank you" said Otto "and please can I ask you to take a look at something else."

Otto went to the carriage and brought his modified toy boat. The professor and manager laughed from their bellies when they saw the contraption that Otto produced. Higginbottom said "don't laugh until you see this. Do you have a pond or a lake near here?"

The manager looked surprised "There is a big duck pond in the village just a few kilometres away, but we are very busy and, with the greatest of respect, is a toy boat really something that we need to see?"

"Oh yes," replied Higginbottom. The three men all got into the carriage with Otto and drove to the village. Otto had brought his kindling wood and matches. He put the boat onto the water and lit the small fire. The professor looked particularly bored watching the tiny boat as its kettle started to steam, but when it

got going both men were amazed by its speed. The professor looked startled "Who came up with this idea?" He asked Higginbottom. Higginbottom replied, like a proud father, "Well the prince did of course."
The works' manager didn't know what to say "Would your royal highness mind if we built a full size prototype of this boat?"
Otto turned to the manager "That was just what I was going to ask you to do. How long would it take?"
"It is a simple enough design, but it will need some thought to keep it stable. Perhaps a month." Once the small boat had cooled down Otto gave it to the manager. "You are welcome to borrow this, but please keep it safe for me."
"I will" he promised.

Two days later Otto and Higginbottom met with the professor in his office in the University of Munich. The professor began his summary as soon as his office door was closed. "I have fantastic news for you. The east-west railway can be built in Bavaria. There is nothing that prevents its construction. There are a number of steep valleys that will need bridges and there are some hills that will need gorges cutting or tunnels digging. To build the railway and install say twelve stations along it, a goods yard and some engine sheds would cost about 140,000 guilders. To build 20 engines will cost around 20,000 guilders."
"How long will the project take to complete?" Asked Higginbottom.
"It seems that about two years would be needed with the workforce we have now."
"What if we need it to be working in less than nine months?" Asked Otto very seriously.
"Nine months!" Exclaimed the professor. "That is a very short time, but it could be possible, as long as we can find and train at least four hundred new workers and build all the gorges, bridges and engines at the same time … it will cost more to do it this way though."
Higginbottom looked delighted. "Thank you professor, you have helped us very much. I am so glad that a railway can be built and

that engines could be manufactured so soon. Please do keep working on this plan and we will work on how to finance it"
"It was a great pleasure. I am delighted to help in any way I can, but 160,000 guilders is a king's ransom. How will you ever find this money?"
"I think that we will be able to" said Higginbottom honestly.

Otto and Higginbottom then made their way back to the castle. It was only a few days before the king and queen were expected back and there was nothing more that they could do now on their grand railway plan for Bavaria. Life in the castle soon got back to normal with Otto's lessons each day and a growing dog needing Otto to play with him each evening. Every night Rufus slept on his small carpet on Otto's floor and each day the servants tried to entertain Rufus while Otto had his lessons. Usually entertaining the dog was impossible and so Rufus ended up scratching at the classroom door until he was let in. Rufus could only stay as long as he slept on a rug on the floor and did not disturb the lessons.

Chapter 10
Winning over the Nobility

It was mid afternoon on a very hot Saturday in early June and Otto was outside playing with a ball with Rufus. Rufus was full of energy and kept on wagging his tail and chasing the ball long after Otto had run out of patience to keep throwing it. The garden was always magnificent in June, the lawn was a vibrant green, the lake shimmered in the sunlight and the smell of the queen's flower beds filled the garden. Otto saw a carriage approaching at a good speed along the driveway. He looked closely but from the distance he could not make out whose carriage it was. As it got closer Otto realised that it was a very familiar coach, it was his mother and father. He ran with Rufus to greet them near to the front door. The king and queen were delighted to see Otto after they had been away for nearly two months and they both grabbed Otto and hugged him.
"I am sure you have grown" said the king.
The queen looked at Rufus and said "I am not sure whether Otto has grown that much but the dog certainly has." The weary travellers went into the castle followed by a young boy and a very large puppy with an endlessly wagging tail.

Once the king and queen had found a comfortable seat and some coffee and cake had been served, Otto told them about everything that had happened and he wanted to know how things had gone in England.
"How long did the return journey take?"
The queen sounded much more refreshed as she spoke, "We spent a week and a half travelling, we wanted to return more gently and see some friends as we travelled across Europe."
"How long were you in England?" Asked Otto.
"Almost four weeks."
Otto continued with his questions, "Did you see Prince Albert and Queen Victoria?"
"Oh yes, we saw them twice and met with many of their

ministers."

"Will they help us? Will they lend money to Bavaria?"

"Well, yes and no." Replied the queen.

"My dear," said the king, "it is time for Otto to learn the truth. We do not return from England with any money or a firm promise of money."

Otto was shocked. "Do you mean that the trip was a waste of time?"

The king looked very calm when he spoke, "Not at all, far from it. We have learned a lot about Mr Stark and we have learned that he is in some way connected with an organisation of nasty individuals called The Club of Europe, who plan to take over areas of Europe and run the continent like a dictatorship. Under their regime no one will be free to do what they want and people will have to do as they are told or face terrible consequences."

"Will they kill people who do not do as they are told?" Asked Otto.

"Yes," replied the king, "that is exactly how that evil organisation works."

"We have to make sure that they don't manage to control Bavaria" said Otto.

The king looked more severe, "I agree. We have to do that."

"So how will England help?"

The king answered. "We need to raise money ourselves and whatever money we find, Prince Albert has a group of business men who will match the investment, as long as the money is invested in industry in Bavaria."

Otto asked, "Why can't they just invest money without needing someone to put in additional funding here?"

"Because they are not living here in Bavaria to protect their investment, they want to see local people funding enterprise so that this investment will be secure."

Otto wanted to see progress, "So what do we do next?"

The king had a cheerful smile, "I have all that in hand my boy. We are going to have a big summit here in a week's time. I have already invited my richest noblemen and a few Bavarian business men to spend two days at the castle."

Otto was curious, "What will you do in that summit?"
"We will plan what we do to industrialise this country and how we can do it with the money we have." Said the king.
Otto looked puzzled, "Will the noblemen all agree to one plan? They don't seem to work together very well"
"I think they will agree if I encourage them" said the king confidently.
Otto was not so confident. The king had to get agreement to his plan, without it they may just as well hand over the kingdom and the keys to the castle to Mr Stark and his evil Club of Europe organisation right now.
"I am really worried about this plan" said Otto after a long pause. The king was still convinced that he could make the summit work "It will all be all right" he said. The king seemed to be brimming with confidence.
The queen turned to Otto, "what worries you?"
"I don't think that the noblemen will agree. If there is anything that my lessons in politics, and the work I have done in Füssen, have taught me it is that getting agreement from people to one plan is really difficult. I don't see why the noblemen will think that a plan is good just because it comes recommended by us. I think they will all want to do different things, they will all want to put in different amounts of money and then we will never get agreement."
The queen could see that her son's lessons were proving to be very valuable. The queen turned to the king and said "I think Otto may be right and we will only have one chance to get this summit right. It is important that you let Otto help you in planning this summit."
The king could tolerate many things, but this was too much. "I am perfectly capable of running a summit on my own. After all I have run a country on my own for long enough."
The queen replied, "I know you are capable, I just think that you must have help from Otto. I am certain that he can help you to make the event even more successful."
The king's mind was closed. "I won't discuss it further. I don't need any help. I am going to my study and I don't want to be

disturbed."

"Perhaps we didn't pick the best time to talk to him," said the queen after the king had gone. "Otto, I think you are right, we need to be very clever about how we run this summit. It will be our only chance to get this county free of Mr Stark and his evil friends."

"Then we had better hope that father sees some sense."

The queen smiled, "I think I can persuade him."

The queen tried everything she could think of for the next five days, but the king would not listen to reason. The king's health was not good just after they returned from England. After two days he was still looking very white. One afternoon the queen sent some tea and cakes up to him and went to his study half an hour later. Neither the food or drink had been touched. "Please take some rest" the queen asked, "you really don't look well."

"There is nothing wrong with me that a night's sleep will not fix."

"At least eat your cake."

"I am not hungry, you eat it or send it back to the kitchen." This really was a bad sign. He was usually able to consume half a cake in an afternoon. Today not one slice had been taken. The king was not in a mood to listen and the queen could see that it was pointless trying to persuade him any more. She asked for his dinner to be sent up to the study when he did not come to the table to eat.

The queen went to bed early that night but was woken by the sound of coughing. She went to the study and saw the king sitting behind his candlelit desk at one o'clock in the morning, still looking very white, coughing and complaining that he was bitterly cold. The fire was well stoked and the king was roasting hot.

"I am sending for the doctor right now."

"It is just a cold, don't waste your time." The doctor arrived an hour later and insisted that the king go to bed with a glass of warm water. The doctor had left some medicine to relieve the symptoms a little but warned the king, "It is a flu, unless you take it easy and go to bed you will be very seriously ill tomorrow."

The queen was exasperated; she turned to her husband "Now will you rest?"

"Yes, yes. I have to be well for the summit in two days, I will go to bed." The queen and the doctor helped to get the king to bed. He soon fell asleep and spent the night either snoring deep loud snores or waking in fits of coughs.

The next day was much worse for the king. He was so unwell he would not leave his bed and things were not improving much in the run up to the summit.

"Should we cancel the summit?" the queen asked Otto.

Otto replied, "When can it be held again?"

"Not until late August, many of the noblemen will be away for the rest of the summer."

Otto looked very worried, "We can't wait that long. Do you think that father will recover in time?"

"Not by tomorrow. If this goes ahead it is just you and me who can host the summit."

Otto asked the queen, "Is there any other way of doing this?"

The queen thought deeply about Otto's question. "I can't think of anything else. I think that we either host the summit ourselves or cancel it until August. Have your lesson's given you any ideas, can you think of anything else we can do?"

"Nothing else comes to mind and we need to decide today. I think we should host it. I will get Higginbottom to start thinking about how we run it straight away."

Otto walked to Higginbottom's suite and tapped on the door. Once Otto had explained what he was planning Higginbottom looked at Otto as though he had told him that they were going to Mars on a flying sledge. "You are going to do what?" Higginbottom said, "If you are trying to manage with less people than you need why don't you just get rid of all the government workers and do all their jobs for them while you are at it."

"I know it is going to be really difficult to do this but I don't think we have a choice." Otto replied.

Higginbottom still looked at Otto in amazement. "But this is the most important summit in the history of your country. If this does not work then you will no longer have a country. Don't you think that it is just a tiny bit risky leaving this to the queen and a twelve year old boy, albeit a very able and clever twelve year old boy?"

Otto looked sad. "I know it is risky, but I just wanted to help and I thought you would be able to help us."

Higginbotten replied, "Of course I will help you in any way that I can, I am just highlighting the obvious point that neither you nor the queen have any experience of running an event like this, and you are planning to get your experience on the highest risk event that your country has ever had."

Otto replied, "We have to decide right now whether we run this summit or we don't. If we delay there will not be time to send out letters to cancel the event and the noblemen will be angry at coming here for an event that is not happening ... please Higginbottom, if there is anything that you can think of. We need your excellent mind now?"

Higginbottom started thinking. "So you can't cancel, you have to hold the summit. Will the king be able to help?"

"Not unless he makes a miraculous recovery."

Higginbottom looked very seriously at Otto, "So if you have to go ahead then you need the best combination of people you can have. Do any of these noblemen know me?"

"I don't think so."

Higginbottom replied, "Well then, let me help you."

"Do you feel happy to do that?"

"Not at all happy, but I can't just leave you and the queen alone with the noblemen."

"Thank you Higginbottom, it is very kind of you to offer to help."

Otto and Higginbottom spent the rest of the day deciding how to get the noblemen to agree to do one thing together. Higginbottom

showed Otto how to get agreement "Above all, the noblemen must feel that if they don't agree they will no longer be noblemen. They must feel the pressure that your family are feeling"
"How do we do that?" Asked Otto.
"That is easy, leave it to me. Has the king given us any guidance?"
Otto replied, "When we talk about the cost of the railways all that he can afford is five percent of the cost, we must not go any higher or the king will run out of money."
"Is there anything else?" Asked Higginbottom.
Otto replied, "Nothing at all, the king seems to be so unwell now that he has washed his hands of it."
"Oh dear," sighed Higginbottom.

The next day the noblemen began to arrive at the castle and were greeted by the queen and Otto. The king was still far too ill even to come downstairs. The queen explained that the king was very ill and that they would start the summit without the king who would join them later. Coffee was served in the library for everyone and the queen introduced Higginbottom to the group as a "Special Advisor." Higginbottom walked around the room shaking hands and talking to as many of the noblemen as possible. Otto was starting to feel out of place with the noblemen. He gazed out of the windows and he saw the island in the lake that he loved so much and occasionally caught a glimpse of Rufus running on the lawn. Otto found a few seconds when Higginbottom was not talking to someone.
"Can't we just get on with it?" Otto whispered to Higginbottom.
"We are getting on with it." Replied Higginbottom.
Otto continued to whisper, "I mean talk about what is important so that we can go out and do something fun while it is still light."
"I don't know about you, but I am talking about what is important." Whispered Higginbottom.
"No you are not, you just asked the count about his journey."
Higginbottom sighed and walked towards the king's study where he could talk to Otto more openly.

Higginbottom said, "Of course I was talking to the count about his journey. That is important for him and it is important for me to know how he feels about his journey, and how he feels about this meeting. I can then understand what matters to him in his own life. Once I understand him I have a better idea of what might happen when we talk about business today."

Otto looked even more frustrated "Good grief, I would much rather just get on with talking and then go for a good run with Rufus."

"When you said that you would rather be a professor than a king, you meant it didn't you?"

"I did" replied Otto with a grin.

"Well," replied Higginbottom, "for the sake of your family you will have to act like a king today. Pretend that nothing matters to you in the world except the people standing in this room and the plans we have for today. That should help you get into the right mindset." They returned to the group and a footman arrived with a plate of cream cakes which were quickly devoured by most of the guests. The cakes provided an amazing transformation, the conversation moved on from the things that the noblemen didn't have and their lack of money to conversations about the best cakes and recommendations about where to buy such things.

At ten o'clock the queen encouraged everyone to go into the dining room. The queen and Higginbottom sat in the middle of the large table with Otto sitting beside Higginbottom, they had their backs to the gently stoked fireplace. The noblemen arranged themselves around the table, the doors were closed and the servants were told not to enter the room. The queen began. "Thank you all for coming to the castle today and welcome to our summit. I am sorry that the king is unable to join us. I hope he will be well enough to join us very soon. To begin the day I would like our Special Advisor, Mr Higginbottom, to talk to you about a situation that is tremendously serious." Higginbottom stood up. "Thank you your majesty. My lords, during the last three months we have realised that an enemy is operating in this kingdom. This is an enemy of anyone who loves the peaceful and happy life that we all enjoy in Bavaria. It is your enemy and mine. The enemy is very good at hiding behind legitimate looking companies and seemingly well connected individuals. The enemy is called the Club of Europe and their plan is to take over Europe piece by piece. One of the countries that they are already trying to drag into their clutches is Bavaria and they are doing this through a man known as 'Ivan the Unstoppable'. Mr Ivan Stark has already taken a Duke's wealth and left his family destitute. He can and will do this to you unless we agree today on how we stop this man and this evil organisation from functioning in Bavaria."

Suddenly lots of discussion began between the noblemen and many of them started shaking their heads saying "this can not be, we have seen no sign of this." Higginbottom passed a letter from Fiona around the table and then a letter from Prince Albert in England, both describing what Mr Stark had done recently. Prince Albert talked about the advice he had received from his foreign secretary that the Club of Europe was on the brink of taking control of several European countries, certainly halting the industrialisation of Europe and this would be likely to plunge Europe into a great war. "My lords, let me read you just the last paragraph from Prince Albert's letter: 'I can not express how strongly I am concerned about what this organisation will do to Europe and I call on all European leaders to work with us to rid Europe of this dangerous organisation'."

The queen stood up "We have asked you to come here because Bavaria is in great danger, I will explain why in a moment, but first, is there anyone who feels that urgent action is needed?" The noblemen talked for a few moments and then the queen asked them, "We need to act together, please raise your hands if you feel that urgent action is needed?" All the noblemen raised their hands.

The queen continued to talk to the group. "I am sorry to tell you that there is more bad news. Our waterways are already in the hands of Mr Stark. This alone gives him to power cripple our kingdom by raising the price of transportation to the point where we cannot move goods around the country. The movement of goods is essential if we are to follow the example of England and become an industrialised nation that is growing in the world. Mr Stark could make us remain a small country with little more than a farming economy. If he does, we will soon be forgotten by the rest of Europe, particularly England. If my husband were well enough he would say that you have the power to change this, the future of Bavaria is in your hands. If you choose today to work with your fellow noblemen on one plan then we can defeat this evil threat. At our last meeting with Prince Albert three weeks ago he said much more than he could write in his letter. He said that countries like ours had 'two months at best to plan their way out before it would be too late to save them'. Gentlemen, we have two months, if we do not find a way out of this then all your land and your lovely homes will become the property of Mr Stark.

The noblemen talked for a few moments and Count von Schwarz spoke up "I don't understand how it is possible for Mr Stark to do this. After all the work we have done to save the waterways in Vienna and Saxony. Can't we just send the army after him?"

The queen replied. "Prince Albert tells us that other countries have tried this. Stark has friends everywhere and by the time that the army arrive at where they think he will be, Stark is no longer there. So far Stark has also not committed any crime, he has just been very clever and lucky at buying things just at the best moment."

Count von Schwarz replied. "If you want to free the waterways why don't you just pass a law saying that they will all become national property in a week's time?"

The queen said "Stark has already thought of this. The waterways are owned 80% by Stark and 20% by the king of Prussia. If we take away Stark's waterways then Prussia will start a war with us."

Count von Schwarz continued "Can't we just give something to Prussia in exchange for their ownership?"

The queen replied, "Prince Albert told us that Stark will have already thought of this. Prussia will not be able to sell otherwise

Stark will do something terrible to them. If we try to unravel the web that Stark has created we will just waste the time that we could use to save our country. Mr Higginbottom will talk about the things that we can do."

Higginbottom stood up and began to talk through all the ways that Bavaria could release itself from this situation. Otto turned to the queen and whispered "Mother, you didn't tell me what Prince Albert said, is all that true?"
The queen replied, "I'm afraid it is. Albert described Bavaria like an animal that had acquired a large group of parasites and would soon die. He said that very soon all of the energy and wealth would be sucked out of the country and ..."
"and what?" Asked Otto.
"You don't need to know about the rest." Replied the queen.
Otto said "Yes I do."
The queen took out her handkerchief and dried her eyes. In a whisper she replied "Albert offered us a home if ever we needed it, he said that he hoped that we could save our country, but he feared that it might be too late already to save Bavaria."
Otto tried very hard to reply in a whisper. "This can't happen ... I would miss the mountains and lakes ... and we can't live in England, it rains all the time there."
The queen tried to smile. "Don't loose heart. I didn't want to tell you because we need to be strong and fight for our country together."

Once Higginbottom had talked about the ways that England was managing its industrialisation he showed the noblemen how this could be a way to get Bavaria out of the trap that Mr Stark had set. The key was transportation, at present Mr Stark owned the only way that large heavy items could be moved around the kingdom, this was Otto's cue and he had rehearsed his part in the summit well with Higginbottom. Otto stood up and began his speech. "In England steam power is used to move heavy objects with great speed across the kingdom. Steam engines pull heavy trains at about 100 kilometres an hour. The railways allow passengers to travel long distances at great speed in comfort and there is talk about a steam train that could travel at over a hundred and sixty kilometeres an hour. Railways are the future for Bavaria, if we can link them up to other European railways they will bring more tourists to our country and allow us to move raw materials around the country to make things in Bavaria and then sell them quickly and easily to people right across Europe."

The noblemen started talking to each other and then began asking questions. "Why not use roads?" they asked.

Otto replied, "Roads are good, but right now we need to move large numbers of people and lots of heavy goods quickly and easily. A steam train can move almost ten times as much as a steam car, and steam trains have proved to be more reliable in England."

The noblemen kept asking questions, "But we have roads, why not use them? A new railway involves building hundreds of kilometres of track."

Otto replied, "the roads we have are little more than tracks. Powered cars need level roads that are not full of pot holes. We will spend a lot of money creating new roads and right now the cost of transporting goods by road is higher. It is more efficient to build railways and benefit from lower running costs."

Count von Schwarz looked puzzled, "So how much will all this cost?" He asked.

Otto answered, "Firstly we want to build an east-west railway this year that will connect Munich to Ulm and Salzburg. The cost of this will be about 160,000 guilders and half of this money has already been secured"

Count von Schwarz looked like he was about to fall off his seat. "You want us to pay for part of this and yet you say that the kingdom is about to be swallowed up by Mr Stark and his cronies … what guarantee do we have that our investment is safe?"

"You will have an act of parliament that will protect your ownership of the railway infrastructure. The money that this railway will generate will free us all from Mr Stark."

As the clock struck twelve o'clock the queen gathered up the papers that had been used for the meeting and put them away. The servants served lunch and everyone loved the vegetable soup starter which was followed by a chicken salad. The group went out to the lawn after lunch and spent a few minutes admiring the lakes and mountains. Otto was nearly knocked over by Rufus who ran out from the castle. Rufus stood on his back legs once he reached Otto, putting his front paws up onto Otto's shoulders so that he could look Otto in the eye. Otto gave Rufus a big cuddle and then said "Later Rufus, I am busy now." One of the servants took Rufus back into his room near to the castle kitchen and Rufus whined and pulled on his lead; he wanted to spend the afternoon with Otto.

Otto managed to find a quiet moment to talk to Higginbottom. "What is holding the noblemen back, they are asking so many questions ... I had a long discussion over lunch about the gauge of the railway. Does the distance between the two tracks really matter to them? Despite this they look as though they really don't want to do this."

Higginbottom replied, "At the moment the noblemen don't want this. Can't you see it, they are afraid of losing their money, they can't see how this venture will work and they would rather just continue doing what they have been doing. Just wait until this afternoon, you will see some anger and then some denial and after that, just maybe we will get them to agree."

Otto smiled. "Higginbottom, thank you. I am so glad you are here."

Higginbottom replied, "I bet you wouldn't have said that a few months ago."

"Well no."

Higginbottom grinned, "There you see, anyone can change."

The queen went to see the king in the hope that he would be able to join the meeting in the afternoon. He was fast asleep and smelled of some particularly aromatic herbal cure. Katarina was looking after him in the afternoon and the queen asked, "Will he be able to get up soon?"

Katarina replied, "It is going to take a while your majesty. He is still very hot and I don't think he will be much better until at least tomorrow."

The queen smiled at Katarina. "Thank you for taking such good care of him. Let me know if you need anything more."

The queen returned to her guests and whispered to Otto, "it looks as though we are on our own this afternoon."

The group of noblemen moved back into the dining room to begin the second part of their meeting. Higginbottom stood up "My lords, welcome back to the summit. Let us just recap on this morning's meeting. We talked a lot about the evil menace that is gripping Europe and our country. You saw that we have a short time to act to save all that we love in this great nation. You have seen the plans that the prince has talked so eloquently about for a railway that will cross Bavaria and establish us as one of the strongest economies in Europe. By building and running this railway we will be the envy of most of the other European nations. My lords, how do you feel about this?" There was some quiet discussion at the table for a few minutes, which was to be the calm before the storm.

Count von Schwarz was the first to speak up "Let me see if I have this right. You are saying that the royal family have let us slide into a position in which this nation is slowly being taken over by some evil dictator and you are asking us to pay to get rid of this menace that we have not seen or heard of?"

The queen took a deep breath before she responded, "We have come to you all as soon as we could to ask you all to join with us. I know that it feels like an invisible threat, but those of us that have witnessed Mr Stark's actions know that he is a real and dangerous threat, as much of a threat as thousands of soldiers shooting bullets at us right now."

The discussions continued for a long time about whether Mr Stark could really do what he had planned and it seemed as though the afternoon would end with no agreement. At ten to four Higginbottom decided to push the noblemen a bit harder.

"My lords, you can be in no doubt by now of the seriousness of this situation. We have very little time left, what do you feel is holding you back from investing your money in this venture?" Again there was some quiet discussion at the table before Count von Schwarz spoke up. "What is holding us back is the amount of money that the royal family is putting into this. You are offering a mere five percent of the total cost and yet you expect us to risk everything we have ... why are you not risking everything that you have too?"

There was a silence in the room. Higginbottom looked at the queen who looked as though she wanted to speak but couldn't. Otto stood up. "Our income has fallen as this country has suffered, we are offering to put in what money we have, an investment of five percent represents a significant amount for any one investor."

Von Schwarz replied, "You would need to raise this much higher before we would commit." The discussions continued with the noblemen wanting the king to commit to at least twenty five percent, Otto hoped that he could keep the investment much lower than this. In the end he said "If you will commit today, we will invest ten percent." The queen and Higginbottom tried to stop him because they knew that the king couldn't afford this, but it was far too late. The group reluctantly agreed and by the time anyone had time to think about how the king was going to raise all the extra money a plan of investment was formed by the group and an agreement signed.

The queen went upstairs and insisted that the king take a bath and dress for dinner. Once he was dressed Katarina brought him a very special tonic to give him energy. Despite all the medicine that the king had he didn't look well when he arrived at the dinner table, he was white and thinner than usual. His voice was faint. The noblemen greeted the king enthusiastically and tried to lift his spirits but the king really did not want to be with them. Dinner was served for all the noblemen and unusually Higginbottom joined the party. The king looked slightly surprised as Higginbottom sat down, but he made no comment. The king had very little appetite, he had a little of his soup and then excused himself before the main course arrived. He went back to bed and slept. The king had asked nothing about the summit and Otto was very glad that he didn't have to break the bad news about the money to his father that evening. Some of the noblemen left quickly after dinner so that they could begin their journey home. A few noblemen stayed for the night. Once all the guests had gone to their rooms Otto, Higginbottom and the queen sat in front of the fire in the drawing room.

"Well, it could be worse" Higginbottom said "we did get the agreement that we needed."

"We did" said the queen.

Otto had his head in his hands as Higginbottom said "It just leaves us with a bit of a financial, um, situation."

The queen knew that something needed to be said "You could, at least have tried to get them to agree to seven or eight percent."

"I know I should have." said Otto.

Higginbottom tried to sound positive "Eight percent would have been easier."

Otto replied, "It would certainly have been easier to tell father about. But I think that we just need a way of raising money quickly, and I'm sure we can find one."

"I hope you are right" the queen replied. "I am going to bed now and we can decide what to do about this in the morning. Thank you Mr Higginbottom so very much for your help today."

Higginbottom turned to Otto. "What have you learned from today?"

"That I am not very good at politics, that we would have been sunk if you hadn't helped and that I really should be a professor not a king."

Higginbottom replied "Why do you think that you should just be able to just walk into something new and do it really well the first time? Do you not think that everyone needs practice before they become good at something?"

Otto replied "I should have pressed the noblemen for what we need harder. How much practice will it take to do that?"

Higginbottom smiled "Very little I should think, you just need to live in the moment a bit more and forget about all the other things that are going on."

Otto still looked sad, "Let's face it, I will never be the kind of king that I should be, look at all the European kings, the mighty Russian Tsar, look at Queen Victoria."

Higginbottom turned to Otto, "Queen Victoria is a very good example, you see a successful lady leading the most advanced empire in the world ... it is hard to believe that her reign almost came to an end just after it had begun because of her choice of ladies in waiting."

"Really." Replied Otto, "I didn't know about that."

"It was a big scandal at the time, it caused parliament to be dissolved ... so you see even such a great queen has made a few big mistakes, so really the only way to not make any mistakes is not to do anything at all."

Otto smiled. "Not doing anything at all seems like paradise at present ... I am going to bed."

Otto stopped in the doorway. "Higginbottom, I really can't imagine how today would have turned out if you had not helped. Thank you so much for everything you have done. This was a momentous day for our kingdom and you saved that day ... I really can't imagine any other tutor in the world being able to do what you did today. Perhaps we should put up a statue in your honour or name a street after you."

Higginbottom laughed a deep laugh from his belly, "Now you are thinking like a king. Good night."

On his way through the hallway Otto's mind was still turning over what he should say to his father about all the extra money that he had committed to. Just then he walked straight into Katarina. "I am so sorry" said Otto, "I was very distracted. Are you all right?"

"Yes, I am fine. Please don't worry about it," she replied.

Otto looked curiously at Katarina. "It is very late, why are you still here, surely you need your rest?"

"I do need my rest but the queen was very worried about the king and I promised to make him a very special night tonic to help him sleep. So why are you so distracted? Is it about the big summit here?"

"It is," replied Otto who looked very surprised, "how do you know out this?"

"All the servants are talking about it. They don't know what is going on but they know it is very important."

Otto asked "Can you keep a secret?"

Katatina replied, "Yes, of course." Otto told Katarina about the plans for the railway and the cost of the railway and how much he had committed the king to. "My biggest problem is that I have to tell the king at some time, but if I tell him now it might just be the end of him ... and then I will have to be king ... and look at the sort of mess we are in after one day of me doing royal things. Heaven knows where we will end up if I am on the throne."

Otto was sure that Katarina was going to give him another good telling off. After all, she had managed to do this every time that they had met before. But, unusually, Katarina was very sympathetic. She replied, "It is so easy to commit to something that you shouldn't. I once got my father to help a poor old man who couldn't afford a doctor. Father was telling me for weeks how much money this cost him. I am sorry that this has happened to you. You shouldn't feel bad, everyone makes mistakes."

Otto replied "Higginbottom told me exactly the same thing ... but it doesn't make me feel any better and I am very worried about telling my father."

Katarina smiled, "You look like you need one of my night time herbal teas. They help you relax and sleep very deeply. Everything will be better in the morning."

"Thank you" said Otto, and he went with Katarina to the kitchen to make tea. They talked for a few more minutes as Otto drank his tea and then he walked with Katarina to the carriage to take her home.

"Thank you for talking to me," said Otto as he squeezed Katarina's hand gently. She smiled and kissed his cheek just as she got into the carriage. "Everything will be better tomorrow," she said as she left in the carriage.

Chapter 11
A Big Secret Revealed

Higginbottom had breakfast with Otto and the three noblemen who were staying overnight. Count von Schwarz had a puzzled look on his face. "Higginbottom, when I saw you in action yesterday I realised that I have seen you somewhere before you started working here, I know I have."
Higginbottom had a nervous grin, "I think you must be mistaken."
"No, I distinctly remember you I just can't remember where I last saw you."
Higginbottom replied, "You have not been to the castle for the last year so I am not sure how we could have met before."
Von Schwarz said "I have never been to England, so we didn't meet there, this really is odd." The group ate a huge cooked breakfast and then spent a few minutes talking about their favourite destinations in the world. Few of them had been to England so Higginbottom spent a little while telling them how great his country was, but no one was persuaded to visit England because of the reports of constant rain. Count von Schwarz said "My favourite place in the world is Italy, I love the warm air, sandy beaches and clear sea. My wife loves the Italian food so we usually spend a lot of time during the spring and early summer in our house near to Rome ... wait a minute" he said turning to Higginbottom, "that is where I recognise you from. I was at a party hosted by the British Ambassador in Rome last year. You were there. I remember you now as if it were yesterday."
"I think you must be mistaken," repeated Higginbottom looking more uneasy.
Otto smiled, "you were never in Italy last year, your wife said that you were tutor to Viscount Hill's children before this job and he never travelled."
Higginbottom replied, "We did take a short holiday in Italy so it is possible that you saw me."

Count von Schwartz looked puzzled again, "so what were you doing with the ambassador?"
"Well we met a lot of English people abroad. I remember meeting the ambassador once."
"I see" said von Schwartz, looking unconvinced.

Very soon the carriages were prepared and the guests left the castle. As von Schwartz climbed into his carriage he turned to Otto. "Something about Higginbottom's account doesn't add up, make sure you tell your mother and father, it would be worth getting to the bottom of this. We don't want to find that after all this work we end up with someone from the Club of Europe working in our midst."
Otto replied "Certainly not. Thank you, I will look into it."
Once the guests had all departed, Higginbottom joined Otto and the queen in the drawing room. Higginbottom got a cup of coffee and sat down. He looked like a broken man. "I have something to tell you, something that I don't think you will be happy about."
"Go on" said the queen.
"Von Schwartz is absolutely right, I am not who you think I am. I work for the British Foreign Office and I was in Italy last year. In January the Foreign Office was told that Bavaria was funding and empowering the Club of Europe. This was terrible news. I was among the group of diplomats that went to Buckingham Palace to tell Prince Albert. Prince Albert was deeply shocked and he said that if we did nothing and left Bavaria to suffer then all of Europe would be taken over by this evil organisation. Prince Albert and the Foreign Office needed to know what was going on.
"So what did they do?" Asked the queen impatiently, as she was already guessing what the answer would be.
Higginbottom said "Prince Albert and the Foreign Office needed to know if the reports were true. If it was true and you and the king were funding the Club of Europe then no British money would have been allowed to be invested in Bavaria."
"I realise that" said the queen who's patience was wearing thin. She repeated "What did the British Foreign Office do?"

Higginbottom replied directly "they selected a tutor for your son. I was the best qualified to tutor a prince, and I had the best range of languages of any of the senior staff in the department. I do have experience of this work. I tutored a relative for a while so I knew what was expected of a tutor. The British Foreign Office selected me to come to Bavaria and established a credible past and references for me."

The queen was red in the face and she looked like she would explode. She could not speak for an entire minute. "You mean to tell me all the time that Albert and Victoria were being nice to us they were actually spying on us ... on our family and on the way that we run our kingdom. What were you reporting back?"

"I reported very little. I sent a few encoded messaged to London just to say that Bavaria was safe and that Stark was not controlling the royal family in any other way than through the ownership of the waterways. I said that you were working hard to get free of Stark. My boss in London wanted to make sure that Bavaria did not fall prey to this evil empire."

"By spying on us?"

"Well, yes, when you put it that way it seems very bad," replied Higginbottom.

"Albert and Victoria knew all about this?" The queen replied.

"Prince Albert certainly did know what we were doing and he helped plan and approve it. I believe that it was just my boss and Prince Albert. No other diplomats knew about this and I don't think that Queen Victoria knew."

"This is absolutely terrible," said the queen.

Higginbottom looked like a man who was ready to give up. "I agree with you your majesty. It is terrible, it was done to protect Bavaria but it was not done well. I have enjoyed every moment I have spent here and I would love to give up all my connections to England and continue tutoring Otto, I have enjoyed this job more than anything else in my life. But of course I will pack my things and leave today if that is what you wish."

"I think that would be best," replied the queen.

"Mother, please think about this more. After all Higginbottom has done for us, you are surely not going to just let him go like this?" Otto pleaded.

The queen replied, as if Higginbottom was not in the room. "Higginbottom is not a professional tutor, he has admitted that himself. How can he stay and be your tutor if he is not qualified and experienced for the job? Also he has fulfilled a devious mission on behalf of the English government and I will not condone that practice."

"Thank you for your hospitality and kindness, your Royal Highness." said Higginbottom as he stood up from his seat. "I am sorry that we have had to part company like this, I have enjoyed every moment of my time here."

He turned to Otto and trying very hard to keep his composure he said "Good luck your royal highness, you will make a fantastic king."

Otto stood up and hugged Higginbottom, and with tears running down his face he said "Mother, don't let him leave like this."

"There is nothing I can do," said the queen.

Otto went straight to see the king, who had more colour in his cheeks and seemed to want to discuss the summit. Otto didn't want to discuss the summit at all, so he began by saying. "Father, Higginbottom is leaving. Mother has told him to go."

"Why on earth would she do that?" Otto told the king about how helpful Higginbottom had been in getting an agreement from the summit. All that Otto said was that Higginbottom was not entirely truthful about the past. "Ask your mother to come and see me" said the king.

When the queen arrived the king began his monologue, "Wasn't it you who said that Higginbottom has kept Otto from being killed? Didn't Higginbottom just run a summit for you? And now you want to behave like the worst kind of employer and throw Higginbottom out like a servant that is no longer useful?"

The queen was still furious about the situation, "It is not like that. Higginbottom lied to us and he has been controlled by England – we have been manipulated by the English government and Higginbottom was the insider who fed them with information. It is no wonder we had such a rapid audience with Queen Victoria, Higginbottom was corresponding with her husband regularly." The king would not accept any thought of removing Higginbottom from the castle, "It seems, from what Otto has told me, that Higginbottom has changed. He is willing to tutor our son and give up all connection with England. We are not in an ideal situation, but my only concern is that Higginbottom is over qualified for the job – he could run a province by himself."

"I still don't like the way that this came about," said the queen.

"Nor do I," replied the king, "but I understand why Prince Albert wanted to keep an eye on us and I can see that no real harm has been done. Higginbottom is clearly a decent fellow and if he is willing to work for us as a tutor we should graciously accept the help of this gifted man. I want no more discussion on this matter, I will tell Higginbottom that we are sorry, that he is welcome to stay and this will be the end of the matter." The king had made up his mind and the queen realised that she had to accept this decision.

Everyone in the castle was delighted that Higginbottom was going to stay. He was a quiet observant man that people took a while to get to know, but once people knew Higginbottom they liked him very much. No one was as pleased as Otto with the news. When the king told Otto that Higginbottom was staying at the castle his face lit up and he gave the king a big hug. "Thank you" Otto said.

The king replied, "You are welcome … now you must tell me about the summit."

Otto smiled. "Please, not just now. You need to rest. I will tell you all about it tomorrow."

Monday morning came all too soon. The queen and Higginbottom waited for Otto in the classroom at the beginning of the day.

"My dear Otto," said the queen, "you really have to tell the king about the summit now."

"I know." Replied Otto.

Higginbottom smiled, "Go on, it will be better to get it over."
"I know."
"Well? Go on then." said the queen. "The king is dressed and we have a short visit planned today so I will be able calm him down during the morning."
Otto went to see the king while the queen and Higginbottom waited and waited in the hallway. They were only a short distance from the king's bedroom and yet neither the queen nor Higginbottom could hear anything at all of the conversation.
Higginbottom was getting very worried. "Perhaps we should have offered to go with him."
"No, it is better that he tells the king himself." Replied the queen.
"What can they be talking about?" Said Higginbottom.
The queen replied, "I don't know, but it is taking forever." Suddenly, a booming resonant voice said.
"HOW MUCH?"
The queen and Higginbottom said together "He has told the king."

The king refused to talk to the queen or Otto about the summit for the rest of the morning. During their lunch the queen said "Otto has got a plan to find the money."
The king was not convinced. "Well, I'm glad he has a plan. That will do us a lot of good when we are cast out of this castle and the country because we can't live within our means."
The queen replied, "I think that you should at least listen to what Otto has to say. You may not see it now, but he did well in that summit. You would not have been able to get a much better deal from the noblemen, and we do have the agreement that we need."

In the evening the king was still not in a mood to listen. The queen told the servants not to serve dinner until she and Otto had finished talking to the king. The king, queen and Otto came to the dining room. "It is eight o'clock" said the king "why is dinner not being served?"
The queen stood up "You must listen to Otto's plan today." The king disliked late meals and was getting more and more agitated.

"I will listen later on, but I want my dinner now."
"No, if you want your dinner you need to listen to what we have to say right now," replied the queen.
The king could see that he had to do this. "All right, just get on with it please."

Otto brought the king a map of Lake Ammersee near the town of Seefeld. "In early September there is a Bavarian boat race held on one of the big lakes, it is usually a small race hosted by the local mayor. This year I have asked the local noblemen to help in making this a really big competition, something that all of the athletes of Europe will want to be part of."
The king looked confused "how does this help me pay for a railway that I can't afford?"
"We will have a fair in the town, sell tickets to the event and have thousands of tourists come, as long as you and mother are at the event, and you ask the best athletes in Europe to take part, this is certain to make a lot of money. If we could also have some royal guests from across Europe that would encourage athletes from those countries to join in the event."
The king looked like he had seen enough, "Yes" he grunted, "If you have the time to make this work I am happy to help. I doubt that it will raise anywhere near the money we need but let's do this as we don't have a better plan. Now can we please have our dinner?"
"At once" said the queen and rang for Mr Benn.

Otto spent July planning the competition with the major of Seefeld. Higginbottom joined them whenever he could and contributed lots of ideas for improving the event. Otto talked to the king about the list of foreign royal family members to invite. Higginbottom joined them and said "you must invite Queen Victoria and Prince Albert." Even Otto was quite worried about this.
"It is just a Bavarian event, why would the British royal family travel all this way to see a Bavarian event?"
"Because they want re-assurance that things are well in Bavaria,"

replied Higginbottom.

The king said, "Well, you know more than I do about the British. If you think it is a good idea I am happy to do this." In total fifty five foreign sailors and rowers were invited to the boat race along with ten European princes, twelve princesses and the queen of England. The king's private secretary was inundated with all the work involved in sending out so many invitations, on top of all his usual jobs. Twice during the preparation for the event the king's private secretary threatened to leave his job. Higginbottom proved to be very good at convincing him that he should stay at the castle.

Otto got another shock, the queen came in to see him just as his classes finished for the day "There will be a dance after the first day of the competition … and you may need to waltz."

Higginbottom smiled "Shall I help you learn to dance?"

"Yes please" said Otto nervously and the dance lessons began the next day. Otto proved to be very poor at learning to dance. It took Higginbottom a week to get Otto to start dancing every time with his left foot. Then things got even more confusing for Otto. Otto could remember anything that Higginbottom drew on the blackboard, he could remember, almost word for word, anything that was said, but he couldn't remember anything about where his arms and legs were at any one time. Higginbottom persevered in teaching Otto the steps of the waltz over and over again. "Why can't you remember these simple steps?" Higginbottom kept asking.

"I don't know," said Otto in a frustrated tone.

Higginbottom was worn out from the activity. He really felt like he was trying to push water up a steep hill. Higginbottom shrugged his shoulders, "I give up with this," he said. "I will just draw out the steps for you." So Higginbottom drew lots of feet on a piece of paper and numbered each foot, marking it L for left and R for right. Higginbottom then drew arrows between the feet and passed it to Otto. "Is that all it is?" exclaimed Otto "all this one-two-three face the window, face the door" you have been telling me is just those simple steps."

"That is all there is to a waltz." Replied Higginbottom.

Otto said "Well that really is simple, why didn't you tell me this at the beginning." Higginbottom shook his head "let's try again.

One-two-three." Suddenly Otto had mastered the waltz, with each step he had his feet in the right place. Higginbottom now felt safe to take the part of Otto's partner without having his feet stood on. Sure enough the prince was dancing a very elegant waltz.

"Well done" said Higginbottom "so, who are you dancing with?" Otto replied, "I have no idea. Mother just told me that I should learn to dance."

Chapter 12
Grand Progress

"Where are we going?" asked Otto.
The king smiled, "you will see when we get there." It was eight o'clock on a sunny August morning and the carriage was already warming up with the heat of the morning sun.
"Will we be travelling for a long time or a short time?"
"Two or three hours," the king replied as they set off from the castle. The king was facing forwards and had a good view out of the carriage window. Otto was facing backwards and could not see as much. Otto's brain started working on where you could get to in a few hours. The great thing about having a mountain range to the south is that there are not so many ways that you can travel in a carriage. For a few moments Otto's mind wandered and he thought about what it would be like to travel in a carriage that could fly, he started to drift off to sleep but was suddenly awoken by a big jolt. The carriage had hit a huge pot hole in the road and the king was almost flung out of his seat, he was not pleased.
"Will you be more careful," bellowed the king to the carriage driver.
"I am sorry your majesty, it won't happen again."

The carriage continued its journey and Otto slept for most of the trip. Suddenly the carriage stopped "Here we are" announced the king "I think you will like this visit." They had arrived in Landsberg and in front of them was a huge construction operation. A station was being built and the east-west railway was taking shape. As they watched from the carriage, sections of metal track were being lifted in place and secured to the huge wooden sleepers that were laid across the railway. Otto quickly got out of the carriage, the work's manager was waiting for them. "Good morning your Royal Highness" the manager said to the prince, and then bowed to the king and said "Good morning your majesty."
"Please can you show us the construction work" asked the king

eagerly.

"With great pleasure." They walked beside the two newly constructed railway lines that were laid beside one another. One track was for trains heading east the other track for trains heading west. There were at least a hundred men working on the construction site, some were laying bricks for the station buildings, others building up platforms while many more men were digging the foundations and installing a stone base for the railway's sleepers. The king was most impressed "How is the work progressing?"

The manager looked pleased "Very well your majesty. We have been working hard on this project for one month and the station construction is progressing well, the men have got used to laying track. We are on target to complete our part of the railway by March next year. We need to finish and test 55km of twin tracks, and build a goods yard."

The king was delighted "I am so pleased. Thank you for showing us this magnificent construction site. When can we come and see it again?"

"You are welcome at any time your majesty, but if you come in October we will have our steam engine and we will be able to give you your first ride on a Bavarian steam railway."

"I will look forward to it" beamed the king. Otto and the king travelled back to the castle.

"Thank you." said Otto to his father.

"For what?"

Otto replied, "For bringing me to see the railway. I always love to be part of what is going on in the kingdom."

"Thank you for coming with me" said the king with a big smile.

Higginbottom took a holiday for most of August and went back to England with his wife. Otto enjoyed every second of his long Bavarian summer. On many mornings Otto got up early and took Rufus for a walk beside the lake for half an hour just after sunrise, he would then go to the tree house for a few minutes to look out over the beautiful lake and see whether anyone was boating on the lake in the early morning. If someone was out in a boat Otto would row over to see them, if not he would go and swim for a few minutes in the cool water. By then it was nearly seven o'clock and Otto would go to the kitchen to get a bread roll or a bun for breakfast which he would eat in the garden. Otto loved to go to the vegetable garden and when he was hungry in the morning he would pick himself a few peas and eat them raw, and pick a few tomatoes. The garden was well kept and in the late summer Otto thought that it would probably be possible not to need a kitchen but to live entirely by grazing on the castle's supply of fruit and vegetables. After breakfast Otto would play with Rufus or go for a walk with one of his friends in the woods, by lunchtime even Otto was getting exhausted and when he got up so early in the morning he would lie down after lunch and would usually fall asleep for an hour. Rufus would sleep when Otto slept and the dog would usually sprawl beside a sofa that Otto was sleeping on, or if no one else was watching Rufus would climb onto the sofa and sprawl on Otto.

Otto still had work to do during his holiday and Higginbottom had left him instructions to study for at least an hour a day, so each afternoon Otto would get his books and with Rufus lying near to his feet he would complete his day's work. Late in the afternoon Otto would again take Rufus for a walk beside the lake and then Otto would get dressed for his own dinner with the king and queen. A gong was sounded every day at eight o'clock to summon the family and their guests to the table. Otto would eat with his parents and then brush Rufus's hair for a few minutes before he said goodnight to everyone and went to bed.

For Otto the lovely summer days, when he was free to do whatever he wanted, passed by so quickly. It was soon early September. Higginbottom had returned to the castle and the weekday lessons began again. In the second week of September Otto's lessons were interrupted for a few days. The king, the queen, Otto and Higginbottom all travelled to Seefeld for the boating competition. As they arrived in the town it looked as if a carnival was taking place. Each building was decorated with flowers, there were musicians playing in the parks and the town square. So many people were already in the town and there were still two days before the competition started. Higginbottom had arranged for Otto to meet the professor that afternoon. They met by a jetty on the lake and the professor escorted them as they walked along the jetty. Right at the end was the most magnificent boat, it was red with white lines down the side and it had four seats. The driver's seat had handlebars for steering and there was one seat behind the driver on the right hand side of the boat. On the left hand side there were two passenger seats arranged one behind the other. "Here is the prototype boat your royal highness" said the professor with a wide smile. Otto was used to adventure but even he was struggling to take this in. The crude contraption of a boat that he had brought to the iron works had suddenly been turned into a sleek and elegant craft. "Can we take the boat out for a trip?"

"Yes" replied the professor "but only if it is driven very gently by me. There is still lots of work to do to make the boat safe for general use. If it is driven too fast it can easily turn over." The larger boat took much longer to warm up. It was an hour before the water was hot enough for it to be driven. "Keep clear of the back of the boat, it is very hot" announced the professor as they all climbed in and cast off. The professor pulled a lever very gently which diverted the steam. Originally the steam was going out from the boiler through a large opening in the top, the lever diverted the steam into a small opening at the back of the boiler which gave the craft jet propulsion. The craft gently pushed forward and gained speed. "There are a lot of waves today" said the professor "we will only be able to go very slowly." They went just a few kilometres into the lake and then turned around and came back to the jetty. The professor looked disappointed "Let's hope for a calmer day tomorrow and then I can really show you what this craft can do."

The two men and Otto met again on the Jetty early the next morning. This time the king and queen came to watch. As the professor had hoped it was an exceptionally calm day and there was hardly a wave on the lake. Otto, Higginbottom and the professor got into the boat.

Higginbottom turned to the king and queen "Would you like a ride?" He asked "You can have my seat?"
"No thank you, we are happy to watch the boat from here," the queen replied. The professor again took the boat gently into the lake but this time he was able to give it some more power. The boat surged forward pushing the occupants back in their seats. Travelling at this speed the wind was blowing through their hair and a white wake oozed out from behind the boat. Higginbottom looked slightly scared, Otto had an ear to ear grin and the professor was concentrating so hard on the controls he seemed to be oblivious to the speed that the boat was moving. Back on the shore the king and queen looked very worried, no boat had ever travelled in the kingdom at that speed, possibly in the world, and soon a crowd of people gathered on the shore to watch. After five minutes the professor eased back on the power and turned the boat around, speeding up again for the return trip. Once they had tied the boat up at the jetty and everyone had got out, the king and queen hugged Otto. The professor said "what an amazing craft your son has designed." He turned to the king "If you wanted to, your majesty, you could open the competition tomorrow from this boat."
"I will let my son do that" said the king "after all, it was his idea that brought us that amazing craft."

The royal family were staying in the home of Baron von Sinder, which was a towering house with huge gardens and beautifully manicured rolling green lawns that that overlooked the huge dark lake. They returned to the baron's house for lunch. The king's private secretary rushed to greet the king. He was all in a muddle. "I am sorry your majesty but neither the mayor nor I are sure who will be coming to the opening of the competition tomorrow. Some mail has been lost from a coach in Munich and we believe that a number of replies to your letter were with that mail bag. We will have to plan for all the invited guests coming to the

event, but there may be far less."
The king replied, "You plan for the maximum number and just make sure that anyone who comes to the competition enjoys the day."
"Very good your majesty."

The next day the crowds around the lake grew throughout the early morning. The competition was due to start at eleven o'clock. By ten o'clock Otto was waiting in the little red boat with Higginbottom for the fire to heat up the boiler. Higginbottom peered at the pressure gauge on the boiler "These boilers are under a lot of pressure and need very good maintenance. Today the pressure is good and we will have a safe trip."
"Thank you for all your help Higginbottom" replied Otto, "I would be lost without you."

Otto went to join the king and queen as they were greeting some guests of the Bavarian noblemen and the visiting royals. Only two princes had so far come to the event, but there was a surprise in store. A familiar looking gentleman stepped out of a very expensive looking carriage "Welcome your majesty." said the king.
"I am honoured to be here" said the well dressed gentleman.
"Please may I introduce you to my son? Prince Albert, this is my son Prince Otto."
"How do you do, your majesty." said Otto.
"How do you do, your royal highness" said Prince Albert who turned quickly to the king to speak, "As I said in my letter, I do apologise that Victoria could not be here. There was an international crisis just as I left."
"We are delighted that you could join us" said the king. Otto was so surprised to see Prince Albert, a man who's picture he had seen hanging on various walls, but Otto thought it was a huge honour to have the husband of an empress at this little competition in Bavaria. Otto wished that he could talk to Prince Albert but he had to excuse himself and walk down to the jetty. Otto got into the little red boat and prepared to set off.

At five to eleven the professor climbed into the boat and drove Otto into the middle of the starting grid of the competition. Otto looked at the thousands of people who were gathered all around the lake and suddenly felt very scared by the size of the crowd. Otto took a deep breath and stood up. He put the small end of a big metal cone to his lips to amplify his voice. Otto spoke slowly and with a rich deep sound to his voice as he began. "Your royal highnesses, my lords, ladies and gentlemen" welcome to Lake Ammersee and the annual Bavarian boating contest, particularly welcome to all our international guests. As you will see over the next few days Bavaria is becoming a leading nation among a group of industrialised countries. We are starting to lead the world in the design of machines such as the boat that I am standing on today." The crowd clapped loudly. Once the applause died down Otto continued. "Now it is my great pleasure, on behalf of the king and queen, to declare that this competition is officially open. Good luck to all competitors from all nations." Otto sat back in his seat and the professor pulled on the boat's accelerator lever. The lake was calm and the waves were small, the crowd gasped as the little red boat sleekly accelerated away getting up to near full speed. Otto was astonished that the little craft could go so fast, the wind was blowing through his hair.
"How fast do you think we are going professor?"
"At least 60km an hour." Replied the professor.
"So this is definitely the fastest boat in the world?"
"Oh yes" replied the professor with a grin. "You are now travelling faster than anyone has travelled before on water, and it is your design that has made this possible." Otto said nothing. He had his ear to ear grin and was enjoying every moment of this journey.

Once the prince's boat was out of the way and the waves from the boat had died down, the rowing races began with 25 competitors all in separate boats, wearing vests with the colours of their region or country. The crowd cheered hard for the Bavarian teams. Otto's boat returned and was tied up at another jetty away from the crowds. Otto was taken in a carriage back to the platform where the king and queen were waiting for him. Prince Albert stood up "what an excellent speech, and what an amazing boat. Who designed that craft?" Prince Albert was astonished when Otto said "I did, I got the idea for it when I watched a boiling kettle move backwards over a fire."

Prince Albert replied, "Well, there are very few people in the world who see a kettle on a fire and manage to design a craft like that. How many have you sold?"

Otto sadly replied, "I believe just two, we sold them to people in Munich as it is very difficult to move the boats over land. You need a very strong cart and at least eight horses."

Albert looked surprised "You can't just transport them on your rivers?"

Otto said "If only we could. So many people in Bavaria have asked how they buy one but we have no way of moving them on the rivers because Mr Stark will charge a fortune for this."

"What a shame, so what will you do?"

Otto replied, "We need either our railway to be finished or Mr Stark to let our waterways be used."

"I see. This is a great pity." Said Prince Albert, then he looked at the wonderful boat with a smile and said "So how fast will your boat go?"

"We believe that it is doing about 60 kilometres an hour at full speed. We have not managed to find a way for the boat to assess its own speed yet. This is something that we are working on," replied Otto.

Prince Albert smiled, "in England our steam engines have built in speed measuring devices, perhaps you should come to England and see them, and meet the people who design the engines. I am sure that they would like to meet you."

"Thank you. I would very much like to come to England."

Prince Albert continued. "We are having a very special exhibition of steam engines in London in January. Please come along to this and meet Victoria, we would also be delighted if you could bring that fantastic boat, perhaps you could drive it on the river Thames if the river is not frozen?"

Otto was amazed and without even casting an eye towards his

parents he replied, "Thank you for your kind invitation, it would be our immense pleasure to come to London and we will find a way of getting the boat across Europe," with a smile he added "and melting the ice if we have to."

Prince Albert smiled back at Otto. "You have so much energy and conviction in you. I wish my children had just one percent of that."

The first day of races ended with a huge meal which was followed by a dance at Baron von Sinder's home. All the royal visitors, noblemen and a few other important guests including Mr and Mrs Higginbottom went to the baron's ballroom. The ballroom was decorated with amazingly colourful paintings of Greek gods on the walls and the room was lit by thousands of candles that were set into hanging chandeliers and some floor standing lights that each had at least a forty candles in them. A small orchestra played as the guests entered the ballroom and just as he arrived, Otto saw a beautiful girl who had long dark hair and was wearing a white ball gown. Otto thought that all she needed was a pair of wings and she would have been an angel, before he fully realised what he was doing he turned to Baroness von Sinder and said "Who is that?"

"That is Princess Helena of Saxe-Coburg and Gotha, prince Albert's daughter. Would you like me to introduce you?

In a moment of unusual courage Otto replied "Yes please." Everything for the next two minutes seemed like a blur in Otto's mind. The baroness quickly walked across the ballroom and Otto followed her "Your royal highness this is prince Otto von Wittelsbach of Bavaria."

Otto felt that his tongue and mouth were so dry he could hardly speak, he managed "How do you do?"

The princess looked up and quickly replied "How do you do?" The baroness left Otto to talk to Princess Helena but it was to be a very short conversation. Otto tried to smile at the princess and then looked awkwardly around the room. He wanted to start a conversation by making some witty remark that would interest his new acquaintance but his mind was blank. Suddenly he caught sight of one of the paintings, "There is someone who must exercise regularly" Otto said as he nodded towards a picture of Zeus. The half naked figure did not amuse the princess and the conversation was developing into a series of awkward silences. Thankfully Otto was saved by the orchestra who began playing a waltz. Otto summoned all of his remaining courage "Would you like to dance?"

"No thank you, I have recently sprained my ankle and my doctor tells me that I must not dance."

Otto had a genuinely sincere tone to his voice when he said "I am sorry about your ankle." and Otto decided to leave his new acquaintance and politely excused himself. It seemed that the dancing lessons were not going to be useful to him that evening.

Otto sat by himself for a few minutes and it was then that he noticed a familiar figure, it was Princess Helena on the dance floor clearly having a very pleasant time dancing with Baron von Sinder's seventeen year old son. Higginbottom saw Otto looking sad and went to sit beside him. "Why do some people tell lies?" Asked Otto as he looked towards the princess and her dance partner.

Higginbottom immediately saw through the question and replied, "Because either they don't have the courage to tell the truth or they want to spare the person that they are talking to some embarrassment."

"I tried very hard to talk to the princess. I think I tried to talk about feelings, although I must say that my mind had never been so blank, the entire time just seems like a blur in my head. I suspect that the princess thinks I am less intelligent than a doorpost."

"I doubt that she thinks that, but you have to remember, you may be a prince but you can't always have exactly what you want in life. If someone else doesn't feel like being your friend then they will not be your friend. We are all different. Suddenly another waltz was played. Mrs Higginbottom saw the prince looking sad and decided to improve his evening, she began, "your royal highness, I am sure that royal protocol does not permit this, but never mind about that today: Would you like to dance?" Otto smiled for a few seconds as he stood up, he then realised that he had not spoken and he replied "Thank you, I would love to dance." Mrs Higginbottom looked at least ten years younger than her age of 29, she was a slim and happy lady, her skin was well toned and her long curly hair seemed to dance whenever she moved. Otto was very happy to waltz with his tutor's wife and at the end of the dance he developed a big smile. The evening was made even better when, out of the corner of his eye, Otto could see Princess Princess Helena gazing at him. Otto decided that his first dance had been very successful. He hadn't fallen over, tripped or ended up in a heap with his partner. He also decided that he had had quite enough for one evening and made his excuses and left the ballroom, Otto needed his sleep as it had been a very long day.

The races continued each day for the remainder of the week. Otto was very interested in the winners of each race. Watching the rowing style of each team Otto asked Higginbottom, "All these rowers seem to row so hard, but what makes a winning team?"
"A game is won in your head" replied Higginbottom with his usual eye for detail and thoughtful mind. "Each time that a winning team sets out to do something they see the end before they have even started and they work together to be better than the people that they are rowing against."
Otto was impressed. "You seem to know such a lot about so many things. How do you manage it Higginbottom?"
"I pay attention" replied Higginbottom. After three more days of watching the races the king and queen very much wanted to go back to their castle. The king presented the last of the prizes and Otto had made the last of his trips in the boat with the professor to show the boat off to the crowd. That evening most of the noble guests had begun their journeys home. Otto, the professor and Higginbottom went to move the boat from its jetty to a ramp about four kilometres away so that some factory workers could load it onto a special cart to travel back to Munich. As the professor, Higginbottom and Otto accelerated into the lake the

professor said "Something strange is happening, the controls have jammed. His accelerator lever would not move and the boat could not be slowed down. Thankfully it was moving relatively slowly. Higginbottom stood up and looked at the boiler. He announced "Oh dear ... the outflow from the boiler is blocked and there is no safety valve. This is very dangerous; the pressure gauge already shows the boiler under too much strain. The pressure will keep on rising until ..." Higginbottom saw the steam trying to escape through the blockage and heard the hissing noise "We need to swim RIGHT NOW!" Higginbottom announced.

Otto, the professor and Higginbottom removed their pullovers, jumped into the lake and started swimming towards the shore. About half way back the professor started to struggle to keep going. Higginbottom pulled him the rest of the way to the shore. Just as they arrived at the shore of the lake there was a huge explosion from the boat, the shock wave passed through Otto and the two men like an invisible bullet. A fireball engulfed what remained of the little boat, which sank almost immediately. "Well I think 'swim RIGHT NOW' was the best advice we could have had" said the professor, "well done Higginbottom you saved us all."
"Yes, well done," said Otto. "It is such a shame about the boat though, I was becoming very attached to that little craft ... and I never even got to drive it. Although we are lucky in one way, thank goodness it didn't go kaboom in front of Prince Albert!"
The professor looked surprisingly cheerful, "Don't you worry, the main thing is that we are alive and well. Another boat can be built very quickly now. The factory have all the tools and material, they have built three already and can to build another just as easily. But this time they should put a safety valve into the boiler, I really don't know why they didn't do that – I told them that it needed one in the first draft of the plans. Well spotted Higginbottom." The two men and Otto walked towards their carriage that was waiting for them at the lake side with water pouring from their clothes. They walked passed the group of

factory workers who were waiting with a cart for the boat. The professor said, with a cheeky smile, "the good news is that we have saved you the job of taking the boat back to Munich. The bad news is that you will need to tell your boss that it is at the bottom of the lake in ten thousand pieces." The workers looked glumly at one another and got into the cart and set off back to Munich.

On the way home the king talked about nothing other than the 30,000 guilders that had been raised from the competition, the queen talked about Otto needing to make sure that his contraptions were safe and Otto caught up on his sleep in the carriage. He was still thinking about Princess Helena as he slept.

As soon as they arrived back at the castle Rufus met the carriage and stood on his back paws to greet Otto, Rufus had now grown to his full height and was easily able to put his front paws on Otto's shoulders and look Otto right in the eye. Rufus demanded that Otto play with him. Otto was very glad that he had had a long sleep on the journey as it was dinner time before Rufus settled down and stopped bringing Otto balls and bones to throw for him.

Chapter 13
Industrialisation

"Tomorrow we are going on a really amazing journey" announced Higginbottom at the end of his lesson.
"Where?" asked Otto.
"To take a ride on a railway, the first ever ride on a Bavarian railway." Otto was astonished, it was only October, work had started less than three months ago and already there was a part of the railway that was working. That night Otto sat up in bed with his eyes wide open, he wondered what he would see the next day. Rufus was also not in a mood to sleep and kept bringing Otto things to play with. "Go to bed" Otto said and Rufus walked to his big carpet, walked around in a circle twice and then lay down like a balloon that had suddenly been deflated. Otto finally fell asleep just before midnight.

The next day Otto woke up at six-thirty. He king, Otto and Higginbottom all had breakfast early and set off in a carriage. Rufus wanted to join them but one of the footmen held tightly onto Rufus's lead and just managed to hold the dog as the carriage set off. Otto tried to imagine having a train station near to the castle. Imagine just getting into a train and then arriving in Vienna a few hours later ... The journey by road had certainly not improved, the summer sun had baked the surface and loosened the upper layers of the road, the autumn rains were beginning to wash more of the stone at the base away and so there were more holes in the road and the carriage veered and bumped along. Thankfully the king, Otto and Higginbottom were all used to travelling in bumpy conditions, but many people felt unwell travelling on these poor roads and some even refused to travel at all. The king occasionally got upset if the driver was particularly clumsy and the king would bellow "be more careful" when they hit a deep pot hole. The roads became more level once they passed Fűssen and Otto caught up on his sleep as they travelled on the much smoother main road. Otto awoke to find

the carriage travelling very slowly on a dark road through the middle of a deep forest. "Are you on the right road?" the king shouted to the driver.
"Yes your majesty, just a few kilometres and we will be there." assured the driver.

Within ten minutes the road had climbed into some hills and on the other side of the hills was a large town. The carriage slowed down just before the town and turned onto a small road that was lined with building material. There were piles of sand, wood and bricks and just ahead of the carriage was a station building that was having its roof completed. The carriage parked beside the station. The king, Otto and Higginbottom all stepped out to be greeted by a very familiar figure.
"Your majesties and Mr Higginbottom" said professor Ritter "welcome to the first complete section of Bavarian railway." There were a lot of soldiers standing with weapons at the station and some followed the royal group onto the platform.

Otto was astonished by what he could see. Waiting for them was a big dark green Bavarian steam train with shiny red wheels and a very luxurious looking wooden carriage with green leather seats. Smoke was coming from the train's funnel and steam was hissing from its valves. They all climbed on board, followed by six of the soldiers, and the train set off. "Where are we going?" Asked Otto.
"To the next station on the line" replied the professor.
"How far is it?"
"Twenty five kilometres."
Otto smiled, "It is great that we have so much of the track completed."
The professor replied, "There should be much more, we should have many more people working here but Mr Stark is managing to slow down our work."
"What is he doing?" Asked Otto.
The professor sadly replied, "Accidents keep happening. Scaffolding collapses occasionally, parts of a station roof

collapse and we have even had a section of a bridge that has collapsed. I supervised the plans for the bridge and I know that this collapse was no accident. Five men have died this month because things have fallen onto them. That is why we have the army on board the train today. We are now having all of the railway construction secured by the army."

The king was furious, "That wretched Mr Stark, can we not just find him and shoot him?"

"It would be good if we do that," said the professor, "it would certainly speed things up, but Stark has proved to be difficult for even the army to find."

Otto turned to Higginbottom and asked, "Didn't England have a similar problem with people destroying factory machines because they thought that the machines were taking away their work?" Asked Otto.

Higginbottom replied "Yes, but the solution to that was to educate the people a little. I think that this is a different problem, Stark is just paying people to damage things. No amount of education will help with this."

Otto spoke up "Stark must have some senior people, just like we have our ministers, Stark surely can't do this all on his own. How about we remove these people?"

Higginbottom turned to Otto "how will you do that?"

Otto smiled confidently, "I don't know yet, but there must be a way."

The train blew its whistle as it set off, heading east along the track. Everyone was astonished at how comfortable the journey was. There were no pot holes, no bumps, not even any shaking in the carriage. The king announced "this is a magnificent way to travel; you could drink coffee while you sit and watch the countryside go by." The train sped up and still the ride was smooth and gentle.

Otto was amazed by the trip "Professor" he asked, "how fast are we travelling?"

"I believe that we were going to get up to 65 kilometres an hour on this trip. The train will travel at at least 100 kilometres an hour at full speed."

"Father" said Otto "this is incredible, we are travelling much faster than we could ever go with our carriage pulled by horses and yet the ride is much smoother." Soon the engine began to slow down and with another whistle it gently pulled into the station. Ahead of the train Otto could see the unfinished tracks and a partly completed bridge, the professor saw him gazing into the distance.

"It should be finished in January and then it will join up with the next section of railway heading for Munich." Everyone got out of the carriage and stood on the platform admiring the steam engine. "Come with me" said the professor to Otto. They climbed into the steam engine's cab and the driver showed Otto how to blow the whistle, then he showed Otto which levers to pull to take the brakes off and finally he showed him how to start the train moving. The train chuffed just a few metres along the platform before the driver said "enough" and Otto shut off the steam and applied the brakes. Otto climbed out of the drivers cab to find that all the builders and soldiers on the platform were watching him. Even the king had stopped to watch. Everyone applauded as Otto stepped out onto the platform, "well done" said the king "it seems we have a budding engine driver."

All the station buildings were complete in Dinkelscherben, the town that they had just arrived in. A large table had been prepared in what would soon become the main ticket hall. The royal party was served a very large and delicious lunch. The king was particularly delighted with the meal and thanked everyone warmly. The king said how pleased he was with the progress of the railways, and then it was time to board the train for the return journey. The king and Otto were feeling very content after their wonderful lunch and both dozed a little during the train trip. The train again arrived very smoothly at Augsburg station. The king, Otto and Higginbottom thanked the professor warmly as they said goodbye, and then it was time to get back into the horse drawn carriage for the return journey to the castle. The king was sitting in the back of the carriage facing forwards while

Higginbottom and Otto sat in the less pleasant seats, at the front of the carriage facing back. The trip felt particularly bumpy after the very smooth and fast train ride. "We have had our experience of modern travel" said Otto as they hit a particularly large bump in the road, "and now it is back to the past. Thinking aloud Otto said "what stops us having a railway built all the way to the castle door?"

The king spoke up immediately "About 20,000 guilders."

It was early evening as the group returned home. Rufus was getting more and more forceful with the footmen and when he saw the carriage approaching in the distance and smelled the royal party Rufus escaped from the footman who was playing with him on the lawn and ran towards the carriage. Rufus had no sense of danger and ran straight towards the carriage, the driver had to brake very suddenly so that he didn't run Rufus over and the force of the emergency breaking pushed the king out of his seat. He ended up face down on the floor of the carriage with his head touching Otto and Higginbottom's feet. The king's nose was bruised as he hit the floor and he was apoplectic with rage. "You clumsy oaf." the king roared at the coach driver.

The driver quickly came into the carriage and helped the king up. He said "I am sorry your majesty, but I had to save the prince's dog, the dog would have ended up under the carriage wheels."

"Rufus" shouted Otto as he dashed out of the carriage door, "you silly dog." Rufus was beside himself to have the prince back, he wiggled from head to toe and his tail wagged so quickly that you could hardly see it move. Rufus stood on his back legs and put his front paws on the prince's shoulders, while trying to lick Otto's face. Otto walked forwards two steps which forced Rufus to walk backwards and go back onto his four paws again. The king leaned out of the carriage window and shook his head "that ruddy dog" he exclaimed.

Otto looked at his father's damaged nose "I am so sorry, I think we will have to find a way of keeping Rufus in the castle while I am away."

"Yes we will" roared the king, who was beginning to calm down

a little, "Come into the castle, I need my dinner."
Otto replied, "It is not far to the castle, you go on ahead, I will walk with Rufus."
"As you wish" said the king, and the carriage set off with just the king and Higginbottom onboard.

There was a guest at the castle for dinner, it was Fiona. The queen had invited her because she thought that otherwise she would be dining alone. As the carriage arrived and the king got out the queen saw him looking dishevelled and with his damaged nose. "Whatever happened to you, was it such a tough journey my dear?"
The king frowned, "You could say that." Otto and Rufus arrived a few minutes later and the footmen took Rufus for his dinner while Otto went upstairs to get changed. Otto was seated next to Fiona and as the soup was served Otto started thinking about all the things that had happened that day. "Fiona" he asked "how would we find out where Stark is and who is working for him?"
"That's a question. I don't really know what he does these days, but he always used to like working from some big buildings in Baaderstraße in Munich, people used to call it his fortress because it was a tall brick building with very few doors and windows. It might be worth looking for him and his associates there."

After dinner Otto asked the king and Higginbottom to join him in the king's study. Otto told them what Fiona had told him about the building in Munich. Higginbottom looked very pleased with this news "it would be worth getting someone to watch that place, just to see whether Stark is still there."
"I agree" said the king "I will get an army company assigned to find Stark and his associates." The king dispatched a messenger immediately to deliver a secret message written in a special code to the army. The king, Otto and Higginbottom then returned to the queen and Fiona. They had a very pleasant evening talking with Fiona and at nine o'clock Otto wished everyone a good night, went to find Rufus and then went up with his dog to his

bedroom. Fiona decided to stay at the castle that night because the journey back to her woodland home was not pleasant after dark and a carriage could only take her part of the way. As she wished everyone a good night she turned to the king and queen and said "You are so lucky to have Otto, he is an amazing young man."

The queen could see Fiona was looking very sad and she said "You would love to have had a child wouldn't you?"

"I would," replied Fiona, "but I am far too old for all that now. Goodnight to you all."

Higginbottom also decided to go and sleep, he looked very thoughtfully at the king and queen "she is right, you are very lucky to have Otto."

"We know we are" said the queen "and he is lucky to have you in his life. Thank you for all that you do for our son"

At seven thirty the next morning an army colonel was waiting in the study to see the king.

"Your majesty" said the colonel with a salute as the king arrived.

"Do sit down" said the king.

The king began, "you obviously received my letter and so you know what I need you to do."

"Yes sir."

The king asked, "Do you have any questions about your orders?"

"Yes I do sir, I don't understand why you just want me and my men to find and follow Stark and his associates in Munich. If they are a threat to your majesty should we not just disarm and arrest them, or just kill them?"

"No. Stark is a very clever adversary and he will have made sure that, unless he and all his associates are removed together, someone will continue the fight. This situation is like being at war but we have no idea who the enemy are or when they will appear. We can't kill everyone in the kingdom who acts suspiciously, so we need to understand what Stark is up to and how he is working. Once you have that information, come back to me and we will plan our next move."

"Very good sir" said the colonel, and he saluted the king and left.

*****

A week later the colonel returned to the castle. He was shown in to the king's study and the king said "Thank you for returning so promptly. I assume that you have news of Mr Stark. Please wait here for a few moments as there are some other people that need to hear this." The king returned a few minutes later. "Colonel meet my son, prince Otto and my political advisor Mr Higginbottom. I trust these gentlemen with my life. Please tell us about everything you have found out."

"Very good your majesty," replied the colonel and he began to tell them about what he had learned. "We spent the first three days and nights watching the building. There was no sign of anyone and we thought that the building was empty. On the fourth day we noticed that there was some noise coming from inside the building, but still there had not been any activity outside. I managed to get a few people in and it seems that Stark does have his headquarters there, he brings people in through tunnels under the building. Inside he is training people to blow up sections of the railway and destroy factories that build parts so that it takes much longer to rebuild the railway after something has been destroyed." The colonel continued, "I managed to find a plan as I was looking through the papers in the building. Stark is planning, what he called a 'spectacular'. He intends to blow up the largest railway bridge in the kingdom. This will set the project back by six months.

The king quickly jumped into the conversation. "How long have we got before Stark blows the bridge up?"

The colonel replied, "From what we could find out they need more explosives than they have. If we are lucky we have four or five days"

Higginbottom looked at the colonel. "These men are a threat to the kingdom. Can you blow up that building in such a way that you remove *all* these people?"

"Yes sir, my men are already planning this. We have men watching the entry points to the building and we have also sent more men to guard the railway bridges."

"You are certain that when you blow up this building you will get all the people in that building, including Stark? Asked Higginbottom.

"Yes sir, everyone in the building."

"What about other people living near to the building, could they get hurt?"

"No sir, at night there is no one within 50 metres of the building."

"That is good news. You have my permission to go ahead with this" said the king. "Make sure that when you blow up the building everyone, including Stark is inside. How soon can you do it?"

The colonel replied, "We have counted that twenty three men are working with Stark on this and, as long as they are all in the building then we will blow it up tonight."

The king wanted to go to Munich so that he would find out what was going on as it happened, but Higginbottom and the colonel persuaded him not to do this. If the king was known to be in Munich this might make Stark and his gang worry that something was going to happen. For Mr Stark they wanted it to seem like a normal day when he could go into his building as he usually did. The next day was particularly long as everyone waited for news from Munich. After dinner the king became impatient. Higginbottom and Otto sat with the king in his study until midnight. The king turned to Otto, "you look like you really need to sleep."

"No I don't" said Otto, trying to hide a yawn.

"Go to bed" said the king "I will go and sleep myself if there is no news soon." Otto soon felt like he had to go to bed. Higginbottom stayed with the king until one o'clock, and then both the king and Higginbottom decided that they were not going to get any news for some while and so they were better off trying to get some sleep.

At ten to five in the morning a messenger arrived and the king was woken. The message was written in code and the king struggled at such an early hour to decode it so he could read it. Thankfully the message was very short and read "The building has been destroyed as ordered. The exits have been blocked and so far no survivors have been found." The king was very pleased and decided to get another few hours sleep. He told his servants to have the carriage prepared for eight o'clock. He was going to Munich to thank the colonel himself. A seven o'clock the king was woken. He went for breakfast and found Higginbottom and Otto waiting for him. The king told them what happened and both insisted on going to Munich with the king. The king had a wry smile when he said to Otto, "You can come as long as that dog doesn't cause any more mischief." Otto promised that the servants would keep Rufus close to the castle and the three of them set off for Munich straight after breakfast.

The king's carriage went first to Baaderstraße so that the king could see the colonel. "Well done" said the king as he shook the colonel's hand.
The colonel looked sad, "I have some bad news your majesty."
"I am terribly sorry. We have only found twenty two people in the building."
"Oh no. Who is missing?" Said the king.
"Mr Stark, sir" replied the colonel.
"How is this possible? You said that you could get all the people in that building. That was why I let you do this."
"I am so sorry sir. We should have been able to get them all, but it seems that Stark had a strong room and a secret passage out from his part of the building. We had no idea that it was there and the way that we had placed our gunpowder meant that the explosion was not strong enough to blow up Stark's strong room."
Higginbottom looked very unhappy, "We are really in a mess now. Stark knows that we are looking for him and he knows that we have no idea where he is now … what are you doing to find Stark?"
"We are doing everything we can sir. We have men watching all exits from the city. We are searching all the local properties."

Higginbottom looked exasperated, "but that is what Stark will be expecting you to do. He won't go anywhere local and he won't leave the city by any exit that you are watching." The king, Otto and Higginbottom arrived in Munich in such high spirits but were they were now wondering what could possibly be done to recapture Stark. They got back into the carriage to travel to the army headquarters in the city.

As soon as they arrived at the headquarters the king went to see the general who was in charge of the country's army and Higginbottom borrowed the latest map that the army had of Munich. After the king had explained to the general just how disappointed he was with the day's events, Higginbottom and Otto joined the king to make sure that all possible exits were really being covered: The drains, the canals, the rivers … everything. The general promised that every available man would be put onto this work and that he would also have more guards available for the king, the castle and the royal family.

The king, Otto and Higginbottom then decided that there was nothing more they could do in Munich that day, so they got back into the carriage and set off wearily for home. "I can't believe that we have lost Stark again." said the king.
"He is a very slippery character" replied Higginbottom "it would have been difficult for the army to know that Stark had put up extra metal in the building to keep his part safe, just in case it ever got blown up. He must have suspected that this would happen … in which case ..." Higginbottom fell silent.
"What is it" said the king impatiently.
Higginbottom continued, "in which case Stark has planned his escape and he has somewhere to stay already. Somewhere in the city there is a building with a hideaway and it is there that Stark has gone to stay until all this blows over."
"How does this help us find him?" asked Otto.
Higginbottom replied, "I am not sure it does. Stark will only come out once he thinks that we have stopped looking for him … but there is not much mischief that Mr Stark can cause from his

hideout, so perhaps a way of keeping everyone safe for a while is just for Stark to think that we are still looking for him."

"Good idea" said the king, who was keen to find any positive news after such an awful day. "I will make sure that the army appear to keep looking for Stark for as long as possible."

Chapter 14
Life and Death

A dull low cloud had settled over Bavaria for days on end. It was November and everyone in the castle was coughing and sneezing, especially the king who was never happy when he was ill. "Bring me my slippers" he bellowed to a footman "and be quick about it, my feet are freezing."

"Try to cheer up," urged the queen "your ministers are coming to see you soon and you don't want them to think that you are a grumpy old man do you?"

"Quite right my dear" said the king, and he tried to put on a smile. When the ministers arrived the king tried for a few minutes to seem cheerful but it was clear from the odd "how terrible" from the king, that things were not going well. The king did not emerge from his library for an hour after the ministers left.

Otto joined the king and queen for lunch. By this time the queen was determined to find out what was going on "has Stark escaped and found some other way to cause mischief?"

The king looked very solemn "this time it is not Stark, it is the ordinary people who are causing more trouble than our evil chap."

"What happened?"

"It seems that people don't like the machines that we are building and our new factories. They think that these machines will take away their jobs and that the machines may not be safe."

Otto grinned "Well, if people saw my boat explode during the autumn then they might know that there is, occasionally, something to worry about … but that is all part of the fun. These are new and exciting machines, we can't get everything right the first time."

The king still looked gloomy "People are actually breaking into our factories in Munich and destroying machines because they see them as evil." he sighed "We will never see Bavaria progress if that is how the ordinary people are going to behave. We have another problem, the men building one of the railway tunnels have hit a wall of granite that is so solid and thick think that they may not get through it, so it certainly means that the costs will increase." Otto was itching to be involved "Let me go and have a look at this wall of granite. Maybe I could think of something. There must be some way through it."

"No," said the king firmly "you have already been far too involved in this railway to be good. You have spent weeks in the spring organising it and weeks in the autumn raising money for it. You need to concentrate on your education now." For the first time in his life Otto was furious with his father, "You need this railway, you know that this is the only way that our kingdom will survive. Of course I want to help with it. I can get my education as I go." For as second the king was speechless, his son had never spoken to him this way. The queen watched in silence as her husband decided to put Otto firmly back in his place."You will do as I say" bellowed the king, his voice getting hoarser as he bellowed, "when you are king you can give the orders, but until then I will tell you what to do." Otto was not prepared to take this for one minute longer, he stood up and looked the king in the eye "your 'orders' are leading our kingdom into a backwater of Europe, if we continue this way there will be little left of the kingdom in another five years." Otto left the dining room before the king could reply and went back to his classroom to find Higginbottom. The queen turned to the king "Would it really have been so bad for him to go and look at a lump of rock for a day, after all he is right, we do need this railway? Otto is doing so well in his studies that Higginbottom is struggling to find work that is difficult enough to keep his attention." The king did not reply.

Otto couldn't find Higginbottom in the classroom and he decided to do something that he had never done in his life, he was going to take some time off to show his father just how far giving Otto orders would get him. Otto wrote a note to Higginbottom "My father thinks that I should never have time away from my studies, to demonstrate that I am someone who does not take orders from anyone, I am sorry to say I will not be in class this afternoon. There is just a little bit of snow in the hills, I have gone out with my sledge to the lower hills. See you tomorrow. Otto."

Otto put on his hat, coat and scarf, collected his sledge and set off with Rufus to walk into the hills.

Higginbottom felt a chill running down his spine when he read the note. He ran downstairs and found the queen alone in the drawing room, as he gave her the note, his hands were shaking. "There are lots of trees in those hills, it is not safe to sledge there" Higginbottom said. The queen would have liked to leave Otto outside in the fresh air for a while and calm down but she could see how worried Higginbottom was. "Don't worry, the servants will all go out and look, we will find him" The queen's reassuring tone was good to hear but Higginbottom wanted Otto found as quickly as possible. Higginbottom collected his coat, had and scarf and set out for the hills himself. The queen flung the library door open and banged the note down on the king's desk, "you see," she said "you see what you have done?"
The king replied, "If I had spoken to my father the way he spoke to me ..." The queen interrupted him, "We are all going out to find Otto. You must come and join us."
The king retorted, "I have a cold, and besides I have lots of urgent business here. I think searching for him is a waste of time, the boy will return when he is good and ready."
The queen said, "Higginbottom has already gone out to find him, if anything happens to Otto I hope you will be able to live with your conscience."

The queen, the servants and Higginbottom all joined the search, shouting "Otto" at the top of their voices. There were two paths that led from the castle into the hills, a shallow path and a steep narrow path. Higginbottom took the steep route as he thought this would be the most likely way that Otto would have taken. Higginbottom had looked for Rufus before he left the castle because Rufus would have been able to follow Otto's smell, but Otto had taken Rufus with him on his sledging trip. The servants were calling "Otto" as they looked for him, but Higginbottom knew that there was no point in looking anywhere near to the castle as Otto was determined to go sledging. The path into the hills was rocky and the climb was getting difficult for Higginbottom. Soon there was a little snow on the path and he saw four paw prints and just beside them two footprints in the snow. Higginbottom followed the tracks up into the hills. Soon he was far enough away that he couldn't hear the servants and the queen calling "Otto, where are you?" The servants had all taken one of the more gentle tracks into the hills. Higginbottom knew that he was on his own.

Higginbottom walked a good distance following the footprints. It was getting colder as he climbed the hill. Suddenly Higginbottom heard an animal sound, but not a sound that he recognised, it was a howl. Could there be wolves here at this time of the day? Higginbottom found a large stick and walked slowly and quietly towards the sound. Another howl came and this time Higginbottom could identify where it came from, the animal was beside a group of trees. He could see that the wind was blowing towards him, whatever animal it was would not be able to smell him. Higginbottom was safe to walk a little closer to the trees. He put his head down and held tightly onto the big stick. As he got closer he was relieved to see that there could only be one animal. He walked from one side to the other and then the howl came again, and after it a slight crying noise. Whatever animal it was, it was in trouble and Higginbottom decided that he was safe to approach it. As the animal heard him, it put its head up and Higginbottom could see that it was Rufus. He ran to him thinking that Rufus had been hurt but Rufus moved freely and wagged his tail a little when he saw Higginbottom. Rufus pointed his nose towards a big tree trunk. Higginbottom turned his head and, for a second he thought he was imagining the scene, but he realised that the full horror of what had happened was real.

Otto was lying near to the tree trunk beside his sledge. He was facing upwards and blood was pouring from his arm, near his left elbow. The blood was settling on the snow and Otto looked white, although not as white as the snow around him. He must have hit the tree at a very high speed. Higginbottom quickly took off his tie and tied it very tightly around Otto's left arm above the injury to stop him bleeding further. He looked carefully at Otto and to Higginbottom's relief Otto's eyes were open and his heart was beating as he was breathing shallow breaths. Otto felt very cold and he was unconscious. Higginbottom looked at Otto's head and felt his legs and his right arm through Otto's cloths. All other bones seemed to be intact. Higginbottom could see that Otto's left arm was badly broken. Rufus seemed much calmer now that Higginbottom was there and Rufus kept trying to lick Otto's face to get him better. Higginbottom gently turned Otto and removed his right hand from his coat. Higginbottom now felt Otto's spine and his ribs, everything else seemed intact He couldn't feel any more damaged bones. Higginbottom now had a dilemma, ideally he would wait until someone else could help him and they would put Otto onto a flat plank of wood to move him so that they didn't damage his broken bones any further. The problem was that Higginbottom didn't have anyone to carry the other end of the wood and he knew that he had to move Otto quickly or Otto was going to get so cold that he would be much less likely to recover. Higginbottom wondered for a second whether there was some way that Rufus could help, but the young dog would never be able to move slowly and steadily so this seemed a very bad plan. In the end Higginbottom decided that the safest way to get Otto down the hill was to tie him to the top of the sledge and pull him along the paths. The sledge was bent and broken, but Higginbottom thought that it should get Otto slowly back to the castle. There was enough rope to tie Otto's body and arm to the top of the sledge, leaving his legs hanging over the back. Higginbottom checked Otto's legs again and they were both unbroken, the plan could work if only there was something that Higginbottom could use to pull the sledge with, now that the sledge's rope had been used to tie Otto safely onto the sledge. Higginbottom found a nearby tree that was covered in ivy, he took out his pocket knife and cut a small section of thick ivy off the base of the tree. Higginbottom tied the ivy around the front of the sledge and tried to pull it, the ivy was strong enough and Higginbottom, Otto and Rufus set off with the sledge on the long journey back to the castle.

The sledge bumped over the rough track on the path down the hill. Higginbottom worried that all the bumping was not helping Otto. He slowed down as much as he could but still the journey for Otto was not smooth. Rufus walked alongside the sledge staying as close to Otto as he could. Rufus knew that something terrible had happened to his friend. Higginbottom was himself feeling very cold after spending such a long time in the hills getting Otto ready to travel. Higginbottom thought about warm places and pulled his scarf around him as much as he could, then he looked back at Otto and stopped for a moment so that he could pull Otto's scarf around him. The slow journey continued and Higginbottom soon realised that the sun had set and the light levels were dropping, he decided that he had to move faster as he knew that they wouldn't get down the hill in the dark. Night had set in when the snow started to clear from the path near to the bottom of the hill. The clouds had cleared. There was some moonlight but the trees and distant hills obscured most of the the light. Once the snow had also cleared it became very difficult to pull the sledge on just earth and stones, Higginbottom pulled as firmly as he could but eventually the strain became too much for Higginbottom's improvised rope and the thick ivy broke. Higginbottom knew that he could not pull the sledge on his own any further. Thankfully he had managed to get near to where the shallow and steep paths met. Higginbottom was sure that from here someone would be able to help him. "HELP" Higginbottom shouted "HELP – COME QUICKLY – BRING LIGHT - I HAVE OTTO." He heard nothing.

Every two minutes for the next half hour Higginbottom shouted "HELP – COME QUICKLY – OTTO HAS BEEN HURT -

BRING LIGHT." Higginbottom was beginning to think that no one would come and help. There were lots of trees on this part of the hill and it was now so dark that Higginbottom could see nothing in front of him. He would have had no chance of getting Otto any further. If he tried to climb down the hill now then Higginbottom would probably end up in a worse position than Otto. Suddenly a faint voice shouted "Higginbottom, are you there?" The voice was so faint that Higginbottom couldn't make out who it was, he almost thought that he had imagined it. Higginbottom stood up and again shouted "I'M HERE – COME QUICKLY – BRING LIGHT. I HAVE OTTO."
The voice replied "I'm coming up the shallow path, tell me where you are."
"I AM NEAR TO WHERE THE SHALLOW AND STEEP PATHS MEET"
The voice replied "I will be with you in about ten minutes, I have a light." Higginbottom was astonished; the voice was definitely the king's.

"Your majesty," said Higginbottom as the king approached carrying a huge flaming torch.
The king looked shocked when he saw the sledge. "Let me see Otto."
Higginbottom replied, "Otto has a very badly broken arm and he has lost a lot of blood your majesty."
The king turned to Higginbottom "We need to get him into the castle quickly. Everyone is out looking for Otto, they returned at three o'clock to get torches and I haven't seen them since. We will have to get Otto down on our own."
Higginbottom could see that they would never be able to carry the sledge down between them because someone needed to carry the large torch. They decided that the king would hold the torch while Higginbottom untied Otto, the king then balanced the torch against a tree and helped to lift Otto onto Higginbottom's back.
"Will you manage to carry him down like this?" Asked the king.
Higginbottom replied, "I don't think I will get him all the way down, but if you can take him part of the way I think we will

manage between us." Higginbottom set off. He was bent over and held Otto's legs with his hands so that Otto would not fall from him. The king carried the torch and they managed to get about half way down before Higginbottom had to stop for a rest. Otto was then placed onto the king's back and the king huffed and puffed carrying Otto for as long as he could. It wasn't too long before the king had to stop and once again Otto was placed on Higginbottom's back. This time Higginbottom carried Otto all the way to the castle and up into Otto's room. Finally the two men laid Otto carefully on his bed, leaving his coat and scarf on as the room was very cold. Rufus refused to leave Otto. Higginbottom tried to take the dog downstairs but Rufus growled each time anyone tried to take him out of Otto's room. Higginbottom gave up and left Rufus to walk around in a circle twice and curl up on the big rug in Otto's bedroom.

The castle was still empty, all the servants and the queen were out looking for Otto. "Thank you so much" said the king gratefully. Higginbottom looked at the empty hearth, "We need to light a fire quickly. Do you know where the kindling wood is kept?"
"I don't know, but I will look for it" replied the king. Higginbottom went to the kitchen to get a bed warmer. The king looked like a man who had been given an impossible assignment. He looked in every corner of Otto's bedroom and couldn't find any small pieces of wood that could light the fire. Higginbottom was starting to get frustrated with the king, "If you can't find anything just take some coal from one of the other fires with a shovel and bring that here along with some wood." The king fumbled around and eventually brought some wood. The coal proved to be even more of a challenge and he nearly dropped the hot coals on the floor as he struggled to carry them with a shovel. Soon the coals had heated the wood enough to start a fire in Otto's room. Both men stoked the fire briefly and then Higginbottom said "Otto needs a doctor quickly, where can we find someone?"
The king said "I will go and get the doctor now."

"Will you be all right doing that your majesty? It is a dark night and you will need to go on horseback as we don't have a carriage driver."
"There is some moonlight and I will be fine. Take care of Otto while I am away, and thank you Higginbottom for all your help."

The king set off for the doctor as fast as he could and as Otto's room warmed Higginbottom took off Otto's coat. It took a long time to move Otto from one side to the other so that he could get both arms out of his coat and Higginbottom decided that he would take a pair of scissors and cut off any other clothes that needed to be removed from Otto's arms. Otto's feet were being warmed by the bed warmer, which was a stone that had been heated on a fire and then left to cool down before being placed inside a soft cushion lining. Higginbottom prepared some warm water and got some scissors ready. Once Otto was feeling warmer, Higginbottom cut off Otto's pullover and shirt so that he could wash Otto's damaged arm, Higginbottom slackened the tie and watched carefully. Otto's arm did not bleed, this meant that the arm did not need to be tied up any longer. The blood had now clotted in the damaged veins. Higginbottom washed all the dry blood from Otto's arm and then got some clean water and washed Otto's face and hands.

Just as he had finished Higginbottom heard a carriage arrive. He went downstairs to see who it was. The king had travelled back with the doctor and they had brought the doctor's daughter Katarina with them. The king introduced the doctor as they walked up the stairs "Dr Fabian meet Mr Higginbottom. Higginbottom. You already know Dr Fabian's daughter Katarina." The doctor was a tall man with a moustache and dark hair who wore a dark blue suit. The doctor explained to Higginbottom "My daughter is now twelve years old and she is very clever at curing people with herbs. Katarina works with me whenever she can so that she can learn more about natural ways of healing."

The doctor looked very concerned when he saw Otto. Higginbottom told him what had happened, "I found Otto unconscious with a broken arm, his arm had bled a lot but I tied it up and it does not bleed now that the tie has been removed. I have only cleaned him and warmed him. I have tried not to move his arm more than I had to."
"Well done" said the doctor "Thank goodness you stopped the bleeding or he would certainly be dead."
"What is to be done?" Asked the king impatiently.
Doctor Fabian replied, "We need to get this arm sorted out and we need him to get well enough to replace some of the blood that was lost." The doctor started work on Otto's arm while Katarina went to the kitchen with some herbs to make a tonic and to prepare some herbs to smell. The tonic was for Otto when he regained consciousness and herbs would create a good aroma in Otto's room to help him get better.

Higginbottom went into the drawing room to sit by the fire. He had been so busy that he had forgotten how cold and tired he was after he got Otto back to the castle. Higginbottom's throat was getting sore, he was sneezing a lot and he felt like he was about to catch the castle cold. Suddenly he heard the front door open and a lot of noise came from the hallway. Higginbottom rushed to greet the queen and tell her about Otto, "Otto is upstairs in his room, he has broken his arm and has lost some blood but the doctor is with him now."
"However did you find him?" Asked the queen.
"I just took the steep pathway into the hills and then followed his tracks in the snow. Rufus helped, he was standing over Otto howling until I arrived."
"Thank goodness that he took Rufus." Said the queen.

The queen rushed upstairs and Higginbottom talked to his wife and the servants about how he found Otto. Higginbottom wondered whether he should have told the queen that Otto was unconscious but he thought that it would be better for her to find out more gradually. Mrs Higginbottom went upstairs to their apartment and prepared a bath for her husband, hoping that the warm water might make his cold better.

The queen was shocked when she saw her son. "Will he die?" She asked the doctor immediately.
The doctor had a very factual tone in his response "it is unlikely that he will die, your majesty. He is breathing and his heartbeat is regular and even, but he has lost a lot of blood and we need him to regain consciousness before we can be absolutely sure that his brain has not been damaged."
"My dear Lord" said the queen as she took Otto's right hand and gently squeezed it "Get well soon my wonderful boy. We love you so much." She then turned to the doctor "Is there anything more you need? Is there anything that we can do for you? Have you and your daughter eaten? Would you like dinner?"
The doctor replied, "Once I have got this arm in the correct position and secured it with bandages we would be very grateful to have dinner. We left home before we ate."
The queen said, "Of course, I will have some food brought up for you both. Is there anything else that we can get for you, doctor?"
"No," replied the doctor, "Nothing else, thank you your royal highness."
"Thank you both" said the queen. The doctor looked like a professional man who was following his usual routine, but the queen could see in Katarina's face that this was not a standard case. Katarina looked slightly frightened.

The king and queen left the doctor to align Otto's arm and secure the arm with bandages. The queen turned to the king "Now you can tell me what really happened." The king retold the story that Higginbottom found Otto, stopped the bleeding and got Otto onto a sledge, pulled Otto on the sledge until he was close to the castle, called for help. In the king's version of the story the king came immediately and it was the king who carried Otto all the way back to the castle on his back... in record time. "Thank goodness Higginbottom had the good sense to walk along that steep pathway. You do realise that if he hadn't Otto would be

dead by now." Dinner was served at nine o'clock that evening. The king and queen invited Mr and Mrs Higginbottom to join them. No one felt very much like eating, even the king only managed a few potatoes and little bit of his pheasant. They all went upstairs after dinner to see how the doctor was getting on. The doctor announced "The arm is now set and I really cannot do very much more tonight. Would you like me to stay?"
The queen was very keen to keep the doctor nearby "Yes please" she said. Beds were made up for the doctor and his daughter and by half past ten the king, queen and Mr and Mrs Higginbottom went off to bed.

The king managed to fall asleep easily enough and began snoring deep snores. The queen tried to sleep but the combination of the events of the day, all the uncertainly over Otto and the deep snores emanating from the king's side of the bed kept the queen awake. By midnight she walked down to the kitchen to make a peppermint tea. On the way back she called in to Otto's room. He looked very peaceful and for a few seconds the queen was gripped with panic as she started to think about what would happen if Otto died. She reassured herself that Otto was going to be fine and that he would wake up tomorrow and be his usual energetic self. The queen gently held his right hand and said "Good night my wonderful boy. Get up and be with us tomorrow." Just as she was leaving the room she bumped into a tall shadowy figure, almost spilling her tea. "Higginbottom!" said the queen "what are you doing here?"
"I … I … I couldn't sleep."
"Obviously." Replied the queen.
"I just wanted to make sure that he was comfortable." Explained Higginbottom.
The queen smiled "I am so glad that Otto has a friend like you. He is very lucky. Now stop worrying, go back to bed, rest and I'm sure he will be up tomorrow."
Higginbottom smiled, "thank you, your majesty."

Chapter 15
Light at the End of a Long Tunnel

The next day after breakfast Higginbottom paced up and down outside Otto's room. There was still no response, although Otto was breathing normally and his heart was beating evenly. The doctor and his daughter came in to see Otto and declared to the king, queen and Higginbottom that all that Otto needed was time.

The doctor left and promised to call in the next day. The king's cold was getting better but Higginbottom was getting worse, he was sneezing and coughing. The king and queen felt very sorry for Higginbottom, he was taking Otto's accident very badly. Not only was Higginbottom having to watch Otto in this terrible state, but he also had no job to do and nothing to take his mind off the situation. "I have an idea" said the queen to the king. "We will ask Higginbottom to go and bring Sebastian to visit Otto. A familiar voice may help Otto recover and a trip out will do Higginbottom a great deal of good." Higginbottom agreed at once. He would do anything that could help Otto. The carriage left late in the morning and he returned with Sebastian in the early afternoon.

Sebastian talked to Otto and patted Rufus while he sat at his friend's bedside. Sebastian said "We all thought you were so lucky getting Rufus. George loves your dog and keeps asking his father if he can have a dog, but his dad thinks that looking after a dog is too much work." Sebastian spent an hour with Otto. The queen came in to see Sebastian a few times and talked to him a little, very soon the castle gong was rung for dinner. Sebastian ate with the king and queen. They all thought it was very strange eating together without Otto. Very little was said during the meal and soon it was time for Sebastian to get back into his carriage and travel home. By the evening the queen found that Higginbottom was pacing up and down again. It had been a long day for everyone as they all hoped that Otto would wake up, but despite all the smelling herbs that Katrarina had installed, nothing worked that day and everyone prepared to go to bed for another night knowing that the next day was critical. Otto had not drunk water for 24 hours and he really needed to get up the next day and drink. Everyone had an uneasy sleep and the queen woke up early and sat by Otto's bed talking to him. The queen said, "My dear boy, you took your first steps on the lawn just outside this window when you were one year old. I held your hand and then suddenly I had to let go and you kept on walking, did you know that?" The queen smiled. "Your first word was 'Whoosh' when you saw your dad's carriage arrive very fast one morning," the queen continued. "We need our wonderful boy back. Come and get up Otto, please," the queen said. As the queen watched an eyelid twitched, she watched closely again and the second eyelid twitched. Otto muttered something but the queen didn't understand it. Then he repeated it "My mouth is so dry." The queen helped him to lift his head up and take a few sips of water. Otto turned his eyes towards the queen. "Thank you" he said and closed his eyes. The doctor said that Otto would need to rest a lot when he woke up and that they should talk to Otto but also let him sleep for much of the day. The queen woke the king and with tears in her eyes she said, "He talked to me. He is coming back to us."

"Wonderful news" said the king and he turned over and went back to sleep.

The queen went to see Otto again and a few minutes later Otto sat up and had a little more water. "What happened to me?" He asked.
"Don't you remember?" Replied the queen.
Otto spoke faintly "No. The last thing I remember was leaving a note for Higginbottom in the classroom."
The queen smiled, "Thank goodness you did that otherwise we would never have found you." The queen told Otto about all that he had been through and how Higginbottom had carried Otto down the hill. She continued "Your father says that he carried you most of the way but looking at the two of them it is

Higginbottom who has a backache and sore legs, your father probably carried you a couple of metres. Otto smiled. "Higginbottom really went all the way up into the hills to find me and then carried me down the hill in the dark" Otto whispered."
"Yes that is what happened." The queen replied. "Higginbottom is an amazing man. How lucky we are to have him here with us." Within a few minutes Otto fell asleep again.

Otto slept for a couple of hours before he woke. This time Higginbottom was in the room "Come here" Otto whispered to Higginbottom and he grabbed Higginbottom's hand with his right hand. "Thank you" Otto whispered. Higginbottom smiled and didn't know what to say, he eventually replied "I am so glad that you are getting better." Later in the morning the doctor called in with Katarina, they were both overjoyed to see that Otto was awake from time to time and drinking small amounts of water. A few days later Otto was able to eat small amounts of food and he managed to get some of Katarina's special tonic into him – it tasted terrible but, as the doctor said, most tonics that do you any good seem to taste particularly bad. Just as the doctor was preparing to leave, Fiona called in to see Otto and was introduced to the doctor and Katarina. Fiona wore an egg-timer shaped blue dress and she suddenly looked much younger, her hair had been coloured brown and was cut into a short and tidy style. Fiona talked to Otto for a little while and was preparing to leave when the doctor offered her a lift home in his carriage.

It was another week before Otto felt able to leave his bed for any length of time. Rufus was overjoyed that Otto was up and wagged his tail very fast from one side to the other. When Otto opened his curtains he had a surprise, there was a fresh blanket of snow covering everything outside, it looked fantastic. Higginbottom didn't have anything to do during the day and he called in on Otto often while he was recovering. Otto talked to Higginbottom a lot about all the things that they had been through on the night that Otto got hurt. One day Otto said to Higginbottom "I still can't believe that I nearly died. I'm so

young, I want to do so many things. It would have been very sad if my life had ended."
Higginbottom looked thoughtfully at Otto, "We can never know when our lives will end, but I think that you have a strong body so I doubt that you will be leaving us any time soon ... as long as you are more careful."
"I plan to be," replied Otto weakly.

Despite it being two weeks since his accident, Otto found that standing on his legs for more than a few minutes was very difficult. Although his legs didn't get damaged the shock and recovery took away lots of Otto's energy and for the first time in his life he felt very weak. The doctor and Katarina called in every day and the doctor kept saying, "You can't expect to recover from this sort of thing in just a week or two. You have had a major accident and lost a lot of blood, you nearly died. It will take months before you are fully recovered, your body needs time and rest. It also needs good food. After Christmas I am sure you will feel much better." Christmas seemed a long way away and Otto was getting increasingly frustrated. Otto replied, "Is there nothing that will speed this up? I feel like an old person who hardly has the energy to walk across a room."
The doctor smiled, "You need to exercise gently. Katarina can help you with that, she is great with herbal medicines and she is used to helping my patients get back on their feet."
Otto turned to the Katarina "Anything that you can do would be greatly appreciated, I need to do so many things and I can't be an invalid." As he was leaving the doctor went to see the queen. The doctor said, "If there is anything that you can do to get Otto's spirits up you should do it, he is getting very frustrated and we need him to stay positive and happy."
"The problem is that Otto's idea of a good time is whizzing down a mountain faster than sound, I hardly think he is well enough to do this now," replied the queen.
The doctor smiled, "No, but just seeing something or being with someone who is doing something great may be enough to get him thinking more positively."

"Just a moment" said the queen. She went to see the king and returned triumphantly. "I know exactly what to do" she said "Thank you doctor for all your help."

The next morning the queen opened Otto's curtains at 9 o'clock. "Wake up." she said "There is something amazing on the lake."
Otto slowly got up and put his clothes on and walked with his good arm on the queen's shoulder down the stairs. The snow had melted for a few days, but it was still cold and Otto put on his thick coat. He hadn't been outside for such a long time that it seemed strange to wear a coat. As they walked towards the jetty Otto saw the most amazing sight – it was a red steam-jet powered boat, but not a small little boat, this was a bigger and sleeker looking boat that had eight seats and a very professional looking control system. The fire was lit, steam was coming out of the boat's chimney, and there waiting on the jetty was a very familiar looking man, it was the professor. The professor greeted the royal family with a big smile, "Good morning your majesties and your royal highness." The professor looked at Otto, "I am so pleased that you are feeling a bit better. The queen told me that you needed cheering up, so I got the chaps to bring this down for you to see. This is the latest version of the boat. It has come straight from the factory. We are very lucky that we can still drive it here as the lake is not yet frozen."
"This boat is amazing" said Otto.
The professor replied, "We are just waiting for a couple of other people and we can go for our trip." Higginbottom made his way down to the jetty with Katarina, they each carried one end of a big picnic basket. "Who is this pretty young lady?" asked the professor.
Higginbottom replied, "This is Katarina. She is a local expert on herbal medicine. She is coming to make sure that Otto keeps taking his medicine while we are travelling."
The professor looked closely at Katarina. "I thought for a moment you might be the prince's girlfriend." Both Otto and Katarina became red in the face.
Katarina quickly replied, "I am just helping him to get better."

The professor smiled "I was only teasing, you are obviously doing a great job with the prince. From what Higginbottom tells me we are lucky that the prince is still alive."

The queen turned to Higginbottom, "You are sure that this contraption is safe? We don't want Otto having to swim back this time like he did before, he wouldn't make it alive."

Higginbottom replied, Oh yes, it definitely is safe. It has a safety valve and the professor told me that he oversaw the entire design of this boat and has inspected the boat from top to bottom before he took it out of the factory."

The professor called "ALL ABOARD." Everyone climbed into the boat and they set off into the lake at great speed.

"Is it safe to do this speed professor? There is a good bit of wind today and there are waves on the lake" said Higginbottom.

"No problem at all. This boat has some special wings that push it down onto the water at speed so it will not lift off." The queen watched nervously as her son and the craft zipped across the water, bouncing over the small waves.

Otto was amazed at what had been fitted into the boat "The seats are warm" he said.

Higginbottom turned around "some of the heat from the fire can be re-directed under the floor and it warms the seats – it means that you can still travel in the boat during the winter."

Otto was so pleased to be out of the castle and having adventures again, he grinned from one ear to the other and settled back in his seat. "Where are we heading today?"

Higginbottom turned around "To the other end of the lake and then we will go to the island for a picnic ... although it looks like someone may not feel like food." Katarina was very quiet and absolutely white. "Slow down" Higginbottom said to the professor, someone is getting sea sick.

"Don't worry about me" Katarina said "I will be all right in a moment or two." Higginbottom passed her some water and Otto gave her a hug. Once the boat had slowed down Katarina began to feel better. They turned around at the end of the lake and returned to the island, tying the boat up at the little jetty. By the time that they got out of the boat Katarina's colour had returned and she was singing a song. "Are you all right?" asked Otto. Katarina replied, "I am fine, it is you that we need to look after."

Higginbottom and the professor lit a fire to keep everyone warm. Otto was quite exhausted after the trip and he just wanted to sit on a blanket near the fire and look at the magnificent view of the castle. Higginbottom and the professor set off to walk around the island for a few minutes. Katarina stayed with Otto and began setting up the picnic. "It is going to be a mixture of breakfast and lunch" she announced.

Otto said, "Thank you for coming on this trip to look after me, I am so glad that I can get out of the castle."

Katarina replied, "Did you really design that wonderful great boat?"

"No, not very much of it" Otto said. "I came up with an idea for a jet powered steam boat and tested it right here on this lake. The engine was my idea but it was the professor who designed the control system ... and the heated seats!"

Katarina smiled, "But then it is your design. Anyone can re-direct some heat into the floor and the seats but the boat is designed by you?"

"Well, yes," replied Otto.

"I bet you are the first prince in history to have done this."

"Maybe." replied Otto. "Higginbottom keeps telling me that I am different."

"Is that boat really the fastest boat in the world?" Asked Katarina.

"Oh yes," said Otto, "and what is important is that we have this boat in Bavaria."

Otto smiled "I love coming here to the island and I have missed this view of the castle ... just a minute. Who is that? We have more company." Otto was surprised. A rowing boat had arrived with two footmen taking the oars and the king, queen and Mrs Higginbottom onboard. The queen stepped onto the jetty "We thought we would join you for breakfast or lunch, whichever one you are eating. Mr Higginbottom and the professor returned and were very surprised that the party had grown in size. It was a cold day and everyone wrapped blankets around themselves and huddled around the fire. They all had a fantastic meal, they tucked into the bread, chicken and vegetables as their main course and then everyone had jelly for pudding. Katarina made sure that Otto had his tonic and was feeling well after the meal. Soon some storm clouds started to gather and they all decided that it was time to return to the castle. "Mrs Higginbottom, do you buy any chance suffer from sea-sickness?" Asked Otto.

"Never, I have sailed oceans and I can say that I have a very strong stomach … why do you ask?"

Otto asked, "Please could you swap boats with Katarina on the way home as she was not feeling well on the way here."

"Oh, my dear, of course I will," replied Mrs Higginbottom.

"Thank you" said Katarina as she kissed Otto's cheek. Otto became very red. The professor called "ALL ABOARD." Mr and Mrs Higginbottom climbed into the jet boat with Otto and they waved as they set off.

"Now we can really find out what this boat is made of" said Otto. "I will look at my watch as we set off and see how long it takes to get to the castle jetty." They set off and the professor took the boat up to full speed, the wind had picked up, it was a very bumpy ride and a good bit of spray was coming into the boat, but everyone enjoyed the trip. It took three minutes and ten seconds to get back to the castle jetty. Otto, the professor and Mr and Mrs Higginbottom walked from the jetty back to the castle. Otto went to his room for a rest and after about half an hour everyone else had arrived by rowing boat and came into the castle. Katarina went up to see Otto to say goodbye for the day and found Otto on top of his bed fast asleep.

The next day Higginbottom took Otto on an adventure that Otto had been dreaming about for a very long time. Higginbottom took Otto to sit in the driving seat of the jet boat. The fire was lit and Higginbottom showed Otto how to start the boat moving. Thankfully Otto could control most levers in the boat with his right arm, leaving Higginbottom just to release the steam lever that was on Otto's left side. Otto spent half an hour driving the boat, Otto's ear to ear grin had returned and Higginbottom was very impressed, Higginbottom only had to say "slow down" once. Otto was clearly more cautious after his accident. When they had been travelling on the lake for a while Higginbottom could see Otto's arm start to shake, Otto was running out of energy and Higginbottom helped Otto out of the driver's seat so that Higginbottom could take the controls and return them to the jetty. "Well done, you drive very well" said Higginbottom, "did you enjoy it?"

"Oh yes" said Otto quietly.

Higginbottom smiled, "We need to get you better so that you can drive this boat more often."

"I would love to" replied Otto quietly.

Higginbottom said "I'm afraid that the boat will need to go back to Munich for a while so we won't have it back here until the lake thaws in the spring, but get yourself well and you can drive it then."

"I will" promised Otto.

The trip and driving lesson had restored Otto's spirits and he was sure that he would soon be back to normal. A routine soon developed for Otto. Each weekday morning Katarina would call in at ten o'clock after Otto had finished his breakfast in bed, she would make sure that Otto had drunk all of his tonic. Otto would then walk with her around the castle for a while and she would steady him on the stairs. Katarina would make him walk more each day than he had the day before and this would take a lot of Otto's energy. He would start every morning in a very positive way but he was so worn out by eleven thirty that he had to ask Katarina to help him into a chair. Otto would then rest for half an hour while Katarina made him some invigorating special herbal tea. They would talk while Otto drank his tea and then he would have another half hour of exercise for his back and his good arm. Katarina left for the day just before lunchtime and Otto had a short rest, some lunch and then he went back to bed for an hour or so for an afternoon sleep. Otto then did a little school work, Higginbottom couldn't wait to give him something to do and they began with one of Otto's best subjects, maths. After an hour or two of work Otto needed to rest again and take some more medicine, soon it was time for dinner. Otto usually managed to come to the dining room to eat dinner but his appetite had still not fully returned and he ate a small portion of the meal before leaving early from the dinner table to go and rest again. On a Saturday and Sunday Otto would spend most of the day resting. One of Otto's friends would call in on Saturday and they would talk or play cards for an hour or two. Each week Otto got stronger but each week he was still getting frustrated about how little he felt he could do. Otto was trying to get back to studying but he could only manage a maximum of two hours a day of lessons.

After his walking exercise one day Katarina brought him his special herbal tea and he asked her why she never mentioned her mother. "My mother died when I was born," Katarina said sadly "I wish I could have know her, my father tells me she was an incredible lady."
"Who looked after you when you were young?" Otto asked.
Katarina replied, "Father tells me that some of the ladies in the village helped when I was a young baby. As soon as I could go to school my father would work while I was at school and he would look after me himself when I finished my school day, I have been travelling on medical trips with him for as long as I can remember. Father likes me to stay close to him. I think he feels very isolated in the world without my mother."
Otto said, "It is very kind of you to find time to help me." Otto smiled "Thank you."
Katarina said, "I am happy to, this is what father wants me to learn. He said that the more I learn about healing the more I can work with him."
Otto looked puzzled, "How do you find time for school?"
"I left school last year. I still have a tutor occasionally, but now I spend my time helping father and keeping the house running."

Otto suddenly began to understand why Katarina was so cross with him for his behaviour toward Higginbottom. Katarina was one of the many people at that time who had no easy way of continuing at school. Her education was finished and she now had to work. Otto asked, "Do you have any brothers and sisters to help you?"
"No, it is just my father and me." Otto thought that it was amazing that Katarina could keep her father's house running and help the doctor with his patients, when she was just about the same age as him.

The weeks went by and Otto was getting stronger but he was also getting more and more frustrated. He looked outside and could see a thick covering of snow. Otto so much wanted to go sledging or skating, the lake was now covered in a thick sheet of ice that certainly looked solid enough to skate on. One morning Otto had caught a cold and he was feeling so weak and tired that, unusually for him, he became very low in his spirits. Katarina arrived at ten o'clock with her bright cheerful smile. Katarina had now worked with Otto for long enough that all the formalities had gone, it was months since she said 'royal highness' to him, and today Katarina began with, "Come on lazy bones!"
"I can't" Otto replied "I have no energy and I think I have flu."
"Flu, you call that flu. This is a very mild cold … coupled with a serious case of laziness." Katarina tickled Otto's feet. "Stop it" he shouted.
"Only when you smile."
"Stop it" yelled Otto again.
"I told you, not until you smile."
"I will … have you banished from the kingdom." Said Otto with a slight grin.
"Go on then your royal highness, send me off to Saxony, I have always wanted to go there."
"I give up" said Otto as he laughed.
"There you see, you look better already." Said Katarina.
"Is that one of your your natural therapies, tickle someone until they smile?"

"No, but smiling and laughter are certainly healing. People always feel better if they can smile at the world. Some people seem to have a gift for being able to smile in the worst hardship. My father could always seem to do that. Meanwhile ..." She saw Otto returning to a frown and started to tickle him again "... other people who own a kingdom, castles and have servants by the hundred seem, strangely, to have nothing to smile about." Katarina said, in amongst some laughter.
"All right, I give up. Stop tickling me" said Otto who was now laughing "I will smile more."
"Well that is much better then." Katarina said.

Otto and Katarina had tea together again that day. Suddenly the conversation seemed to get into a very deep subject. Katarina asked "Do you have to marry a princess?"
Otto replied, "I don't know, I don't have the slightest intention of marrying anyone."
"The king and queen have not asked you about marriage? They don't have a princess or a duchess waiting to marry you in a few years time?"
Otto said, "No, I hope not. Why do you ask?"
Katarina said, "My father keeps hoping that I will not marry. I think he feels that he will be completely alone if I marry someone and leave the town, or even the kingdom."
"Well, he would be. Surely you don't want to do that?" Asked Otto.
"No," Katarina said, "but I am not sure that I can say that I would never marry. I mean what if a nobleman's son asked me to marry him. Would I turn down living in a grand house and having a maid?"
"But who would look after your father when he was old?" Asked Otto.
"Well, I would look after him, I mean I wouldn't go and marry someone who would not let me look after my father. Father would come and live in the grand house with me." Katarina replied.
Otto again looked puzzled. "Do you have a particular nobleman

in mind to marry?"

"No, I don't mean that I would want to do that, I am just daydreaming. If I married I would probably just marry a carpenter's son."

Otto felt that they had exhausted the subject. "What do I need to exercise today?"

"We need to get your back properly exercised," said Katarina.

Otto replied, "Let's get to it then."

Otto got up the next day and could smell a very familiar smell, it was freshly cut pine wood and the smell filled the castle. Katarina arrived and the first thing Otto said was, "Let's go downstairs quickly, I must see it." There in the hallway was the most magnificent Christmas tree. The servants were working on decorating every part of the hallway with candles and wooden figures from the nativity scene. In amongst everything that was going on Otto had almost forgotten that Christmas was approaching. Very soon the castle was filled with the smell of fresh baking as Mrs Gott prepared the cakes and pies for Christmas day. Otto took Katarina to the kitchen as part of one of their walks around the castle, Otto's appetite was returning. He managed to eat two pies and one thick slice of cake with his herbal tea. "Have more." He kept saying to Katarina.

"I'm full" she said. "I have absolutely no more room."

Mrs Gott looked at Otto "your strength is returning isn't it?"

"Oh yes" Otto said "I feel much better now."

Chapter 16
A Trip to London

A letter arrived in the Christmas Eve post. The king handed Otto a very important looking envelope that was addressed to Prince Otto von Wittelsbach. The letter was from London and had Queen Victoria's official seal on it. "Open it quickly" said the king who was very surprised that Queen Victoria would be writing to his son. Otto looked amazed. The letter read "We would be delighted if you could join us in London for an exhibition called 'machines for the next century'. Prince Albert tells me that you have invented the most splendid steam powered boat. We would be honoured if you would be able to bring this boat to London with you."
Otto could hardly contain himself "This is incredible," he said. "They are inviting me to London for the exhibition that is opening on 28th January, just as Prince Albert mentioned back in the autumn. This is our chance to take the boat to London and show the world what Bavaria can do."
"You can't go" said the king sternly.
"Why not?" Asked Otto.
The king looked puzzled, "Look at you." he replied, "You are not well and a trip like that would slow down your recovery."
Otto said "I am getting better and better every day. By the end of January I will be as fit as a fiddle." The queen also looked very concerned, "We are happy for you to go to London but don't you think that this is too soon. It is only two months since your accident and it sometimes takes years for people to fully recover from such a serious injury."
"I am going" said Otto determinedly and left the room.

Otto almost bumped into Katarina as he walked across the hallway "What's wrong" she asked. "Nothing, at all" Otto replied "I am fine."
Katarina followed Otto up to his room and threatened to tickle him if he didn't tell her exactly what had happened. Otto told her

about the letter and his chance to go to London and show people in the world the new boat so that they could see what Bavaria could make.

Katarina replied, "Someone else could do it, you don't have to go yourself."

Otto said, "But I want to go. The kingdom is in trouble and I am not any use here. We need investment and we need people to realise that Bavaria is not a country of farmers and stupid bear hunters."

Katarina asked, "What will you do if you get ill in London?"

"I will come home."

"How will you travel 1,000km if you are really unwell?" Said Katarina.

"I will find someone to get me better."

Katarina was starting to get very frustrated with Otto "Honestly, can't you see that this is not sensible."

Otto looked more stubborn than he had ever been in his life and said, "It is sensible, I am getting better and I am determined to go to London." The queen came in to Otto's room. "My dear" she said to Katarina "Please can I talk to you?"

"Of course your royal highness."

"Katarina, please will you be honest with me. You have helped people like Otto to recover from all sorts of problems. Do you think it is a good idea for him to go to London?"

Katarina replied, "No, not at all. I think in another three or four months he will be well enough but he is only just on his feet and he will get very tired from such a long journey. Goodness knows what he will have to do in London. If he needs to stand a lot he might exhaust himself and faint."

The queen smiled. "Thank you, I really appreciate how you feel and I quite agree with you, but I fear that there will be no talking Otto out of doing this. The reason that he had his accident was that we didn't listen to him and I don't want to make the same mistake again. Can I ask for you to think about something, I know this will be a very difficult request. If Otto insists on going to London then I will go with him for a month and probably take

Mr Higginbottom. Higginbottom is proving to be a better political advisor than any political advisor we have ever had. My dear." the queen said to Katarina "I will need someone to keep Otto well, and I think you would be the person to look after him. I know it is a huge request and I know that your father relies on you, but please at least think about it."
Katarina replied immediately "I will go, happily."
"You are sure?" Asked the queen.
"Yes, my father now seems to spend most of his time with one of your relatives, the duchess Fiona. I don't think he will miss me all that much."
The queen looked relieved, "Well, that is fantastic news. Thank you for that. I hope that we can talk Otto out of travelling but I suspect that he has already made up his mind."

Christmas day came and the royal family went to church in the morning and entertained a large party of noblemen in the afternoon. Otto joined the party briefly but went to his room after half an hour as he was feeling very tired. For the rest of the week the king and queen tried relentlessly to talk Otto out of going to London but he would not be persuaded and in the end they let Otto write back to Queen Victoria and accept the invitation.

After that, the weeks flew by and Otto found the energy to do more and more of his lessons in January. In mid January Otto went with Higginbottom to Munich to make sure that the boat was being prepared properly for its long journey to England.

The day before the trip there was an air of nervous excitement in the castle. Higginbottom had packed his trunk by six o'clock that evening, meanwhile Otto was still trying to decide what to pack and what should stay. The queen had filled four trunks with gowns and Katarina was dropped at the castle by her father with a small trunk of clothes. The trunks were loaded onto the carriage by the footmen early in the morning. Everyone had an early breakfast and at eight o'clock the carriage set off. It took five days for the group to reach Calais in France. At six o'clock in the

morning the carriage was loaded onto a ship and the party sailed to Dover. The sea crossing was a bit rough and the waves started breaking across the bow of the ship. Otto went to find Katarina who was standing on one of the outside decks with a bottle of smelling salts. "This is excellent" Katarina said. "I knew that we were going to have to sail and this blend of herbs really does get rid of sea-sickness."
"I am so glad" said Otto and gently squeezed her hand. "Perhaps one day people will even be able to travel across seas like this on a train."
Katarina replied, "I am sure that this will never happen, you would need a fifty kilometre bridge."
"Well, maybe they will fly instead." Said Otto with a big smile.
Otto had felt very well throughout the journey so far. As the boat approached the English cost he was delighted to get a look at Dover's white cliffs, something that everyone talked about in Europe.

Once they arrived in Dover the carriage was unloaded and coupled to a new group of horses. The royal party again got into the carriage as they set off on the last leg of their journey to London. Everyone was so glad when they finally reached Buckingham Palace, which was Queen Victoria's brand new home.
Otto and the queen were greeted at the palace by Prince Albert and Queen Victoria. The servants unpacked their trunks and everyone went to their rooms for a rest before dinner.

Dinner in Buckingham Palace was a grand affair with gold cutlery, beautiful glasses and lots of flowers arranged in the middle of the table. Otto was told that today was going to be a small dinner and there would only be thirty guests. Higginbottom and Katarina could not join the royal family for dinner and so they were served dinner in their rooms. Otto found himself seated for dinner with Prince Albert on one side and his mother on the other. Queen Victoria sat next to Prince Albert. Soon a lively conversation developed. Albert loved innovation and very much wanted to know what had inspired Otto to design the jet propelled steam boat. He listened intently when Otto described the boiling kettle on the stove and the simple experimental boat that Otto had built and tested on his lake. Albert roared with laughter when Otto told him about the early prototype that blew up and that he, the professor and Higginbottom had to swim for their lives. Otto didn't tell Albert that it was the very boat that he was admiring in the autumn that blew itself to smithereens. Within half an hour Otto felt like Albert was one of the family, he seemed to be such a genuinely kind and generous man who talked about helping poor people and getting them better places to live and work. Albert talked with great sadness about his eldest son. Albert said, "My son does not want to live the way that a prince should." Otto remembered all that Higginbottom had taught him and replied, very sincerely "I am so sorry that you feel that way about your son."

Just as they finished their main course of the meal, Albert turned to Otto and said "My dear friend, I am so sorry, I didn't ask you how you are feeling. Victoria and I were very worried when we heard about your accident. What happened?" Otto talked about the accident and how he was saved by Higginbottom and Katarina. Otto talked about how Higginbottom had carried him on his back for almost one kilometre to save him and how Katarina had come to see him every day when he was recovering and refused to leave the castle until Otto smiled. Albert nodded "You are very fortunate to have such good friends."
Otto's mother added, "Otto is very fortunate indeed. Higginbottom and Katarina both adore Otto. For Higginbottom Otto is the son that he never had and for Katarina he is the knight in shining armour that she will never be allowed. Victoria smiled but Albert looked very serious and asked "Why would Katarina never be allowed Otto?"
Otto's mother replied, "Katarina is not of noble blood." Otto was very surprised by this comment. He had never thought of people that way. Otto asked, "Why should it matter at all whether someone is or is not of noble blood?"

Albert smiled "Indeed, why should it matter at all?" he asked Victoria.

Victoria looked very seriously at Albert as she replied, "You know perfectly well why. No member of a royal family can marry someone who is not of noble birth. This is the way that it has always been." Otto's mother nodded.

"And what if they do?" Said Otto provocatively. Victoria turned to him sternly "THEN the person who marries inappropriately would forfeit their crown."

Otto smiled, "So if I don't marry the daughter of a nobleman, I can't be king."

"Exactly," said Victoria.

"So who would be king if I marry a servant?" Asked Otto.

Seeing that Queen Victoria was now getting tired of Otto's questions, Otto's mother quickly replied "Your second cousin would be king if you marry a servant my dear, but I think we have exhausted the subject for tonight."

Albert turned to Otto with a sparkle in his eye and whispered, "Everyone thinks that being a prince or a king is easy, but I'm afraid that it is not always that way. You sometimes have to make choices that are not ideal."

"I am beginning to see that." said Otto wearily.

The conversation moved on and Otto's mind started to wander. Suddenly he turned to Albert, "Thank you so much for all the help that you have given my family in dealing with Mr Stark."

Albert smiled. "You are very welcome my young friend. I was not sure how much you knew about this so I didn't want to mention it to you."

Otto replied, "I know everything about Mr Stark and his ways. My father was very unwell just after he returned from England and I helped to get the barons to work with us to pay for the railway."

"You did?" Said Albert with an astonished look.

"Yes, we needed a way of solving this problem quickly and I did as much as I could to help. Higginbottom was also fantastic, mother and I would never have got there without him."

Albert smiled and replied, "I am so glad that you could help with this. My eldest son is much older than you and I wish he would show just a little of the interest that you show in the future kingdom."

"Do you know about the work Higginbottom used to do in England?" Asked Albert.

"He worked for you I believe?" Replied Otto.

Albert smiled, " Higginbottom certainly did, and he was one of the best diplomats we had. I am sorry that we had to send him to Bavaria to keep an eye on your family but we could not be sure whether Stark was controlling your family without someone there."

Otto looked very sincere and replied, "I completely understand and so do my family. We know that you are doing everything you can to help us and we are deeply grateful to you for all your help."

Albert was very pleased with Otto's reply and he said, "It seems that Higginbottom has been able to help you, and I understand that you are enjoying having him as a tutor now that he has resigned from his job in England."

Otto replied, "Yes I am enjoying his lessons. He is absolutely fantastic, the best tutor and friend in the world, and the best political advisor we have ever had."

Albert began to ask Otto about the following day, "Are you looking forward to the opening of the exhibition tomorrow?"

Otto replied, "Yes, I certainly am looking forward to it. I believe that the boat arrived last week?"

Albert reassured him, "That super craft is here and I personally went to see it to make sure that it had arrived safely."

The next day, at the opening of the exhibition, Otto was amazed at the size of the crowd that had gathered. Albert began the day by welcoming everyone to the event and he walked around the exhibits with Otto, Queen Victoria and Otto's mother. When they arrived at the jetty on the Thames Higginbottom and Katarina were already waiting beside the boat for them. The red steam boat with its gleaming chrome chimney had created a great buzz of activity on the dull January morning. The Bavarian flag was flying on the boat and it looked, to all the people who admired it, like a machine that belonged 100 years into the future. Reporters from the national newspapers were asking Higginbottom and Katarina lots of questions. Albert announced that he was about to travel in the fastest boat in the world with its inventor Prince Otto von Wittelsbach. The reporters pushed their way onto the Jetty to get the best view of the boat. Otto climbed into the driving seat and Albert sat beside him, Victoria and Otto's mother sat further back, a few of Queen Victoria's children joined the group and Higginbottom and Katarina waived them off as Otto pulled the leaver and set a course for the centre of the Thames. Albert had arranged that there would be very few barges coming up the river that day so that Otto could take the boat up to a good speed, but Otto had promised that he would go nowhere near the boat's full speed. The boat had been fitted with a windscreen and water deflectors to keep the river water away from the inside of the boat as the Thames was very dirty. Just as they set off Albert turned to Otto and said "It is not going to blow up is it? I can't imagine having to swim in that filthy water."

Otto smiled, "No, I promise you will be safe."

Albert nodded, "Good, although we will be a great deal safer in any boat once the new sewerage systems are completed so that all the muck is taken out of the river." Otto took them on an exhilarating ride up and down the river. Everyone was amazed at the acceleration of the boat and the power it had to turn and stop. Otto did a splendid job of showing everyone what the boat could do but he was also very gentle with the controls, just as Higginbottom had taught him to be, so that he didn't scare any of his important passengers.

After the trip Albert talked to the reporters and said how he had admired the original boat in Germany and how much he had enjoyed today's trip in this bigger boat. Albert, Victoria and the rest of the royal party continued on their tour around the exhibition. Then all eyes in the crowd were fixed on Otto. Higginbottom had prepared Otto well. This was Otto's moment to let the world know about Bavaria. Otto delivered an excellent short speech and then the newspaper reporters began their questions. "How does it feel to have invented this splendid craft your royal highness?"

Otto replied, "It is amazing to have had a part in the development of this incredible Bavarian boat."

"How soon can we expect to have boats like this that we can buy in England?"

Otto said, "We can take orders today and the boats will be delivered in the autumn."

"You seem a bit young to be driving the fastest boat in the world. Should that worry anyone who travels with you?"

"Not at all" said Otto seriously "I am almost thirteen and, while I may be young, I have already driven a number of vehicles very safely."

There was almost a party atmosphere developing among the reporters. One reporter decided to have a bit of fun with Otto, "We heard that your last trip on a sledge did not end so well?"

Otto decided to play to the crowd just as Higginbottom had taught him, Otto replied "Since you mention it, that was entirely the tree's fault. That tree was in the wrong place at the wrong time, and the silly thing was just standing still at the end of a ski run. It is amazing that the tree hadn't been hit before." The reporters all laughed.

"You have convinced us it is safe, can we have a ride please?"

"Of course" said Otto "seven at a time please." Otto set off with the boat full of journalists and gave them a good ride up and down the Thames. He repeated the trip three times just for the press so that all the reporters who wanted to try out the boat got a ride.

Otto stayed seated after the last trip and wished the reporters well as they left. Higginbottom and Katarina could see that Otto was completely exhausted. Higginbottom looked at Otto "You have done very well, but now it really is time to take a rest."

Otto looked very sad, "Albert is expecting me for lunch."

"I will explain why you can't come." said Higginbottom, "Now get into the carriage with Katarina and go back to Buckingham Palace for a rest." Otto knew he had no choice and reluctantly he did as he was told. Once they were back at the palace Katarina found Otto's tonic. "Ugh" exclaimed Otto "is this a different tonic?"

"No."

Otto said, "It seems to taste much worse today."

"You just need to rest," Katarina replied. She asked the servants to bring Otto some lunch. Once he had finished it Katarina told him to go and rest for at least an hour. She looked in on him fifteen minutes later to find Otto fast asleep while sitting on the sofa in his room. He had really worn himself out. It was three o'clock when Otto woke up and he insisted that they go straight back to the exhibition. Otto was very pleased to see that Higginbottom was driving the boat on the river to demonstrate its power to the crowd. Otto talked to Higginbottom for a few minutes and they agreed that Higginbottom and Katarina would stay with the boat for a while and Otto would go and find the royal party. There was an awkward moment when Otto left Katarina, he said "thank you" and reached to squeeze her hand gently just as she tried to put her arms out to give him a hug. "Look after yourself." Katarina said.

It didn't take Otto long to find the royal party, the largest crowd was always around Victoria and Albert. Otto made his way through and apologised to Victoria and Albert for not joining them for lunch, "Don't give it a second thought." Albert replied, "We know you are still recovering, and it is fantastic that you can be here." Otto walked around more of the exhibition admiring the engines and locomotives that were being displayed. He talked to some of the exhibitors and they were amazed at how much Otto knew about the way that steam engines worked. Albert listened to some of the conversations and one person that Otto was talking to expressed great surprise at Otto's knowledge, Albert turned around and said "don't be surprised, young people are becoming more and more clever, this young man has just invented the world's fastest boat and it is here on the Thames

today." By five o'clock the royal party went back to Buckingham Palace and Otto went to find Higginbottom and Katarina. Both Higginbottom and Katarina looked exhausted as the boat had drawn huge crowds. Otto smiled "At least we have a crew of people to drive the boat and answer questions tomorrow so we don't have to do this much work again."
"That is very good." Higginbottom said "I don't think any of us could do two days in a row like this."
Otto looked up "Thank you both for everything you have done today, this was a magnificent day for Bavaria."

The exhibition ran for a further three days, but there were fewer royal guests during the following days and the crowds were a little smaller. Otto still drove the boat once a day to do a bit of playing to the crowd but he only came to the exhibition for a few hours each morning. Higginbottom took Katarina to see some of the sights of London and she was amazed by the theatres, vibrant markets and large buildings. Katarina had grown up in the country and so any city seemed large to her but London really was vast. On the final day of their stay Otto and his mother were invited to Windsor Castle to a large formal dinner. Otto was surprised to find himself again sitting next to Albert. Prince Albert turned to his left "Otto, you got off your sick bed only a few weeks ago and now you are here in London helping to draw a crowd and showing off your amazing boat. I know your mother was unhappy about you travelling. All this must have taken every bit of spare energy that you have. Why did you not let someone else come and show off that fantastic boat?"
Otto looked at Albert very thoughtfully. "I wanted this done really well. It is so important for Bavaria that we grow more industry in our country and that people across the world see us as another industrialised nation, just like England."
Albert looked very seriously at Otto and said, "You are prepared to greatly sacrifice your well-being for your country?"
"Well yes." Otto replied. "Wouldn't anyone who loves their country do that? I understand that you have done the same."
"In what way?" Asked Albert sternly.

"Queen Victoria tells me that you worked through the night many times in preparing for the Great Exhibition seven years ago in London."

"And she is absolutely right," laughed Albert. "You are a very good observer of people, my dear young friend ... and you have an excellent memory." Albert suddenly looked sad. "I fear that we may soon need all of your skills and more just to save ourselves."

Otto leaned forward and whispered, "I presume you are referring to Mr Stark."

Suddenly all the kindness and gentleness in Albert's face had gone and he looked white and tense. "We have to stop that evil man before he inflicts more hardship on the poor people of Europe."

Otto paused for a few seconds to think. "I believe that father is doing all he can."

Albert replied, "Yes, your father is doing all that he can, we are so pleased that he is helping us to rid Europe of this menace. If there was anything more I can do to help with Mr Stark you only have to ask."

"Thank you." said Otto.

Albert continued, "We need to be rid of this man, he has proved to be as slippery as a barrel full of eels."

Otto giggled, "That is the first funny thing that anyone has said about Mr Stark."

Albert smiled briefly, "Well it is certainly true." Albert paused for a second. "Victoria and I will be leaving tonight to go to Canterbury and we won't return to London until after you leave. I am sorry that we have to go as I have so much enjoyed your company. You are such a talented young man.

"Thank you" said Otto. "I have so much enjoyed my visit to London. Thank you for your hospitality, your kindness and particularly your advice."

"It is my great pleasure. I do hope we will see you again soon." said Albert.

There was a pause while Albert discussed some arrangements with Victoria. Finally Albert turned to Otto at the end of the evening, "Goodbye for now my young friend. Do keep in touch, keep on inventing and I hope that we will meet again soon. I would really like Victoria to see Bavaria. Perhaps I shall bring her while the mountains look so impressive in the snow."

Otto smiled, "You are, of course, welcome to stay with us at any time."

Just before they left London Otto had one final place to go. He went to one of the big railway locomotive builders. Prince Albert had arranged for Otto to talk to their Chief Engineer. The engineer was very surprised when such a young man arrived, but the moment that the two of them started talking the older man could see exactly why Prince Albert had asked him to meet Otto. Otto had a fascinating afternoon being shown around the factory and particularly looking at whether you could adapt the speed measurement system from a steam engine onto a boat. Otto had some good ideas when he left and he had a few days to think about them during the journey home.

The journey home to Bavaria seemed to take longer than the journey to London. Everyone was exhausted after all the activities and a bumpy carriage is not a comfortable place to spend even one day, let alone five. Finally the carriage arrived at the driveway to the castle and everyone got out feeling like caged animals that had just been released. Otto raced down to the kitchen, he had arrived just as Rufus had been given his dinner. Poor Rufus didn't know what to do first. He ate a few mouthfuls of food and then ran to Otto and then ran to his bowl and ate, and repeated this process until all the food was gone. All the servants made a fuss of Otto, making sure he was all right after his long journey. Meanwhile Katarina had already prepared Otto a special herbal tea to help him relax.

Just a few weeks after everyone arrived back from England it was the 24th February, Otto's thirteenth birthday. The king and queen had invited a lot of guests this year and Otto was to have an evening birthday party. All the candles had been lit in the ballroom. The dining room and the hallway were also awash with candle light. George, Sabastian and Katarina all arrived together and then Fiona arrived accompanied by Dr Fabian. Even Professor Ritter made it through the snow from Munich to join the party, and each guest brought Otto a beautifully wrapped present. Everyone wished Otto a very Happy Birthday and soon a group of four musicians started to play. Some of the guests began to stand up and dance, a waltz began and Otto walked straight towards Katarina who was sipping a drink in the corner of the room. "Would you like to dance?" Asked Otto with a big smile.

Katarina replied, "I would like to, but it is a long time since I learned to dance and I worry that I won't get my legs in the right position at the right time ... and then we will end up in a heap."

"Have no fear," replied Otto as he took her hand and led her to the dance floor, "you will remember your steps perfectly." Katarina began the dance looking down nervously at her feet and saying "1-2-3" over and over again so that she didn't miss the timing of the music. They danced the waltz very professionally. "Well done" said Otto at the end of the dance, "I told you there was no chance of us ending up in a heap."

Katarina did not look so relaxed "That was very stressful. I need one of my special herbal teas." Otto walked with her to the kitchen to make tea. "Otto, do you mind everyone looking at you all the time?"

Otto replied, "I think I have got used to it, people just seem to be interested in what I am doing."

Katarina looked surprised, It is odd. When we danced I could feel so many eyes watching me."

As Otto walked back with Katarina they saw Fiona in the hallway. "I have some some news for you, come with me she said."

The king, queen and the doctor were waiting in the king's study. Fiona said, "I have found Katarina now and I will tell you all about my great news." Fiona paused and looked around the room. Everyone was intrigued, Doctor Fabian looked uneasy. Fiona continued "My marriage to Ivan Stark has been annulled."

"Well that is excellent news" said the king.

"What is annulled?" Whispered Katarina to Otto.

"It means that the marriage never took place, it was as though it didn't happen. It is very rare that this happens."

Katarina looked puzzled and whispered "why would you want to do that?"

Fiona continued "John Fabian and I are pleased to announce that we are going to be married." Doctor Fabian smiled nervously as he awaited a response from the king and the royal family.

"Well that is fantastic" said the king and shook Dr Fabian's hand. "Welcome to our family" said the king. Everyone in the room seemed to be delighted by the news, except for Katarina, who quickly left the room and went down to the castle kitchen. Otto followed her and found that, unusually, the kitchen was empty. Most of the servants were busy upstairs and Mrs Gott had decided to have a rest for a few minutes. When Otto got to the kitchen he found Katarina crying. He put his arm on her shoulder and she turned and hugged him, "Why would dad do that without telling me anything about it?" she sobbed.

"Perhaps he just couldn't find the right time." Said Otto helpfully.

"I never had a mother and feel like I have lost my father now. You are so lucky growing up with two parents."

Dr Fabian came in to the kitchen and said "Would you mind if I talked to my daughter for a few moments, your royal highness." Otto left Katarina to talk to her father.

Katarina returned to the party ten minutes later and squeezed Otto's hand. "Thank you" she said as Otto turned around. "How are you?" Asked Otto.

"I am a bit better. At least I know what we will do and how we will live after the wedding."

"I think that the musicians will stop playing very soon, but would you like one last waltz this evening?" Asked Otto kindly.

"Yes, I think that a waltz would be very good." Otto asked the musicians to play his favourite waltz and he took Katarina's hand and led her to dance.

Katarina looked around the room, "I am not sure whether it is

just the calming effect of my herbal tea, but I am not so worried about all the eyes looking at me now."
Otto grinned, "Maybe you are getting used to it."
"Perhaps," said Katarina with a smile.

Chapter 17
Trapped

Otto, the king and queen were in Munich at the new central railway station which was built from white stone with dozens of columns holding up the elegant tiled roof. The building looked magnificent in the April sunshine. The king addressed the crowd that was gathered near to the entrance to the platforms. The king glowed with pride "My lords, ladies and gentlemen" he announced. "Today is a great day for Bavaria. Just over eight months ago work started on this amazing railway line. Today all this hard work means that we have a complete railway running from Ulm in the east to join with the railway in Salzburg in the west. This railway will very soon link up with other railways in Austria and throughout Europe meaning that we are no longer dependent on slow river boats to transport our goods." What the king didn't say was that he was no longer dependent on Mr Stark. The king liked to make a speech and he went on to talk about how this railway would connect Bavaria with Europe and bring in more tourists. The king's speech ended with "Three people have made this railway possible, their enthusiasm and vision have led to this amazing achievement. Firstly my son, Prince Otto, also our excellent Professor Ritter and then last, but certainly not least, our fine Mr Higginbottom, an Englishman who has been as good a friend to my family and to this country as anyone could wish for. I offer you three gentlemen the opportunity to open this railway that you have made possible."

A ribbon was placed at the entrance to the platforms. The king passed Higginbottom a pair of scissors, Otto held one end of the ribbon and the professor the other. Higginbottom cut the ribbon and the king, queen, Otto, the professor and Mr and Mrs Higginbottom walked onto the platform. Waiting for them was a green train with gold decoration, pulling three carriages. The royal party got into the luxurious royal carriage of the train that was furnished with leather seats, wall paper and portraits of the royal family. A group of noblemen was also shown into the next two first class carriages, including Barron von Staig and his son Sebastian. The train blew its whistle and set off. Another train was waiting behind to take a selected group of people who had helped build the railway.

Once the train had reached Ulm the king gave another speech to open the station. The king then went to a grand lunch, given by the town major for the king and all the noblemen who had travelled with him. Mr and Mrs Higginbottom sat with the professor. Sebastian managed to join Otto during the lunch.
"What did you think of the railway?" asked Otto.
"It was amazing" replied Sebastian, "To think that we have covered a journey of 150 kilometres in just two hours, imagine trying to do that speed with a horse and carriage."
"You would be shaken until your bones broke." Added Otto.
"Exactly."
"So just how fast can a railway train travel?" Asked Sebastian.
Otto replied, "Ours will do almost 100 kilometres an hour. In England there is talk of getting a train up to 100 miles an hour, that is about 160 kilometres an hour. Imagine if you could travel at that speed all day, you could have breakfast in Vienna, lunch in Munich and maybe even dinner in Paris. Just think, when trains were first tested in England people thought that they would die if they went faster than 30 miles an hour."

After lunch there were more speeches and the group went back to the station to catch the return train to Munich. Otto walked with Sebastian and the boys talked about how magnificent the trains were as they walked back to the station. The station itself was very busy. Trains were arriving and goods being unloaded. There was so much to do that it looked like the railway staff were struggling to cope with all the work. Otto saw one station porter trying to move a pile of about 100 boxes from the platform, but before he could finish the next train arrived and more boxes were taken from the incoming train and put onto the pile, people struggled to walk past the pile of boxes and guards and porters couldn't easily move with all the people who were moving around the platform. In the middle of this Otto heard a voice "Your royal highness, Mr Higginbottom has fallen and broken his ankle, I will take you to him." A tall man was standing just behind Otto.

"Who are you?" Asked Otto.

The man replied, "I am Mr Fabel, the major's assistant." Otto and Sebastian followed Mr Fabel into a dark horse drawn carriage. Suddenly they felt someone hold a handkerchief with something smelly in front of their faces. Both boys immediately fell unconscious and when they woke up their hands and legs were tied together and they had a scarf tied over their eyes and mouths. The carriage was moving but the sounds of the town had gone and it seemed that they were somewhere completely different, in the countryside. "What is the meaning of this?" Otto tried to say but his words were muffled by the scarf.

"Don't worry your royal highness" the man said "You will be returned to the king and queen, just as soon as they have given Mr Stark what he needs." Otto remained calm throughout the trip but Sebastian kept struggling to get free. Otto tried to tell him not to worry, in a muffled voice Otto said "These men wouldn't dare to hurt us, they know what the king would do to them if they did."

Soon the sounds outside changed and the horses' hooves clopped on cobble stones, people were walking near to the carriage and other carriages travelled alongside. Otto was trying very hard to listen for a church clock, if only we had some idea of the time, he thought, we could work out which town we may be in. Otto listened carefully but could not hear any clock chime. The carriage travelled on and seemed to be taking a very long time to get anywhere. It was obviously a very big and crowded town, and there were not many of those in Bavaria. After a few more minutes Otto's concentration paid off, a clock did indeed strike six o'clock, so they had been travelling for about four hours. The clock was a big clock, not a town clock but probably a city clock, so it was likely that they were back in Munich. Soon they arrived at their destination and the boys were quickly taken from the carriage and carried into a building. Once they had been put into a windowless room their blindfolds and scarves were removed by a large unshaven man. He then walked away and locked the door to the room as he left.

As soon as the boys were alone Sebastian turned to Otto "what are we going to do?"
Otto replied, "We will think of something. I am fairly certain that we are in Munich so it won't be too difficult to hide once we can get out of here."
"How do you think we will get out, we are tied up, and we would need to dig through the walls of this place to escape?"
"I don't think it will be so difficult" said Otto confidently.

Back in Ulm the king, queen, Mr Higginbottom and Sebastian's father, baron von Staig were beside themselves with worry. They had not boarded their train and were waiting with Mrs Higginbottom and the professor at the major's house for news of Otto and Sebastian. They had initially thought that the boys had gone off on some adventure on a train on their own, but this seemed less and less likely as the afternoon went on. The staff at the station were doing their best to find the boys, among their other work. The station staff tried to ask people whether they had seen two boys. One family saw two boys getting into a very distinctive dark horse drawn carriage with the black blinds drawn on the windows and gold writing on the doors. "Is it possible," bellowed the king, "that my son could be kidnapped in broad daylight. What is going on in this world?"
"Calm down," said the queen, "we can't be sure it is a kidnapping, perhaps there is something more to this."
Mr Higginbottom looked very thoughtful "The coach is distinctive, perhaps this will help us."
The king dismissed the idea, "It will be difficult to search the whole of Bavaria for one coach."
"Anything distinctive can help us." said the professor, and the queen nodded.

The king, queen and Higginbottom were still with the mayor and at seven thirty that evening a hand delivered letter arrived in the mayor's letterbox. By the time that the mayor saw the letter it was too late to follow the man who delivered it.

The letter read "*I have the prince and the baron's son. Do exactly what I tell you or you will never see the boys alive again. Firstly you must not get the army or police involved, they will not be able to help you and I will kill the boys if my informants tell me that you have involved these organisations. Secondly you will pass a law granting full ownership of the new railway to me within 48 hours from today. Thirdly you will agree to sell me any new railway that is built at any time in Bavaria.*" The letter was signed by Ivan Stark.

"Oh no." said the king, "Just when we thought we had got rid of that wretched man."
Higginbottom looked carefully at the letter, "If only we had some idea of where Stark is we might be able to find the boys before his 48 hour deadline."
The queen looked dismayed, "We don't have very much to go on, just one short letter. If Stark really does have people working for him in so many areas of the country it is going to be difficult for us to get help from the police or the army."
Mrs Higginbottom took a look at the letter. "It is a very white paper," she said, "an unusually white paper, if I am not mistaken this paper is made by Keller and Voelter in Saxony and is still mainly sold by one shop in Munich." Dinner was then served, even though no one had much of an appetite. The king managed to eat half of his food, while everyone else ate just a few potatoes from the main course. "After dinner I am going to Munich" announced Higginbottom. "We have less than two days to find the boys and it seems possible that Stark is in Munich, it is also the only place within eight hours of here where they could hide the boys without someone finding out, imagine if they were held in a town like this." Higginbottom turned to the mayor "You would find out within a couple of hours if a strange carriage

arrived in your town and two boys were carried out of it … someone would see. The people that have the boys know what will happen to them if they are found. I don't think that the boys can be held in any town. Only a city is big enough. Who will go to Munich with me?" Mrs Higginbottom and the professor nodded. The queen agreed to join them and then everyone looked at the king, who was just finishing his beef. "Why are you staring at me?" he asked the queen. "We want to know whether you are coming with the rest of us to Munch?" she sighed "or whether your dinner is more important than your son."
"Munich … yes I will go." replied the king, "I don't think we have thought of a better plan."

The royal train was still waiting in the station. Everyone boarded at nine o'clock and within two hours they had arrived in Munich. The best suites were rapidly organised at the Grand Hotel and the next morning the search started. Higginbottom and the professor went out to ask people whether they had seen the dark coach the night before. Higginbottom bought a gun. He was convinced it was going to be needed if they were to get the boys back in one piece. Despite hours of searching that morning it seemed that no one in that part of Munich had seen the coach the day before. Mrs Higginbottom joined them for dinner. Mr Higginbottom was beginning to think that he was wrong to come to Munich. Mrs Higginbottom could see how sad her husband was, "You will find the boys. It is just a matter of time."
Mr Higginbottom replied, "Time is something that we don't have at the moment."
"They must be within a mile of here. You just need a good way of searching the area." Mrs Higginbottom pulled out a small map of the city that she had bought, "Why don't we divide the city centre into three areas and each try to search one of the three before nightfall." They all agreed to this and after lunch they set out to continue the search. Mr Higginbottom asked about the coach in each inn he passed, Mrs Higginbottom asked people she passed about the coach and the professor tried both approaches. They met for dinner in the hotel, the professor found one person

who thought that he may have seen the coach, but he couldn't be sure. "We will all go to that part of the city tomorrow" said Higginbottom. They decided that there was nothing more that they could do that night and they were so hungry and exhausted that they went to the hotel restaurant for dinner.

Otto and Sebastian were not going to enjoy such a pleasant dinner. A girl unlocked the door and as she entered the room she looked straight at Otto for a second and then looked away. She had brought two small plates of beef and potatoes for Otto and Sebastian for dinner. Otto looked directly at the girl "Thank you" he said as sincerely as he possibly could. The girl silently untied his arms so that he could eat with a spoon. "Thank you" Otto said again. Otto could see that the girl's face was blank. She kept trying not to make eye contact with him. "I'm prince Otto" he said in a deep voice while holding out his right arm for the girl to shake his hand." She looked very uneasy, but after a short pause she held out her right hand and they shook hands. For Otto all the things Higginbottom taught him about understanding what people were thinking and feeling came back to him and now he was sure that this girl would help in some way. Otto was willing to persevere for as long as it took to build any kind of friendship with her. With a big smile Otto asked, "What is your name?" Again there was a pause.
"Anna." Came the faint reply.
Otto replied, "What a lovely name, my grandmother was called Anna. When she was young her hair was very long and brown just like yours. Sebastian was getting bored with this "I had such a sore back earlier today" Sebastian complained. "It must be this cold floor."
"Well done" muttered Otto. Anna walked to Sebastian, untied his hands and gave him his lunch. Anna looked sincere as she spoke "I am sorry about your back, I will try to help."
Sebastian started to enjoy having someone besides Otto for company "Thank you so much for untying my arm" he said "It is great to be able to move a little more."

Anna came back ten minutes later to tie the boys' arms up once they had finished their dinner. She came again an hour later with some cushions. "I am sorry that you are here." said Anna in her quiet voice.

"I am sorry too." Said Otto." I felt very angry when I first arrived but now I think I am accepting this more as something we have to go through."

Anna looked directly at Otto and said, "I don't know how you can think this way. I think that my uncle has been forced by the devil to keep you here. Look at what they have done to you, why do you not hate us all?"

Otto smiled gently, "There would be no point in hating you or anyone else, and anyway even if I wanted to I could not hate you, you have done nothing but be kind to me and Sebastian."

Anna replied, "If I really was kind I could have taken the key to this room from my uncle, but I feel so scared of what will happen to my family if I do."

"What will happen to them?" Asked Otto sincerely.

"They will be imprisoned, or worse."

Otto replied, "But you said that they have been forced to do this, presumably by a man called Stark who only wears black."

"You know him?" Said Anna.

"Oh yes."

Anna looked scared, "Do you think he is the most evil man in the world? I know this is what people say about him."

Otto smiled again, "I don't know, Mr Stark is certainly not good to people …but who are we to judge who is good and bad?"

Otto asked Anna to sit with him and Sebastian. "Why do you feel that any harm would come to your family if they are being forced to do this?"

Anna said, "Because the king won't understand … he won't wait for an innkeeper to tell his side of the story. The king will just look at what was done and have us all shot."

Otto replied, "You have nothing to fear from my father. I can promise you that he will not be angry with you when he understands what has happened."

"And who will explain it to him?" Asked Anna.

"I will." Said Otto.

"What if he doesn't listen?"

Otto insisted. "I will make him listen. You have nothing to fear from my family. I promise you that with my life."

Anna started to shiver, more from fear than from the cold. "I know what you want me to do … you want me to let you out of here … but I feel so scared."

Otto summoned all his skills at dealing with people. "You are a good person and you feel scared because you know that keeping us here is wrong. You know that letting Sebastian and me go is the right thing to do don't you?"

"I have to go" Anna said as she held back her tears. "Be careful. I will come back soon."

"What was all that about?" Said Sebastian with a sigh after Anna left.

"I think she will let us out of here." Replied Otto.

"Why don't you just say 'My father is the king, now let us out of here or you will all be shot'?"

"Because we might get out this way." muttered Otto. In a louder voice he said "Did you know you win at many things with your mind. Higginbottom taught me that. All you have to do is really believe that you will achieve what you want; and I really believe that we will get out of here unhurt very soon."

Anna came back at nine o'clock to check that the boys were tied up. "Will you help us?" Asked Otto.

Anna paused, "Yes, but you have to be ready to leave tonight."

"We will be."

"I will come in the night when the house is quiet. Anna returned ten minutes later. She untied the boys' legs and then re-tied them with a knot that was easy to undo. "If anyone comes in make sure that they see you tied up otherwise I won't be able to get you out of here tonight."

"We will" said the boys together. When they were sure that no one was likely to come in, the boys brought their coats near to them. The hours passed by slowly for Otto and Sebastian that night. They knew that they had to stay awake and keep quiet but it felt like they were waiting for weeks. Finally Anna arrived. "Don't say a word" she whispered as she slipped the knots down from their arms and legs. They followed Anna out of the door to the room, the three of them walking as quietly as they could. They walked up a flight of stairs and into a hallway, Anna reached for a key to open the outside door, she got the key into the lock. Suddenly a voice came from a room at the back of the building, "Anna, what are you doing?" Anna started to shake so much that she couldn't turn the key. Otto turned the key and flung the door open. Anna was blocking the exit so Otto grabbed her arm and pushed her through the open door, Sebastian followed him. "Who is that man?" asked Otto. "My uncle, he is the man that works for Mr Stark. Mr Stark will probably kill me for this" said Anna.

Otto replied, "No one will hurt you because you are coming with us" said Otto and pulled Anna by her hand into the road. Anna's uncle rushed out of the building but one of his legs had been damaged and his limp, even at full speed, was not a match for Otto, Sebastian or even Anna as they were running away. Otto, Sebastian and Anna kept running from one street into another in a zig zag pattern to make sure that no one could follow them. They kept looking back just to make sure that there was no one behind. Actually by the end of the first road Anna's uncle had given up the chase, he knew that with his limp he had no chance of catching three athletic young people. Soon Otto realised that they had lost their captor and they slowed down.

"What do we do now?" asked Sebastian as they were catching their breath.

Otto was convinced that they needed to keep moving, "We need to move around until we find somewhere safe. It must be about six o'clock and the city is starting to come to life, Stark and his friends will already be looking for us. It is not safe to go into any official building, Stark has friends everywhere. Do you have any place we could go to?" Otto asked Sebastian.

"No we don't have a house in Munich."

Otto asked, "But do you have any friends here that would hide us?"

"None," replied Sebastian.

Otto turned to Anna, "Do you know anywhere that is safe here?"

"No, my family own the inn that you were held in. Apart from my uncle's house I don't know anywhere else in the city."

Otto looked puzzled. "I know of a few places we could go. There is the professor's office, but that is the first place that Stark would look. We could go to a hotel, but I don't have any money and if we make very much fuss about who we are then the whole city will know very soon. We could go to the Iron Works, but Stark will probably look there as well. We really are stuck. Does anyone have any idea about what we do next?"

"What will your family be doing?" asked Anna.

Otto sighed "They will probably think that Sebastian and I have gone off for a trip on the railway by ourselves."

"No they won't." Replied Anna.

"How do you know? Said Otto.

Anna replied, "From what I heard today Stark wants the railways, that is why he has captured you. I think that the king and queen will have been asked to sign over control of the railways to Stark in return for your life."

Otto became very angry, "just as we had got rid of that despicable man, let's hope they haven't signed anything. If they know we have been captured Higginbottom will have worked out that we are in Munich."

Sebastian looked intrigued "How will he know."

"It is the only place big enough for Stark to hide us. Anyway, they will have come to Munich. I know they will, at least Higginbottom will, so if we go to the Grand Hotel I think we will meet up with Higginbottom there."

"Extraordinary." said Sebastian, still trying to keep up with Otto's reasoning.

Anna smiled, "This seems sensible to me, so how do we get to the Grand Hotel?"

Otto turned to Anna, "You live in Munich, don't you know the way?"

"Not to the grand hotel your royal highness, it was always full when I wanted to stay there," Anna replied with a fake posh accent and a broad smile.

Otto was getting impatient, "Sebastian and I could be recognised if we ask, but if you ask the way to the city centre we should be able to find the hotel."

Anna was getting her sense of humour back, "Very good your royal highness" she said with a courtesy.

Otto was not impressed "Come on, there is no time to lose."

Anna managed to find a man who explained how to get to the centre of the city. They had a few kilometres of walk ahead of them, but at least they were heading in the right direction. Otto and Sebastian turned the collar of their coats up so that they would be more difficult to recognise, they turned away from the road every time a carriage passed by and separated slightly so that they were unlikely to be recognised together. As they walked, the streets became more crowded, more and more people were walking to work in the city and so it was easier to hide from passing traffic. They finally reached the city centre. It took Otto a few minutes to work out where the hotel was, but soon they were standing in front of the building. "I will go in." said Otto boldly.

"What will we do?" Asked Anna.

"Wait here until it is safe," replied Otto. He then walked into the hotel, his coat collars were still up and he tried not to look too regal.

In a quiet voice he said, "I am here to see Mr Higginbottom, he will be staying in one of the suites."

"What is your name please?" Asked the receptionist.

"Otto von Staig" replied Otto. "I will be waiting in the restaurant."

Otto positioned himself so that he had a good view of the main doorway leading in to the restaurant. There was a second entrance to the restaurant at the other side of the room, but this was usually used by guests so Otto hoped that, if Stark appeared, he would use the main entrance. It took just two minutes for the tall thin profile of Higginbottom to walk through the main entrance.

"How ever did you get away?" Asked Higginbottom.

"It is a long story." Otto replied, "But quickly tell me, do you think Stark could be following you?"

Higginbottom replied, "I don't believe ..." Suddenly there was a loud bang; someone had fired a gun at the back of the room.

"OUT, Get out" shouted a loud voice from the back of the room. Everyone in the restaurant got up to leave. A dark figure grabbed Otto and Higginbottom by the shoulder, "not you two" he said. Once the restaurant was almost empty the dark figure pointed his gun at Otto. "You thought that you were being very clever meeting in a public place ... but you were wrong. Do you think that this was not the first place I started to watch when you went missing from that fool of an innkeeper?"

"What do you want Mr Stark?" Asked Higginbottom.

Stark replied "Oh, you know what I want and you know that I will get it. I want to own the railway that is taking the livelihood away from my rivers and canals."

"You only have yourself to blame for that. You put your prices up so high that no one could afford them, what did you think would happen?" Asked Higginbottom.

Otto could see two young people peeping around the small door at the back of the restaurant. Stark was looking the other way, facing Otto and Higginbottom with the gun in his hand. Otto decided that it was time to get Stark to focus on him. Otto began to tell Stark exactly what he had done wrong. "You made a real mess of this didn't you? You bought a canal system and some rivers, you lost money on all of them and now you have been outmanoeuvred again. How stupid can you be?" Higginbottom gently kicked Otto to try and get him to stop but Otto wouldn't. "I met your wife Fiona, she is such a great person and yet you walked away from her to make money, and now you have lost all that money and you are pointing a gun at us because you are so desperate that you will do anything to try to get your money back. You know what the king will do when he catches you, don't you Mr Stark?"

Stark smiled, an evil smile, "The king will not catch me," he said in a deep voice, "not while I have two hostages."
Otto replied, "Really. I think you are going to be shot very soon." Stark was at boiling point, he cocked the gun. Higginbottom stood on Otto's foot to get him to stop. Suddenly a big rock thrown by Sebastian just missed Stark's head. Stark began to turn, he tried to point the gun at Anna and Sebastian. Thankfully, an even bigger rock thrown by Anna hit Stark right between the eyes and he fell backwards slightly. Higginbottom wasted no time and took out his own gun shooting Stark's right foot. Stark fell to the floor in agony. Otto grabbed Stark's gun and Higginbottom kept pointing his gun at Stark's chest while Anna went to find the hotel manager to get some rope to tie up Mr Stark.

The king and queen, the professor and Mrs Higginbottom appeared after all the action was over. They saw Stark tied up and being taken away by the police. Otto realised that Anna had not been introduced. "Everyone, this is Anna, she has looked after Sebastian and me and saved us several times from Stark and his evil men." Anna did not like everyone looking at her and her cheeks began to glow red. Otto continued "Anna, meet my mother and father, the queen and king."
"Your majesties," said Anna with a genuine deep curtsey.
Otto said "Anna, meet the most splendid tutor in the entire universe, Mr Higginbottom, his wife Mrs Higginbottom and of course our excellent professor Ritter." Anna smiled and shook hands with them all, her hands were still cold and shaking after the excitement of the morning.

"What are we going to do now?" Asked the queen.
"I am going to have my breakfast" said the king with the tone of someone who had spent a morning fighting an evil intruder, rather than arriving after Stark had been disabled.
"After breakfast I think we should all go home" said the queen.
Otto nodded "I agree. But there is one thing that we have not yet worked out." He turned to Anna. "Until the police catch Anna's

uncle it is not safe for her to return home, so I think that she should come to the castle with us for a few days for her own safety." Anna looked at the ground and shuffled her feet, her cheeks started to glow red. She said "I... I will be safe enough here, I am sure that my uncle will not do me any real harm."

The queen interrupted, "My dear, we can't thank you enough for what you have done. We have our son safe and well because of you. If you would like to come and stay in our castle for a little while you are most welcome." Eventually Anna agreed to join the king and queen but only for a few days, until her uncle could be found.

Chapter 18
Some Things Will Never Change

The royal party had only just arrived back at the castle when Dr Fabian's carriage stopped on the gravel driveway. The doctor passed his hat to Mr Gott and was shown in to the drawing room where Otto and Sebastian were waiting. "I was asked to come and make sure that you and Mr von Staig were well. How are you both?" He asked Otto and Sebastian.
Otto turned to the doctor "Thank you for coming, I am well. How are you Sebastian?"
"I am also well."
Dr Fabian looked very seriously at the boys "You have both been through a long ordeal."
The queen joined them, "Thank you for coming to see the boys, doctor, we just want you to check them both to make sure that they are in good health, particularly after Otto was so badly hurt in the autumn." The doctor gave both boys a thorough check up and pronounced to the queen "They are both in excellent health your royal majesty."
"Thank you, doctor." Suddenly the queen looked towards the stairs. "Please can you have a look at someone else, doctor?"
"I am happy to." The queen went upstairs and returned with Anna. "Anna saved my son and Sebastian." Anna's cheeks began to glow red again. The doctor talked to Anna and took a look at her. He declared that she was fit and healthy. Mr Gott then brought coffee and the conversation moved on to how well everything was growing in the garden this year. Just as the doctor was preparing to leave the castle the queen asked him, "Doctor, do you think you might have some relatives in Munich?"
"Yes I do, why do you ask?"
The queen replied, "Because Anna's surname is also Fabian, I wondered whether you were related?"
The doctor asked. "Anna, did you know my great uncle, George Fabian, he was a very well respected business man in Munich?"
"Well, yes," said Anna is surprise, "he was my grandfather."

"My goodness," replied Dr Fabian, "that makes us second cousins. So your uncle Maximilian must be George's rebellious son that we always called mad Max?" Anna thought that calling her uncle mad Max was very funny.

"How extraordinary that you should meet your second cousin like this," said the queen. "You and Katarina must get to know Anna while she is staying here. I always think that families should stay together."

"I agree completely." said the doctor, turning to Anna he said "We will see more of you while you are staying at the castle and you really must come to my wedding next month. But now I really have to go as I am running late and I still have a lot of patients waiting to see me."

That afternoon Otto was busy working through a mathematical problem in the drawing room when Mr Gott announced "Miss Fabian has arrived."

"Show her in" said Otto excitedly. Katarina dispensed with the formalities of greeting a prince and rushed up to Otto giving him a huge hug. "I came as soon as I could - how are you?" she said.

"I am very well," replied Otto.

Katarina said, "Father tells me that you have survived your ordeal well."

Otto smiled, "I don't think I would call it an ordeal. Being tied up as a hostage was just a matter of dealing with a bad situation in the way that Higginbottom recommended, a game that you play in your mind. As long as you tell yourself that you are well and that everything will be good, then somehow it will be."

Katarina looked relieved. She smiled at Otto, "I am so glad that you are well and safe."

"I am glad that it all worked out too." replied Otto as he got up from his seat. "Come with me, I have someone that you should meet." Otto knocked on Anna's door and as they entered he said "Katarina Fabian meet Anna Fabian your father's second cousin from Munich. It was Anna's ability to lead an escape and throw rocks that got us away from Mr Stark." Otto left the two girls to get to know each other. Katarina was very excited to meet Anna

and the girls found that they had a lot to talk about. Otto went back to his mathematical problem. After half an hour both girls came to the drawing room and Katarina asked, "We were just going to make a herbal tea, would you like to join us?"
"I would love to join you for tea, but why don't we have our tea brought up here?" Otto rang the bell and Mr Gott came to ask what he could bring them. The girls thought that it was very funny to have someone bring them their drinks. Once Mr Gott had gone Anna said "I would not have believed it, last week I was working for my uncle bringing people drinks at the inn and now this week I am sitting in a castle with a prince having someone bring me my tea. Life is amazing."
Katarina smiled at Anna, "I still can't believe that of all the people in Munich that could have held Otto hostage he just happened to end up with my father's second cousin."
"Girls, what do you need to do to prepare for the wedding?" Asked Otto.
"I don't have to do very much." replied Katarina, "Father bought me a new dress last week. What would you like to wear?" she asked Anna.
"I have nothing that I could wear to a duchesses' wedding" replied Anna. "Perhaps it is better if I do not go, I wouldn't want to look out of place."
"Nonsense" replied Katarina. "You will come to the town with father and me this week and we will find you something to wear."

Throughout the week Katarina called in to the castle every day, just as she had done when Otto was ill. Otto enjoyed her visits, it was a bit like the times when she used to call in to help him get better after his accident, but now Otto had his lessons each day and he only managed to slide away from his classes for a few minutes to talk to Katarina. Anna and Katarina became great friends and throughout the week they talked about the preparations for the wedding. Dr Fabian did find Anna the most wonderful light blue dress which matched Katarina's light green dress.

On the Saturday of the wedding the king, queen and Otto arrived at the majestic church in Füssen that was decorated with huge arrangements of beautiful yellow and purple spring flowers. The large church was almost full, Otto was sitting near to George and he could see Sebastian and his family. Right at the back of the church Otto could just see Mr and Mrs Higginbottom taking their seats. The sun shone brightly as Fiona walked down the aisle while the great organ played. The wedding mass was a very happy celebration. A meal and party in a large room in the town hall followed and everyone enjoyed the short walk from the church to the town hall, people in the town stopped what they were doing to watch the wedding party walk by, it was unusual for the royal family to walk but the queen insisted that it would be silly to get into a carriage and be driven just a few metres across the town while everyone else walked.

Once the meal had finished and the musicians were preparing to play, Otto found a moment to talk to Katarina. "We haven't really had time to talk since the wedding announcement. How are you?"
Katarina replied "I am well. I am much happier now that I have spent more time with Fiona, she is a wonderful lady and I will be very happy living in a house with her. I don't think of her as a mother but I am sure that she will be a good friend. The main thing is that father has promised that he will always find time to be with me and work with me in the way that he used to. I think he got very distracted when he first met Fiona, but now he is a bit more like the man he used to be."
Otto smiled "I am so glad that things have worked out well for you, and I am really pleased that you have made such a good friend in Anna."
Katarina grinned and talked very openly with Otto, "Anna and I are so much alike, we like the same clothes, the same stories, and the same sort of people ..." she paused and then looked at Otto briefly. Katarina continued "... I really must get back, father will be wondering where I have gone." Katarina went back to her table,

Otto rubbed the back of his neck "What was all that about?" he said to himself.

Very soon musicians started to play and some of the guests began to dance, Otto looked around the room and he knew what he should do, but this presented a big problem. "Higginbottom," Otto whispered "What can I do, Katarina and Anna look uneasy and I think I should ask one of them to dance, but I can only dance with one and the other one will then feel uncomfortable."
"My goodness," replied Higginbottom, "how you have changed. Last year when I met you, you would never have worried about how someone would feel in that way. Well done Otto."
"Thank you ... but what about my dilemma?"
Higginbottom replied, "Oh yes. Just get George or Sebastian to dance with whoever you don't ask, and then make sure that you dance with the other girl."
"Thank you" said Otto, "I knew you would be able to help." Now the only problem Otto had was convincing another boy that he should dance. This was going to take all the persuasion that Otto could muster.

Otto walked directly towards Sebastian. "My dear friend," Otto began "you know how you have always wanted to drive my boat?"
"Yes?" Sebastian replied eagerly.
"Well I am going to let you ... I just need a small favour in return." Otto said this as positively as he could.
"I will do anything for that. What do you need? You want me to look after Rufus, mow the castle lawn. I would even clear the castle drains for a few minutes at the controls of that boat." Replied Sebastian. He really looked like he meant every word.
Otto smiled at Sebastian, a genuine happy smile. "My friend, I don't ask for anything like this, just five minutes of your time. I want you to dance with my other dear friend Anna Fabian, and then have the next dance with Katarina Fabian."
"DANCE?" said Sebastian "you want me to dance, here, with all these people watching me?"

"Yes" replied Otto.

Sebastian started to look very white, "but, but" he stuttered "I can't remember any of the steps, and what if I stand on the poor girl's toes."

Otto quickly replied "Then you will do what the rest of us do, apologise and keep dancing."

Sebastian really wanted to drive Otto's boat so he knew that he was going to have to do this. Quietly he said "Go on then, let's get this over with ... but given a choice I really would rather sort out the castle drains."

Otto grinned "Sorry my friend, the drains are not an option." Otto went to ask the musicians to play two waltzes one after the other and then Otto walked straight to Katarina and Sebastian followed him and stood in front of Anna. "Would you like to dance?" the boys said together.

Both girls anxiously replied "Yes."

Katarina asked Otto, "Are you just trying to see whether we do eventually end up in a heap?"

"Not at all." Otto replied. "You looked like you needed to dance." Katarina and Otto both smiled when they looked at Anna and Sebastian dancing together, both of them were looking at their feet and seemed to be trying not to stand on one another's feet rather than dancing. The first waltz ended and Otto thanked Katarina and then went to dance with Anna. Sebastian began to dance with Katarina. This time Sebastian looked more professional as he danced with Katarina confidently following his lead. Otto had become experienced enough in dancing a waltz that he could lead Anna very well and Katarina was able to convince Sebastian to stop looking at his feet for long enough that he began to enjoy his second waltz. "That was great." announced Sebastian at the end of the dance, "Shall we carry on?" A polka began to be played and Katarina had no idea of how to dance a polka so she said, "I am very tired and my legs need a rest. Do you mind if we sit down for a few minutes."

Otto tapped on Sebastian's shoulder "Well done old thing" he said.

Sebastian replied "It was great fun, but don't you forget about me

driving that boat."
"I won't" replied Otto.

A week later Otto had arranged for the jet boat to be delivered to the lake from Munich. It was a Saturday morning and Sebastian had arrived at the castle before breakfast to make sure that he didn't miss his chance to drive Otto's amazing boat. The fire had been lit by one of the men who brought the boat from Munich and by ten o'clock in the morning the steam pressure was high enough that it could be driven. Katarina and Anna gathered on the jetty to wave to the boys as they climbed into the gleaming red craft. Katarina had warned Anna that it could be a bumpy ride in the boat and so neither of the girls wanted to travel. Higginbottom joined the boys to make sure that they stayed safe on their journey. The agreement was that Otto would take the boat gently into the lake and then pass the controls to Sebastian. As they set off Higginbottom began explaining how to control the boat to Sebastian, "The most important thing" explained Higginbottom "is to drive gently and slowly. The boat will turn upside down and crash if we take it too fast so you must be very careful."
"I will" promised Sebastian. Otto stopped the boat once they were away from the jetty and in deep water. Otto got out of the driving seat and Sebastian got in. Higginbottom repeated his message "You must drive gently and slowly." There was very little wind and the lake was smooth so it was possible to travel quite fast.

At first Sebastian did exactly as Higginbottom had asked, he drove the boat very gently and pulled carefully on the control levers but after a few minutes at the controls Sebastian began to go a bit faster, and then he went faster still, "Slow down" said Higginbottom and Sebastian obediently reduced the steam outlet pressure and the boat slowed down. Sebastian set a course for the other side of the lake and, in what seemed like a few minutes they had reached their destination and were turning around and heading back to the castle. Sebastian loved driving the boat. The green of the scenery flew by so fast it almost seemed blurred. Higginbottom suggested that they stop at the island for a few minutes on the way back, Higginbottom took the controls himself to bring the boat safely up to the jetty. After a short walk on the island they all decided to go to the other end of the lake near to the wear. The boat was excellent fun when it was close to the weir. It had so much power that it was safe to travel very close to the edge. Higginbottom took the controls and drove to within five metres of the edge of the waterfall, as the boat began to be drawn towards the waterfall Higginbottom turned the boat so that its back was facing the waterfall and then he put full power on the boat for just a couple of seconds, the boat shot away from the waterfall pushing the two boys back in their seats. "Who wants to drive back to the castle?" Asked Higginbottom, once they were well away from the weir. Both boys wanted to drive but Higginbottom said that Otto should take the controls as he had not driven the boat very far that day. Otto enjoyed every second that he drove, he was very careful with the controls and Higginbottom didn't need to say "slow down" at any time. Just as they approached the jetty Higginbottom asked "do you want me to take the controls? We need to fit the boat through a narrow space to get it tied up?"

"No," Otto said "I will be fine." Otto gently manoeuvred the boat between the rocks and then turned the boat so that it was lined up with the castle's jetty and just as he was turning the control column his sleeve knocked the steam leaver putting full power on the boat. Otto grabbed the lever but it was too late, the boat shot forward towards the castle beach and they came to rest with the boat half in the water and half on land. Katarina and Anna rushed to the boat to make sure that everyone was all right. Higginbottom looked at Otto and with a grin he said "Oh dear, you do have a habit of speeding at the wrong time."

Otto smiled, "the lever has a design flaw." He replied.

"I can see" said Higginbottom. "What a good thing that that didn't happen when you were driving Prince Albert in London."

"So how are you going to get the boat out of here?" Asked Anna.

"Good question" replied Higginbottom "any ideas boys?"

"We just need a few more men to push it" said Otto.

That afternoon they assembled all the footmen, gardeners and delivery men that they could find. Each man pushed as hard as they could and after half an hour the boat was finally back in the water and Otto tied the boat to the jetty. "Thank you" he said to all the men who had helped.

Anna, Katarina and Mr and Mrs Higginbottom joined the royal family for dinner that evening. It had been a long day and everyone was very tired, suddenly the king announced "Mr Stark has been given the death sentence for treason."

Otto was upset by this news. "Father, you know that I am unhappy about us having someone killed. Of course I know what an evil man Stark is, but why would we kill another human being? We need to set an example and show that every human life is valuable? Surely we should just put him in prison."

The king was surprised "After what he has done, he needs to be killed, that is the way we have always done things."

Otto was determined "No, he is another human being. He needs to be imprisoned, but certainly not killed." The discussion went on and on and Otto would not move, he was determined that Stark should not be killed. Katarina whispered to Anna "Have you ever seen Otto so insistent?"

Anna replied, "Only when I saw him confronted by Mr Stark. He really wouldn't back down, even when Stark was about to shoot him."

Eventually the king could see that he would have no peace if he didn't back down. The king looked at Otto "If you are convinced that this is the right thing to do I will spare Stark the death sentence but I know that we would be safer if we killed him."

Otto nodded "I agree, perhaps we would be safer, but it would not be the right thing to do. Thank you father. We need to make sure that he is imprisoned for life in a very strong prison cell, but we will show the people of Europe that Bavaria will not kill anyone."

At the end of the meal Katarina said, "it is still light outside, would anyone like to join me for a walk?"

"I would like to go for a walk up there" said Otto as he pointed towards the hill at the back of the castle. Higginbottom, Anna and Katarina decided to walk up the hill together with Otto. They all knew what Otto wanted to do. They walked slowly up the steep path just as Higginbottom had done seven months before to save Otto. Rufus loved the walk, he was the only one of the group that bounded along happily. Higginbottom remembered all about what happened the day that Otto was so badly hurt. When they arrived at the top of the steep path they found the sledge still where it had been left on that winter's night six months ago. Otto stopped and for a moment, he couldn't quite bring himself to get close to the sledge again, a chill ran down his spine. "We need to decide what we do with it. Should we get rid of the sledge?" Asked Higginbottom.

Otto looked at the bent and slightly rusty red sledge. "I loved that sledge and I was nearly killed because of my own stupidity. I should never have gone sledging near to the trees. I would like to have it brought back and cleaned up so that I can use it again next winter."

Higginbottom understood, "I am sure that the footmen could organise that very soon."

Anna stood and looked out towards the castle, she couldn't believe her eyes. "It must be at least a kilometre to the castle from here." She turned to Higginbottom, "did you really carry Otto all that way on your back in the dark?"

Higginbottom replied, "Yes, most of the way, and I would gladly do it again if it meant the difference between Otto living and dying."

Anna turned to Katarina and said, "I think we have found someone else who likes Otto as much as we do." Both girls hugged each other and this time it was Otto's turn to get red cheeks. They all started walking back down the hill again. Once the girls were out of earshot Otto looked at both girls walking in front of him and said to Higginbottom quietly "I think that your lessons in understanding people's feelings and quickly making friends may have worked too well."

"Nonsense," replied Higginbottom with a big grin, "I am sure

that you are just the first prince that they have ever met."
Otto thought deeply about this, "That may well be true, but all the same I am planning to enjoy my summer with my dear old friends and my two new friends."

Lightning Source UK Ltd.
Milton Keynes UK
UKOW06f2332040516

273593UK00001B/15/P